ONE
GOOD
REASON

ONE GOOD REASON

SUSAN STAIRS

HACHETTE
BOOKS
IRELAND

2

First published in 2018 by Hachette Books Ireland
First published in paperback in 2018

Cataloguing in Publication Data is available from the British Library.

ISBN 9 781 47361 813 8

Typeset in Cambria by redrattledesign.com
Printed and bound in Great Britain by Clays Ltd, Elcograf S.p.A.

Hachette Books Ireland policy is to use papers that are natural, renewable and
recyclable products and made from wood grown in sustainable forests. The logging
and manufacturing processes are expected to conform to the environmental
regulations of the country of origin.

Hachette Books Ireland
8 Castlecourt Centre
Castleknock
Dublin 15, Ireland

A division of Hachette UK Ltd.
Carmelite House
50 Victoria Embankment
London EC4Y 0DZ

www.hachettebooksireland.ie

For my children

Let everything happen to you
Beauty and terror
Just keep going
No feeling is final

–Rainer Maria Rilke

It's warm up here. And dry. So dry. The wind makes sure of that. It comes in from the north, clearing the sky of cloud, the air of dust, and ridding the place of moisture. So the earth on these hills is poor. A loose mix of clay and limestone and gravel that crumbles underfoot and yields to even the slightest pressure. Rain rarely falls. But all this dryness doesn't stop the vast acres of vines thriving. Their roots are adventurous, pushing hard through the soil, searching groundwater to feed their fruit to ripened plumpness. Like the aged and plentiful fig trees in the sloping grounds of Notre Rêve. Clustered in the sunniest corner of the villa's garden, their broad, open-handed leaves flitter down daily at this time of year, coating the parched grass in layers of crispy, curling husks. No one bothers to clear them any more. And no one gathers the fruit. It thumps to the ground at summer's end, an unwanted harvest-carpet of sticky, boozy pulp. Over time, leaves and fruit combine, disintegrate, become part of where they fall. Come winter, the human remains that lie half hidden under the shady figs will be covered completely.

Next year, it will begin all over again. And the next. And slowly, slowly, the earth beneath will subside and the shrinking mound will be swallowed. That's what will happen.

Unless someone comes looking.

And they know what they're looking for.

ONE

March 2015

Before Laura joins the lengthy queue for Security, she glances back. Her mother still stands where she left her, one pale, veined hand clutching the mauve scarf at her throat, the other held chest high, palm out, ready to wave. Laura raises her arm over her head and moves it through the air, but the woman she's looking at remains static and unseeing, like a life-size cardboard cut-out, a 2D version of her real self. Any doubts Laura may have had evaporate. Her mother is not the person she used to be. It's time for action.

Laura has no idea if this trip will be successful. If it will make things any better. Perhaps when she returns home she won't feel any different from the way she does now. The way she's felt ever since what happened.

What happened.

That's how her family refers to that night. The night when everything changed. They skirt around it, try not to talk about it. But they do. And, invariably, it ends up in a fight.

Laura shouting. Amy crying. Richie punching his fist through a door.

And their mother, Angela, silently watching. Helpless, as yet another fragment falls from what remains of her shattered world.

Before last October they'd all been under the impression they'd get justice. That sentences would be served as some kind of exchange for the damage done. For the mental and physical scars. For the gaps that had opened between them. For the way doubt seeped into the bones of their house and all trust in its safety disappeared. But that's the thing with hope: it's so fucking unreliable.

Their father had tried hard to help them through it, to remain calm and rational whenever his family got upset, confident that justice would prevail. He'd wade into their squabbles with spirited words of reason and inspiration: 'Don't let what they did define us,' he'd say. 'Don't let it destroy us.' And then, gathering them into the muscle of his tight, musky embrace, the hot whispered words of his mantra: 'We have to let it strengthen us. Strengthen what we have, who we are. Don't let them win. For Jesus' sake, don't let the buggers win.'

But they did.

And when it finally became clear that all those involved had walked away, unpunished, it had been too much to bear. Perhaps he'd set too much store in a positive outcome but Laura couldn't blame him for that. Then the wound had been salted by a triumphant V outside the court and the rage he'd been keeping at a simmer had instantly leaped to the boil. Against the grate of his ribs, Karl Pierce's heart had turned into a flaming ball. Alive with a fire he couldn't damp down.

One that had taken just a week to burn itself out. In the end, their father had been brought down by the very emotion he'd urged his family to disdain.

Laura boards the plane. For the first time in months she feels . . . purposeful. Like she matters. Like she could spit in the face of anyone who might rub her up the wrong way. Confrontation. Once, it was the air that she breathed. But since what happened, she's learned to be a little less dependent. She'd given as good as she'd got that night but when the price for defiance is a dislocated jaw, well . . . it kind of colours your thinking. Makes you question who you thought you were, throws all certainties into disarray. Whoever said trauma brings people closer together was telling a stinking great lie. In the case of Laura's family, it's doing its best to pull them apart. It's as though they've each retreated to their own private corner to grieve, like starving dogs with lumps of rotten meat.

Take Amy – she likes to put her grief into words. Her counsellor encourages it and, being Amy, she does what she's told. Laura often hears the sounds she makes, late into the night after she's had a session: the rhythmic *tap-tap* of her fingers on the keyboard, the clunky whirr of the printer belching out page after page. Her sister says the process allows her to 'contextualise' her suffering. Where's the sense in that? Who wants to spend time making a place for pain in their life? Surely the idea is to move away from it, put something else in its place. Laura tried therapy a couple of times but all it did was make her angrier so she stopped attending. Richie never went at all. He preferred to deal with his feelings another way, wanted to find someone to beat the shit out of the scumbags. But Karl said they had to stick to the rules; they had to allow justice to take its course. Jesus, Dad, would you think that way if you were still alive? Laura wonders, as the plane speeds down the runway. You put your faith in the system and it failed us. It would've been better if we'd taken the law into our own hands.

She looks down on the rain clouds, satisfied that she's on top, like she's getting the better of them. It's not a feeling she has very often now. Her father is dead. Her mother has been left as one half of the whole the two of them made together. The bond she once shared with her brother and sister is weaker than it was. She and Amy were once inseparable. Though they have distinct – almost opposing – personalities, the bond they'd shared had been tight and fast. Richie was their baby. The little boy they'd practically smothered with love since the day he'd been born. Now they are all different people.

After that night, their father had tried. His endless reassurances, his attempts to calm his family's rage . . . It all seems so ineffectual now. Like pissing into the wind. Laura didn't cry when he went. Not that she'd expected to. She's always thought about sadness more than actually feeling it. Her brain understands the purpose of sorrow, but anger, jealousy, deceit, they just seem more . . . useful. As a pig-headed teenager, the sit-down talks her father forced her to endure the countless times she stepped out of line did nothing but make her realise that he loved her. Unconditionally. That knowledge gave her permission to continue her defiance. She's probably supposed to feel bad about that but, hey, who can be held responsible for the person they used to be? What matters is who you are now and what you're going to do about things today, right?

She might not have cried when her father died but she'd held his cold, stiff hand as his lifeless body lay on the hospital trolley. He hadn't been at peace. Maybe some people let go of their troubles when they leave this world but that hadn't happened to her dad. The anger was still there. His chest was swollen with it; she'd seen it bulging behind his eyelids. 'Don't worry, Dad,' she'd told him in her head. 'I'll see to it. You can count on me.'

She orders a coffee, leafs through the boring in-flight magazine. Thankfully the middle seat is empty – she doesn't have to worry about unwanted human contact. But the bald guy sitting in the aisle seat keeps throwing glances, without any attempt to disguise his interest. When he becomes seriously annoying she gives him a 'back-off' stare. He gets the message, and a few minutes later, he dozes off.

An hour and a half into the journey, the clouds begin to break up and soon, through the gaps, she can see the snowy peaks of the French Alps thousands of feet below. The sky brightens, sunlight bursts into the cabin and the attendants go through their routine of collecting rubbish and flogging scratch cards before they start preparing to land. Laura fastens her seatbelt and gets that woozy sensation in her stomach as the plane begins its descent. She thinks about her mother, wouldn't be at all surprised if she's still standing where she left her, that vacant expression on her face. They'd been silent on the drive to the airport; they'd already done all the talking.

At the departure gates, her mother's eyes had filled with tears. 'I'll be fine,' Laura had said. 'This is something I have to do. For Dad. For all of us.'

Her mother had nodded, tried to raise a smile. 'You're sure? You don't have to. You can still change your mind.'

'I'm sure.'

'Knowing you, you'll get what you want,' her mother had said, with a weak smile. 'You usually do.'

The plane comes in low over the bay, glides steadily over the clear blue water. The wheels hit the runway, the engines roar, and Laura grins to herself.

Yes, Mum, I'll get what I want. Just not in the way that you think.

TWO

Driving home from the airport, Angela takes a wrong turn. Instead of stopping as soon as she discovers her mistake, she keeps going, even as her heartbeat quickens and heat prickles up through her body. She knows she should pull over but crazy panic overrides common sense and she caves under its influence, allowing it to take over. A voice in her head is calmly telling her what to do: Stop, turn around, take a right, right again. But Panic tells her not to trust it. What would you know? Panic says. You stupid woman, you're the one who has us here in the first place.

Her breaths shorten as she swings round a large circular green, sails past a string of plastic-fronted shops – a butcher's, a launderette, a takeaway – and a terrace of pebble-dashed houses. Laura had suggested taking a taxi but Angela had wanted to drive, to be responsible for her all the way to Departures. Angela's cheeks flame. Pressure builds behind her eyes. Panic propels her further down the unfamiliar road, takes her past a flat-roofed school building disgorging a grey-legged centipede of uniformed teenage boys. Slow down, the voice tells her, there's a way out of this. You're in control. Those are your hands on the steering wheel, your foot on the accelerator. But . . . maybe I want to be lost. Lost lets me make excuses. Down back roads and side streets and in dark corners. Places where I won't see a soul I know. Lost is vague and comfortable. It's where I want to be. It's . . .

The menace of something tall and shadowy looms up ahead, monstering over her. She swerves left into a tarmacked yard and presses her foot on the brake. Slow, slower, until she comes to a stop inches from an arched wooden door. A church. Not since Karl's funeral has she been inside one. And not for a very long time before that. Richie's christening? No, not that long ago. Not more than eighteen years. Haven't there been weddings? And First Holy Communions? Of course. Ceremonies. The compulsion of them. The having to. All that expectation. People like that, don't they? They seem to find it reassuring. But nothing is as certain as waking up to find your husband lying dead in the bed beside you. As always, Angela had listened out for her husband's breathing that chilly autumn morning, a habit she'd formed over the years. Straining hard for the familiar grainy rasp, her world had collapsed when the only sound she'd heard had been silence.

Half of her is gone and everything is less than it was. Especially time. Months, weeks . . . they mean nothing. Today is a bagful of blurry moments and tomorrow a ribbon of smoke. But the past, there's sense in that still, isn't there? In what came before.

Laura. Now there was a demanding baby. First-born, she'd had a soft landing. Her rounded form had sat easy into the shape of Karl and Angela's warm embrace and there it stayed.

Angela recalls the nights spent rocking her to sleep; the days passed staring into the perfect beauty of her amber eyes. Oh, how she'd thrived on it. The privilege of that sole attention. So good while it lasted. Until the dilution. From one hundred per cent to fifty on Amy's arrival. From fifty to thirty-three and a third on Richie's. The cruelty of it!

She'd been born eight days early. Angela hadn't known she was in labour until her waters pooled onto the quarry-tiled kitchen floor of the Leeson Street house in which they were living. A dark, rain-sodden Friday evening in mid-December, one year almost to the day since Karl and Angela had met. The house they were living in was a dilapidated Georgian four-storey-over-basement owned by about-town auctioneer Frank Butler, whom Karl had met while working as a bar boy in a Baggot Street pub. Frank had taken a shine to the six-foot twenty-one-year-old who served him his Irish coffees. Karl was fully aware of the attention and was quick to detect the opportunity it presented. When he'd heard Frank dramatically lamenting his inability to find someone trustworthy to oversee the renovation of his recently purchased period townhouse, Karl hadn't hesitated to put himself forward. He'd reckoned an ongoing mild flirtation with suede-coated Frank was preferable to spending smoky nights squeezing beer-sodden cloths, emptying butt-congested dregs and hoping the contents of his tips jar might make up for his scabby wages. He'd told Frank he had first-hand experience of building work, though the closest he'd ever been to anything of the sort was when, aged fourteen, he'd helped his late father build a concrete shed in the back garden of their terraced cottage in Kildare. Had Frank known the truth, doubtless he would have hired him anyway. 'I'm positive you'll be perfect,' he'd said. 'When can you start?'

It was Frank who'd driven them to the maternity hospital that evening. Karl, white-faced, was waiting on the granite steps when he'd pulled up in his maroon Jag at five on the dot to deliver the ivory envelope containing Karl's weekly wages. 'Lucky for you I'm punctual,' Frank remarked, as they sped through the slick city streets. After twenty hours of indescribably painful contractions, Angela pushed their baby girl out into the world and Karl cried for the first time since the long, slow death of his mother. He told Angela later that when he'd looked at their daughter for the first time he'd felt a shifting, a physical jolt, and instantly the world was more defined, as though he'd spent his life until that point peering through a veil. And that when he'd taken Laura into the crook of his arm, he'd known for sure that there'd never be anything more important than her protection.

Frank had been the natural choice for godfather. They'd asked him on Christmas Eve. He'd accepted immediately, saying, in his own dramatic way, that it was the best present he'd ever received.

Who would have imagined it? Not Angela. All those years ago when she and Karl had first met, he'd told her that this was for ever. And she'd believed him. If there was, somehow, to be an end, she'd thought it would be so many years up the road she'd hardly be able to count them. It would come at a time when the future they'd planned had become their past, when their children's children had children, when the world had become a place she and Karl didn't understand. And she'd always trusted that they'd go together. That some force – whatever it might be – would see to it that neither of them was left alone for long. Or at all. When Karl died, she got sick of people advising her to count her blessings, telling her she should be happy they'd been together for more than twenty-five years. How can she be grateful for what she's missed out on? For being robbed of all the time they should have had left? Where's the happiness in that? Celebrate Karl's life? I'd rather mourn his death, if you don't mind. There's sense in sorrow – it's what I can understand. You know what I mean, don't you, love? You wouldn't want me to deny how I feel? That would get me nowhere. Would make what we had so much less than it really was.

She pulls up in front of the house, turns off the engine and sits for a moment, wondering how it is that she's home when the last thing she remembers is an empty church carpark. Obviously there was a journey in between but she has no recollection of the detail. Thoughts of Karl had brought her home while she'd autopiloted through traffic lights and corners and right-hand turns.

Sleep. She hungers for it. For its blissful, ignorant safety. She unlocks the front door, heads straight up the stairs to the bedroom, throws her coat onto a chair. She lifts the padded lid of the blanket box that stands at the foot of the bed and takes out the sheet that Karl died on. It hasn't been washed since. She lies down, wrapping it tight around her body. The smell. Is it the death of him or the life? Everything is upside-down now. Nothing is as it was. She rolls herself tighter in the sheet . . . so tight she finds it difficult to breathe.

THREE

Along worm of vermilion crawls from the tube as Paddy Skellion squeezes it with some force. It lies next to a buttery blob of titanium on the sheet of plate glass that serves as his palette. Two pigments side by side: cardinal red, immaculate white.

Like blood and salve.

He drizzles the paint with linseed oil, then, with the mini-trowel of his knife, he swirls the colours together. The action never fails to remind him. Early mornings – feet laced into oversized steel-toe boots, his breath a freezing white mist in front of his face – mixing mortar for his father, a bawdy hulk of a man whose shovel-sized hands could lay five hundred bricks a day. Forty-odd years ago that was, when Paddy was a fluffy-lipped pup who thought himself too smart to bother with school. Being a brickie like his father was his sole ambition back then. Nothing wrong with that. Great money in it . . . when times were good. He'd learned that the hard way. Working fast and getting paid per brick was fine when there was building going on. Then the bad times hit and it was the ferry to Holyhead, the coach to London and a decade working the sites round Canary Wharf. His father's death had brought him home. It still stings that he didn't live long enough to see how Paddy's fortunes had changed.

He looks up, feeling his heart lift, as it always does, at the view. What would you think of me now, Da? Not bad, yeah? The three huge windows here in his upper-floor studio frame nothing but blue: cloudless skies over untroubled waves dotted here and there with the pale smudge of a super-yacht. Another world. You would've called me a jammy bastard, wouldn't you, Da? Inner-city Dublin to the French Riviera. And all by way of canvas and paint.

He adds another drop of linseed, slicing his knife over and back through the oily pink mass. Colour is his thing. He's never been hung up about the technical stuff. He's self-taught and proud of it. The critics might not rate him but what does he care? His popularity enabled him to buy this place with cash. Cost him every cent he had – a view of the Mediterranean doesn't come cheap – but he's already back in the black after his most recent show. For the moment, the plan is to spend winters out here. Long term, a permanent move is on the cards. Life isn't bad. But there are things that could be better.

'Swear to God, Simon Keyes thinks you're a bloody machine.' Marie pads, barefoot, across the sun-warmed floorboards. She's not dressed yet, still wears her striped cotton pyjamas, her grey fleece dressing gown. She hands Paddy one of the mugs of coffee she carries, then sits in the leather chair that faces the view. 'He's looking for fifteen by the end of next month.'

Paddy takes a sip and studies the back of his wife's head.

From this vantage point, she could be any age. But face on, time is beginning to take its toll. She's forty-nine now and, in the last few months, she's begun to . . . deteriorate. The light shows up her crow's feet, her crêpy neck, the brittleness of her hair. Maybe it's the glut of smooth flesh that's available for free viewing on the beaches, in the streets, at every turn, it seems. It keeps happening. He sees some firm young thing in a café or a shop and the artist in him can't help but admire her golden skin, her full lips. The perfection throws Marie into stark relief, makes her age so much more apparent. It's not Paddy's fault that he thinks this way. It's what he's about, what art is all about. Beauty. Creation. Permanence in the face of decay. Twenty-five years. He's had slip-ups. She knows about some of them. But lately the urge to tell her about all the others has been strengthening.

'Fifteen? I can manage that. Did he mention sizes?'

'Sizes? Um . . . God. Did he mention sizes?' She glances at him over her shoulder. 'I'll have to read the email again. Senior moment.'

Marie looks after Paddy's admin – the workaday stuff: ordering stretchers, rolls of canvas, packing materials; fielding requests for work, many of which get turned down. He supplies three galleries on a regular basis – one each in Dublin, Belfast and London. Between them, they take everything he's able to produce. There are no contractual obligations; Paddy can afford not to tie himself down. And it's cash on delivery. You want a Skellion, you pay for it upfront. It's an arrangement they're happy to go along with. Skellions don't stay on the wall for long. Paddy is in the enviable position, therefore, of knowing that every painting he produces is already sold.

'You can let me know.' He puts down his mug, squeezes a glob of Naples yellow onto his palette, and another of ultramarine. 'And what time is that, um, meeting on Friday? Eleven?'

Marie nods. 'As far as I can remember. I'll check.' She turns back to the view. 'For what it's worth.'

Paddy selects a flat brush and directs his attention to the prepared canvas that sits on his paint-spattered easel. 'No harm in giving it a shot, see what she's about.'

'Well, if you ask me, it'll come to nothing. As usual.'

'More than likely. But I'm curious.'

'Suspicious, you mean,' Marie says. 'Like she just *happens* to be in the area?'

'I know. But it's possible.' Paddy loads his brush with the thinned-out pink and sweeps it over the virgin canvas in wide, bold strokes. 'Plenty of bigshots out here have personal art advisers. We know that.'

'True. I suppose if her client's as big a deal as she says he is it could turn out to be lucrative.'

'Remains to be seen. For sheer brass neck she deserves the benefit of the doubt.'

Laura Karlson, Art Adviser. He'd googled her after he'd received her initial email but had found nothing. Not entirely surprising. A lot of these types operate under the radar. They earn their money by being discreet. But it had sounded an alarm bell. He'd wasted time on 'big collectors' in the past, before he'd started to enjoy his present success. Agents and dealers promising the sun, moon and stars and delivering, ultimately, zero because they didn't have the connections they'd boasted about. He'd told Marie to send a thanks-but-no-thanks reply. But this Laura had been persistent. Had got back to say she'd be in the area and would like to meet with Paddy in person this Friday, prior to introducing him to her client – a 'gallerist with a successful space in Lower Manhattan'. He'd be in Nice only until this Sunday, she said, and, all going to plan, would be free to 'take things further' on Saturday evening. Dublin, Belfast, London . . . *New York*. That had clinched it. Scepticism aside, there was enough there for Paddy to take the chance. If nothing came of it, at least he'd get to spend a half-hour or so in the company of a female other than his wife. And who knows? She may even be attractive.

FOUR

*L*ara Peers. Laura rolls her eyes at the misspelling. The guy holding the sign in Arrivals is probably late thirties: black skinny jeans, muscle-hugging black T-shirt, collar-length thick, sandy hair. He makes eye contact. She nods, and he turns, on the presumption she'll follow. She watches his barely there arse as he leads the way, sloping through the glass doors and out into the heat, like a cocksure panther. Would she? Probably. She knows she could have him. She's sure. Sure she could take him. But sure that she could leave him too. Sometimes no action is required – the certainty is enough.

He clicks open the boot of a shiny black Mercedes, lifts her wheelie case with one finger and tosses it in, catching her eye. What? Like, she's supposed to think he's Thor? It's practically empty. She packed light. Shopping on rue Paradis tomorrow. Chanel, maybe. Armani, Louis Vuitton. Not that she's into that crap but it'll be necessary in order to achieve the right mix: in command yet attractive. It'll be challenging. But fun. Even more so when she won't be the one paying.

She slides into the back, sits behind the passenger seat where she has a pleasing view of the panther's profile. He steers with his left hand, resting his right arm on that raised bit between the front seats, whatever it's called. Richie would know. And make out Laura's an idiot because she hasn't a clue.

At least, once upon a time he would have. But he's not that kind of Richie any more.

Her body relaxes into the soft leather seat as they speed along the promenade des Anglais. Nice is a city that gets straight to the point. Laura likes that. Barely twenty minutes off the plane and already she's in the middle of it, watching those in denial of the ageing process stroll, jog, skate, basically flaunt themselves against the backdrop of the Mediterranean. Plenty of skin on display for a Wednesday afternoon in late March. Topless bathing on the pebbles just a few feet from the city traffic – she's always found that hard to get her head around.

They drive alongside the harbour with its rows of moored yachts, their glossy hulls and brass hardware shining in the sun. As the road climbs, the panther floors it, holding her gaze in the rear-view mirror. Laura stares him down until he's compelled to look away. Up here, the view is amazing. The Bay of Angels, glittering and sparkling like it's been sprinkled with diamond dust. At least, that was how Amy described it in a What I Did For My Summer Holidays school essay she'd won a prize for at the age of about nine. Their father had been so proud when she'd read it out to the family, handing her a fiver as a reward. True, he'd slipped Laura the same later on, but she'd still been a bit miffed.

Amy has a way of viewing things that other people seem to appreciate. She condenses stuff in an orderly and attractive way, making fully rounded stories out of events that Laura finds routine. Amy gives people what they want, always anxious to be liked. Instead of standing back in reflection, measuring out her feelings like her sister, Laura feels more comfortable being right in the thick of things – bringing on the future as opposed to looking back and dissecting the past. Not that she's averse to contemplation. It's hard not to think about things like life and death. How fragile one is, how certain the other. She's not convinced there's anything out there after we die but sometimes she wonders where her father is, where the essence of him ended up after the body of him gave out. He can't be just 'gone'. There was too much to him for that. Her mother thinks the same. She talks to him. Laura has heard her. Is that normal or might she be going crazy? Can it really be a good idea to be attached to one person for such a long time?

They're on the confusing part of the drive now, where it's all twists and turns and sharp bends, and it's easy to lose your way. But this guy is familiar with the route. His speed has been constant, even when rounding corners; he seems confident he has ownership of the road. Should Laura be surprised he hasn't said a word to her? Fair enough, his English might not be great, and the only French she could use in reply is the smattering that made it into her memory despite years of inattention at school, but complete silence? Amy says Laura exudes negativity. That she incites confrontation. Or is it *invites* confrontation? Whatever.

The panther swings a sharp left onto the narrow forest track, driving about a hundred yards, through open gates, and on to the circular gravelled clearing at the end. With an exaggerated sigh, he stops the car and gets out.

Laura follows. 'Thanks,' she says, '*merci*', when he takes her case from the boot.

She thinks about smiling, just to let him know his silence hasn't pissed her off, but before she can make up her mind she hears, 'Welcome, darling! Welcome, welcome!' and along the path skips her godfather, his precious Persian, Trudy, at his feet. 'Here in one piece! How wonderful to see you!' He kisses both her cheeks, gives her a long, tight hug. 'How was the flight?' he asks, pulling away. 'And the drive? Bruno was his usual talkative self?' He laughs. 'Our little joke, isn't it, Bruno, dear?'

Bruno? Laura suppresses a smile. Truly, a dog of a name.

'You are lucky I am not a sensitive man, Frank,' he answers.

His voice, his accent, find their way in under Laura's clothes. The sensation is pleasant, if a little rough. Like sandpaper on itchy skin.

'Now, don't be selling yourself short,' Frank tells him. 'A brute you may be, but not one completely without feeling.'

Bruno gives Frank the laugh he's expecting. 'Be careful. Perhaps next time I don't remember the way.'

Frank waves his hands. 'Off you go. Shoo now. Your job is done for today. I'll be in touch.'

Laura's head doesn't turn but her eyes swivel to see Bruno slide into the car and roar away. Frank takes her case and together they walk towards the villa.

'Don't worry, darling,' he says, linking his arm through hers. 'Bruno will be at your disposal for the length of your stay.' Laura rounds on him, eyes widening, eyebrows raised. 'What?' Frank asks, feigning indignation. 'He's your type, isn't he? Why else do you think I had him collect you? Oh, stop making faces.'

A gulping laugh escapes Laura's throat. 'I'm not five years old, Frank! I don't need to make faces. If I want to say something, I'll say it.'

'So say it, then. I'm right, aren't I? Or should I have asked for a female driver? Where do your preferences lie, these days?'

This is why Amy has always been jealous that Laura has Frank as a godparent. Though Amy has a godmother *and* a godfather, Laura would never trade her one for her sister's two: weird Willie and his horror of a wife, Yvonne – old friends of their parents who seem to have forgotten Amy's existence. Frank and Laura . . . they have something special. And neither of them is afraid to speak their mind.

'Okay, so he's hot,' Laura says. 'I admit it. And if you'd chosen a "female driver", as you put it, no doubt she'd have been cute too. But what's with a driver anyway? Not up to collecting me yourself this time?'

'It's a little luxury I've gifted myself,' Frank replies. 'Having a chauffeur was a lifelong dream.'

'You mean you've given up driving?'

Frank stops, turns, hugs his goddaughter again. 'You have no idea how much I've been looking forward to you coming. This last week, time has practically stood still.'

'I can understand that,' Laura says, noting he's chosen not to answer her question. She pulls away, squinting against the sun. 'Must be unbearable at times. Stuck in this shithole. All-day sunshine. Panoramic views. Fuck-all to do.'

He shakes his head, smiles. 'Laura, Laura. Light of my life. So much your poor father will miss out on.' Then his face gets serious. 'Angela. How is she?'

Laura pauses, thinking of a way to describe her mother's current state. 'A bit all over the place, to be honest.'

'Pity she couldn't come.'

'More wouldn't than couldn't. Just didn't want to leave Richie.'

'Poor boy. No change? Still spending most of his time in his room?'

Laura nods. 'Refuses help. Hardly speaks. Generally makes Mum's life a misery.'

'He's had a hard time of it. It's not his fault.'

'We all have. He doesn't have a monopoly on grief.'

'Mitigating factors, though. He was exceptionally close to your father. He's the youngest. And he's a boy.'

'Jesus. If you're looking for a fight you're saying all the right things.'

'You know it's true, my dear.' He starts walking again. 'I wouldn't say it if it wasn't.'

'The mental confusion of an old man,' Laura teases.

Frank laughs. 'Seventy is the new fifty, or haven't you heard?'

Laura follows his lead. 'You keep telling yourself that.'

They reach the front door and Frank climbs the four steps, a little falteringly, Laura notes. He stops on the top one. 'It's not going to be the same, without your father here, is it? He was so looking forward to the party.'

'Looking forward to calling you an elderly gent, you mean.'

Frank smiles. 'That too.' He gazes out over Laura's head, his eyes pale, almost transparent in the sunshine. 'I do hope your mother will be all right.'

'She'll be fine,' Laura says. 'I'm over here now, amn't I? That's what she wants.'

He turns and enters the cool, tiled hallway. 'I know. I just hope she gets some comfort from the outcome.'

Frank lives full-time in the villa now, enjoying the solitude and privacy it affords him, generally only returning to Ireland for 'ceremonial reasons', the last time being for Karl's funeral. When he'd bought the property, he'd named it 'Notre Rêve'. *Our Dream.* That was about fifteen years ago and, ever the romantic, he'd thought the dream would last for ever. Or at least for a lot longer than it had. The dream was that he and his partner, Lee, would retire and spend their days as grizzly old gays on the Côte d'Azur, somehow die together and have their ashes scattered over the Bay of Angels. Or something like that. Then Lee went and fucked it up four years ago by falling down the basement stairs of Frank's Dublin townhouse, smashing head first into a glass door and bleeding to death. He'd been known to down several bottles of wine in an evening, and Frank blamed himself for leaving him overnight while he flew to London on business. If he'd been there, called an ambulance, Lee might possibly be alive.

Laura had never understood what Frank saw in Lee. His awful dress sense, his perma-tan, the jungle of hairs on the back of his hands – to her, he and Frank didn't go together. Lee was brash and loud, grabbing attention wherever he could find it. He worked – sporadically – as an interior designer but it was Frank who paid all the bills. He'd cheated on Frank too, several times, even bragged about it during their regular raging arguments. Though, in the months leading up to the accident, he'd claimed he'd turned over a new leaf. When he died, Laura did her best to feel sad, but part of her still thinks that Frank's better off without him.

'It looks different,' Laura says of the vast, sunny living room. 'You've taken down the drapes.'

'So much better without them,' Frank says. 'Kept out so

much light. And must you say "drapes"? Whatever happened to "curtains"?'

'Sorry. Mollie. I guess it rubs off.'

'How is the American psycho?'

'Still around.'

Frank sinks down into the deep velvet couch, his body half disappearing into the row of plump scatter cushions. 'That's a pity,' he says. 'I was hoping you might have fallen out again.'

'Sorry to disappoint you, but no.'

'I preferred it when she was off radar.'

'Look, I know you've never liked her but she's okay. Seriously.'

'What was it you said about her when you ended it?' He beckons Trudy, who jumps into his lap. 'You said she was a bit bubble-gum. All juicy at first and then nothing. How come the renewed flavour?'

'She gets it. Just friends now. She's not pushing for anything more.'

Trudy makes herself comfortable, rolling onto her back. Frank strokes her pinkish stomach. 'Well, I'd advise caution. Lee used to say she had more money than sense.'

'The same could be said about you, where Lee was concerned.'

'That was different. Lee and I were in a long-term relationship. She was splashing the cash all over the place, even when you'd only just met her.'

'I didn't hear him complaining when she took the four of us to Shanahan's that time. In fact, I seem to remember he ordered the most expensive steak on the menu. And a bottle of Dom Perignon.'

'That was a little over the top, I agree. And I had words with him about it. But that's not really the point.'

Laura flops down in a fancy swivel armchair. 'Okay, let's just leave it. I didn't come all the way out here to talk about Mollie Teller.'

Frank's only looking out for her, doing his concerned-godfather thing. He's probably right about the money. Coming into a fortune at eighteen is not exactly ideal. Especially when it's because you lost both your parents at the age of twelve. But hey, who'd turn it down? Mollie has it, she may as well spend it. Regardless of what Frank thinks, she's happy she and Mollie have renewed their friendship. It's going to make the outcome of this trip all the more successful. Laura will let Frank in on that side of things soon. But not yet.

Only when she's sure she has him fully onside.

'Hope you've something fabulous planned for dinner,' she says, spinning around. 'And something equally fab to drink.' She catches Frank's eye as she flies past, noticing the disapproval, which grows as she comes round again. 'What?' she asks, turning one more time before using a foot to brake directly opposite him.

'The spinning. It was annoying.'

'God, who's grumpy today?'

'Oh, don't be ridiculous. I'm entitled to express an opinion.'

'I never said you weren't. But you'd want to know if you're coming across all granddad-y, wouldn't you?'

'Likewise. When you're behaving like a bratty teenager all over again.'

They stare at one another for a moment before Laura takes the lead and grins. 'Jesus. I'm here literally five minutes. What the hell?'

Frank's features relax. He smiles. 'I know. Listen to us. What're we like?' Trudy raises her head, alert to something outside in the garden. She darts to the floor in a graceful leap, shooting through the open French windows in a flash of silvery grey. Frank crosses his legs, lays his arm along the back of the couch. 'So. You're all set, I take it? For the visit to Skellion?'

Laura's breath catches in her throat. She coughs. 'I need to talk to you about that. There's been a change of plan.'

'Oh dear. Why don't I like the sound of that?'

Laura looks around the room. The increased light makes the wear on the parquet and the threadbare patches in the Chinese rug more noticeable. It shows up new lines on Frank's forehead, the amount of white in his hair and beard. And the cloudiness she'd detected in his eyes on her last visit, not long after her father died, is more apparent now, lending a certain detachment to his gaze. Perhaps it's not fair to rope Frank in. Mentally, he couldn't be fitter, but physically? Still, she can keep his involvement to a minimum. It's not as if he'll have a major role.

'Well,' she begins, 'tomorrow we're going shopping.'

Frank frowns. 'For?'

'I need some new clothes.'

'Okay, but—'

'Good stuff. Designer, probably.'

'I see,' he says, after a pause. 'Should I be afraid?'

'Of?'

'You tell me. Your mother sent you over here to talk to the Skellions, yes? Though what she's hoping to achieve from that, I'm not sure. Paddy Skellion is not a reasonable man.'

'You think I don't know that? If he was, I wouldn't be here, would I?' She gets to her feet. 'I wouldn't have to go to this trouble.'

Frank looks away. 'I don't know . . .'

She stands over him now, hands on hips. 'What? You don't know what?'

He sighs. 'If all this was such a good idea. Some people would say it's sheer madness. That you should just . . . let it be.'

'Oh, my God. Are you for real? You're saying this *now*?'

His eyes turn to hers once more as he pats the seat cushion beside him. 'Sit down. Stop hovering. You're making me feel like I've done something wrong.'

'Well, you're doubting me and that's as good as.'

'Not doubting. Questioning. And I've a bloody right to. I thought it was all in train. Now you're telling me you have something else in mind.'

'Chill. I have it all thought out.' She sits down beside him. 'Well, kind of.'

He takes her hand in his. 'You're scaring me.'

She rubs his bony fingers. 'You might have to surrender your Visa card.'

His head slumps on his chest. 'So it's going to cost me?'

'Well, I have to look successful. And smart. And sexy.'

'I'm not sure that'll be possible.'

She digs him in the ribs. 'Very funny. Looking the part is essential.'

'The part? You mean you'll be . . . pretending to be someone you're not?'

She lifts his chin. 'You know me, Frank,' she says. 'When did I ever turn down the idea of a little fun?'

FIVE

Here. Laura's text means she's at the villa now and the tightness in Angela's chest fades. She's in good hands. Frank – Karl had known what he was doing way back when. Angela had protested a little at his choice of godparent. Not much, but enough. 'I know he's not family,' Karl had said, 'but trust me, Lala, he's as good as.' He'd always called her Lala. Right from the very beginning. 'Angela-la,' he'd said, then shortened it to Lala and it had stuck.

It was dusk on a drizzling night a few weeks before Christmas of 1988 when they'd first met. Karl had been walking back to his canal-side bedsit, having spent the day installing a crystal chandelier in Frank's drawing room when he'd spotted her. Over the years, he'd recounted the story over and again to the kids; it became a bedtime favourite. He'd describe how he'd seen her, standing under a frilled black umbrella, looking through the tinsel-bordered window of an electrical shop on Camden Street. 'Something about the stillness of her among the bustling, frenzied shoppers made me stop,' he'd tell them. 'That and the way she was dressed:

purple velvet coat, laced leather ankle boots, the black corkscrew strands of her hair licking her cheeks. Like she'd come from another century.'

He'd pressed his damp sleeve against hers, breathed in the air she'd breathed out and boldly planted a soft kiss on her chilly pink cheek. She'd turned, smiling, offered him her elbow and they'd walked slowly through the crowds, dodging puddles reflecting the Christmas lights that were strung across the street. Karl had taken charge of the umbrella and, at Kelly's Corner, asked if she'd like to go for a drink. They'd found a place – dark oak walls hung with shiny brasses, a smoky log fire burning in the snug – and sipped hot whiskey while they shared their stories. Angela worked in an art-supplies shop on Camden Street back then. She lived with her family – mother Rita, father Pat, brother Brian – in a bungalow off the Dundrum road. She'd considered becoming a nurse, she'd told Karl, but had changed her mind when she realised the training hospital was run by nuns – she'd already had her fill of them at school.

They were both twenty-one, she a Gemini, he a Capricorn, facts that seemed important back then. Karl was keen to impress. He told Angela that Frank's house was only the start, that after he was finished there, the contacts he'd made were going to lead to all sorts of exciting projects. That he had his finger in many pies. That he was going to be a wealthy man. Angela could tell from the slight flicker at the corner of his mouth that his feelings weren't as sure as his words. But she didn't care. She'd found a home in Karl's face, a full stop to the unfinished sentences that whirled around her head whenever she thought about her future. Now, there were no more questions to be posed. 'And as for me,' he'd tell his listening children, 'I felt like I'd known this girl all my life. She'd never been a stranger. She'd always been there, waiting for the perfect time.'

Angela unravels the sheet from her body then lies still, staring at the ceiling. She shivers. This room is no longer a shared space, it's simply a place where she attempts to sleep, a portion of square footage in this house where they live. This cavernous, detached Victorian red-brick called The Haven. Back in the early days, this was the kind of home they'd dreamed about but never imagined they'd be able to afford. The twists and turns in their fortunes had seen them pack up and leave several houses before they'd settled here. Laura, Amy and Richie – they each have childhood memories of books and board games squared into cardboard boxes, of favourite soft toys pillowed into black plastic bags, the other-people smell of strange rooms and having to memorise yet another new route to school.

The Haven was supposed to have been their for-ever home. A place their hoped-for grandchildren would visit. When they'd bought it, though they knew it was draughty, impractical and would require constant maintenance, they'd fallen in love with its charm, its character, and planned never to leave. But after what happened . . . their ardour had cooled. Karl had stopped caring. In the months that followed, he'd let things slide. The annual jobs he'd previously never failed to attend to remained undone. That winter, leaves went un-gathered, trees un-pruned, and the roof tiles turned green with algae. Coming up to Christmas, chimneys went un-swept, the boiler un-serviced, the planned repainting of the hall forgotten.

When spring arrived, he'd brought in an estate agent – a pencil-heeled blonde with a foghorn voice – who enthused about the detailed plaster mouldings and original marble fireplaces. She'd left happy at having so easily secured such a beautiful family home for her firm, but slightly puzzled at the dispassion shown by the owners at its disposal. She wasn't to know, of course, that what had happened almost a year before had severed the emotional bond; that, for Karl and Angela, the consequences had been instrumental in reducing the comforts of their home to those of an elegant but soulless hotel. When The Haven was put on the market, they had no plan as to where they might move, they were simply hopeful that not having to traverse the spaces where they'd been violated would mean they might think about what had happened somewhat less than twenty-four hours a day.

Months passed, and soon it appeared to Angela that the place was cursed. Eventually, a substantial price reduction had unearthed two eager bidders and a sale had been imminent. Then Karl had taken his leave of the world and Angela, unable to comprehend life as a widow in some strange new place, had called a halt. How could she leave? Hopelessly bereft, she'd made the decision to stay, convincing herself that there was life still in the withered vine of sentiment that attached her heart to the house. But the shoots were weak, they couldn't hold. It wasn't long before they were ravaged by the malignant memory, and she'd ended up hating the place once more. But by then Amy had moved home from the city-centre apartment she shared with college friends, and Laura (who'd never officially left home but who rarely spent more than a couple of nights a month at The Haven) was now back on an (almost) permanent basis. Angela hadn't had to ask – neither of the girls had been able to bear the thought of their mother being there with only Richie for company. By that stage, he wasn't really much company at all.

Angela closes her eyes. She pulls the sheet over her head, hoping for sleep, for its deep, velvet softness. The room falls around her. The walls crease and fold. The ceiling bows until it feels as though it hangs just inches from her face. How long she will stay in this house now, she has no idea. She's not sure if she cares. Her family. She thinks about how their lives have been shaped by the places in which they've lived, the rooms in which their histories were made, the journeys they took, the people they met. Their children's very personalities were formed, moulded and pressed into substance by the spaces she and Karl had chosen, or had been compelled, to reside in. She pictures it as she falls asleep: the first place they'd called home. *Cosy basement flat. Rathmines Road. Twenty pounds per week*, the *Evening Herald* classified had read. 'Cosy' had meant cramped and 'basement' cave-like, with a curtained corner for a kitchen and a cupboard-sized bedroom that had never seen daylight. Happy doesn't begin to describe how they'd felt when they moved in. Though she and Karl had been grateful for Frank's generosity in allowing them to live in the townhouse while it was being renovated, they'd yearned for a space of their own and, once the townhouse was almost finished, they'd set about finding it.

Laura was seven months old then, chubby, demanding, and sleeping between her parents every night, having already mastered the art of manipulation. For the first few weeks in their new home, she was hard to settle, screaming herself sick unless she was in Angela's arms or lying slumped across Karl's warm chest in the evenings. Her parents thought nothing of giving in to her whims, rapt as they were by the prettiness of her round face and the wide smiles she gave them when she got her own way. To leave her crying for more than thirty seconds not only resulted in pint-sized Miss Reidy in the flat above thumping loudly on the floor, it also brought about a metamorphosis in Laura that neither Karl nor Angela could bear – her soft cheeks red and blotched, her soulful eyes glassy with tears, her beautiful rosebud lips downturned in a grimace. And so, at her slightest whimper, Miss Laura Elizabeth Pierce was hugged, rocked, fed, watered, changed or entertained in whatever manner allowed for the preservation of the peace. Sometimes Angela would watch from the shadowy recess of the chilly kitchen as Karl waltzed around the dated furniture with his baby daughter snug in the tight fold of his arms. She'd marvelled at how her life had turned, how, in such a short space of time, she'd become someone else, with someone else, and how both of them had created another someone else between them.

'He's an . . . entrepreneur,' Angela had told her mother, when she'd first met Karl and was attempting to explain what he did. She knew it sounded pretentious, incredible even, but in her heart she believed it. Karl would go on to greater things, would take the risks needed to realise his dream of becoming a wealthy man.

'Is that so?' her mother had said, cigarette bobbing between her lips. 'En-tre-pre-neur, is it? That's another word for gobshite in my book.'

'Sounds a bit dodgy, if you ask me,' her father had said, peering at her over his bifocals. 'No place of his own, no family to speak of, no proper job.'

'Not everyone wants to work in the civil service, Daddy,' she'd replied. 'There's more to life than a guaranteed pay cheque every week.'

Her father had turned red in the face. 'Is that so? Well, you might want to try surviving without one, young lady. You'd know all about it then.'

Her parents hadn't taken to Karl. He wasn't the accountant, solicitor or doctor they'd imagined their son-in-law would be. No matter that he loved their daughter and she loved him. That wasn't important to them. 'Love never paid any bills,' her mother had said, when Angela announced she was moving into the townhouse with Karl. 'You barely know him. It's a recipe for disaster.'

'I'll save a fortune,' she'd told her mother, eager to emphasise the financial advantages of the arrangement. 'I'll be able to walk to work. And if I'm not living at home, I won't have to be giving you any money for my keep. I'll even be able to start saving.'

Rita had taken a deep drag of her cigarette and blown a long ribbon of smoke into the air. 'Sure what will you be needing to save for?' she'd said, eyes narrowed. 'Won't the en-tre-pre-neur be raking in the millions?'

And then, when Laura had come along, well, Angela was sure she couldn't have been made to feel any more of a failure if she'd said 'I'm to be charged with murder', rather than 'I'm pregnant'. Rita had stared at her. 'There,' she'd said after several long, silent moments. 'What did I tell you? I knew no good would come of it.'

And now the tears come. Angela curls into the invisible shape of her husband, hugging his absent body. It was good.

It was right and perfect from the very beginning. Their tiny girl had taken hold and, if not for her, for her helpless cry and the sharp urgency of her hunger, there would be no strength in their tale, no ending to live for, no lives that would be worth defending.

SIX

Paddy is an hour into his latest piece and he stands back now to survey progress. He squints, moves his head from left to right, nods. This one's good. Really good. He might have to increase his prices. Marie still sits in the chair by the window, flicking through the pages of an exhibition catalogue that arrived in the morning post. She'd annoyed Paddy earlier by puncturing the precious silence with some unnecessary remarks, but she hadn't been offended when he'd asked her to be quiet. That had pissed him off even more than her talking. He finds her understanding so bloody irritating sometimes.

He steps closer to the canvas, flicks a stray lock of hair from his eyes, loads his brush with more pigment.

'Oh, forgot to mention,' Marie says, and he grits his teeth at the sound. 'Got a text from Tory. He's coming over at the weekend.'

Paddy zips an angry stripe of paint across the middle of the canvas. Like hell she forgot. 'Nice of him to acknowledge our existence,' he says in reply.

'Paddy, would you stop? Give him a break.'

'Isn't that what we've been bloody well doing all his life?' His chest tightens. He feels heat rising to his face.

Marie closes the catalogue, drops it to the floor. 'Don't be getting all upset,' she says, getting up from the chair and walking over to him. She rubs his arm. 'Remember your blood pressure.'

He shrugs her off. 'A nice little holiday for himself. And need I ask who'll be paying for his flights?'

'A hundred euro or so, Paddy. It's not going to break the bank.'

'On top of everything else I pay for. Couldn't he go out and get a part-time job? Loads of other kids seem to manage to pay their way through college.'

'We've been through all this before. It's an intensive course, he doesn't have time.'

'Ah, don't give me that rubbish. It's no more intensive than any other business course. And how do we know he's even going to his classes? He could be swanning up and down Grafton Street every day for all we know.'

Marie takes a deep breath. 'Paddy. He's our son. We have to trust him. He's nineteen now. And he promised. If he hadn't started that course . . . Well, he knows what the alternative might've been. He's learned his lesson.'

'That's exactly my point! I had to jump through hoops to get him onto it. And fork out a fucking fortune for it too. Never mind the cost of his food and rent. The least he could do is show his appreciation and contribute, make it look like he's even *marginally* grateful.'

'He is. I know he is.'

Paddy swishes his brush round a jar of turps, clacking it

noisily against the rim. What had he expected? That Tory would fall at his feet in worship? That he'd have a sudden personality change? Allowing himself to get mixed up with those lowlifes, what the hell had he been thinking? 'You really think so?' he asks. 'You can honestly swear he's grateful?'

'He's got a whole new circle of friends,' Marie says, as if that proves her point. 'He's forever sending me pictures. And a girlfriend too, by the looks of it.'

A new circle of friends? That's a laugh. Hadn't they already tried that? Six years in a private school, but Tory had preferred the company of that gang of troublemakers who roamed the streets, most of whom probably hadn't made it past third year. The guts of fifty grand it had cost, all told, and hadn't Paddy busted his balls making sure it'd happen? All that wasted effort. Marie thinks Paddy only has himself to blame, he knows she does, though she's never exactly said so. She'd have been happy sending Tory to the local secondary. But Paddy was never going to allow that redneck culchie headmaster, Keane, get the better of him. He didn't care how many fucking degrees he had. To him Paddy was just a shitty labourer, one of a team working on the new art room for Hillford College the year Tory had been born. Keane had wandered on site and struck up a conversation with some of the lads, blathering on about the importance of the 'creative arts'. Paddy had mentioned that he did a bit of painting himself, whipping out a couple of photos he had stuffed in the back pocket of his overalls. 'Ye might do better to schtick to the bricklaying, boy,' he'd told Paddy, with a snide laugh. Twelve years later, Tory had walked through the doors of Hillford as a new pupil, Paddy having paid the first year's fees upfront from the proceeds of the sale of just two of his latest works. And had he reminded Keane of their previous encounter? Bloody sure he had. Keane claimed he'd no recollection of it but his blank expression hadn't fooled Paddy.

'All that stuff is behind him,' Marie is saying. 'He's moved on. He has a bit more growing up to do, but that'll come with time.'

Paddy can hardly bear to look at her face. Why does she have to be so bloody *reasonable*? Sitting on the fence, seeing things from all sides . . . Nothing would ever get done if we were all like that. Whenever Tory was being a little bollocks as a kid, she'd always have a justification, some kind of excuse for his behaviour. Her rationale for this latest trouble was that Tory had been under the influence of the gang he was associating with, which Paddy largely agreed with, though not to the extent that he didn't question why Tory hadn't had the cop to just walk away at the time. At seventeen he might've been a minor but he wasn't special needs. But then she'd gone and muddied the waters by suggesting they contact the family involved, the family whose house Tory and his scumbag friends had broken into. Didn't they deserve an apology, she'd asked, after all they'd been through? Paddy had been against it. It had been bad enough that Tory had admitted he'd been involved – Paddy didn't know why he hadn't just denied it, would've saved them all a shitload of trouble – but to go grovelling for forgiveness as though he'd been the fucking ringleader? No way. And then, when they'd found out the identity of the family, that the father was, of all people, Karl Pierce . . . By God, Paddy had been glad they'd offered no apology. 'Whatever you thought about him back then, it's water under the bridge, surely,' Marie had said, using that *common-sense* tone of hers. 'What about his wife, his kids? Your ancient grudge has nothing to do with them.'

Paddy has never told her the full story of his history with Pierce but, Christ, whose side is she on? The whole business still rankles, even after fifteen years. Karl 'aren't-I-the-big-man' Pierce. Jesus. He'd almost felt like congratulating Tory for getting one over on him. Call it coincidence, call it karma, call it whatever you like but, to Paddy's mind, there's a kind of justice to the whole affair.

Pierce had been in court for Tory's sentence hearing, along with his wife, a son and a daughter. He'd glanced at Paddy at the start but there'd been nothing in his eyes that had suggested recognition. That had come only when it was over. Marie had stared straight ahead, avoiding eye contact with anyone, her way of pretending she wasn't there, that it wasn't happening. Tory had been cocky: he'd had the stance of someone unburdened by any threat of punishment. Even though Paddy hadn't been one hundred per cent sure of success, he'd told Tory he'd nothing to worry about, that it was all sorted. Tory's solicitor, Vincent Frayne, is a long-standing client of Paddy's. He has an impressive collection of his work and, on the promise of a gift of several more and a sweetener of six grand, had promised to deliver a quiet word to the judge prior to proceedings.

He doesn't like to admit it, but Paddy's heart had thundered in his chest. Sitting there, waiting for the outcome in the small, stuffy room that was designed to be less intimidating, more 'welcoming' than an adult court room, he'd been forced to contemplate the years-old memory of a dirty back street in Hackney. Beer-breath in the midnight air, boots slippery with blood, and a slight he has no recollection of now. He hadn't really read about it in the next day's evening paper, had he? *Man found with head injuries, now on life-support.* No, it had just been his drink-addled brain making it all up. That's what he's told himself ever since. And that's what he's chosen to believe. He hadn't hung around after that. Had packed his stuff, stuck a note on the fridge for his flatmate and taken the boat home from Holyhead.

Marie, of course, had been all teary-eyed with relief when Tory had walked free. Then, surprise, surprise, after a week or so, when the dust had settled, she'd started to waver. The family's tears that day in court had got to her; Pierce's wife and kids making sure the judge could see they were in bits. But it was over and done with. They didn't need to start opening up any 'lines of communication', as Marie had put it. Not with Karl Pierce. Marie might've fancied herself as a peacemaker but Paddy knew she wouldn't go against him. She'd learned from experience that he would've made her life unbearable for a long time if she had.

'I'll leave you to work,' Marie says quietly, casting an eye over the canvas. 'Not sure I'm mad about that pink, though,' she adds, as she walks out of the room.

As he hears her feet on the stairs, Paddy puts down his brush. He walks over to the middle window and opens it wide. The air is only slightly warm; it'll be into May before it really hots up. But it's still a lot more pleasing than the cold and damp of a typical March day back in Dublin. Coming out here, Paddy had hoped for distance. But, in truth, there's no real escape. Tory has been a disappointment, has made some unbelievably bad choices. But Paddy has his reputation to uphold. People are fickle. A painting by Paddy Skellion might be one thing but a painting by the father of a violent thug . . .

They'd been so lucky that Tory's age had meant his case was dealt with in the children's court. As a result, he couldn't be named in the media and the whole thing went no further than the court room. All along, Vincent had told Paddy he was pretty certain Tory would walk. First offence, good family and all that. But if Vincent had been wrong and there'd been a sentence, or community service, or a fine . . . it could've leaked out. Paddy hadn't been prepared to risk the rumour mill. And, despite his son's failings, he didn't want that for him. He'd pulled out all the stops.

He narrows his eyes as he tries to focus on the pale strip of beach in the distance. Their only child. What had they done wrong? How had it happened? They'd given him the best of everything, right from the start. They'd laboured long and hard over his name, giving him one sure to make him stand out from the horde. By the time he was three, he was able to answer anyone who remarked on it, chanting by heart that Mammy and Daddy had called him after the Tory Island painters. And even before Paddy had hit the big-time, he'd made sure that his son had wanted for nothing. Then, when the boom came, well, he'd earned the money; he could spend it however the fuck he liked. Tory was a kid other kids were envious of. One who had the latest whatever: skateboard, games console, sports gear, mobile phone – you name it. Paddy couldn't be blamed for splashing the cash, could he? He'd come from a family of ten where it was first-up-best-dressed and eat what you're given or else go hungry. Being able to buy his son the kind of stuff he hadn't had growing up makes Paddy feel good. Gives the two fingers to those who'd written him off when he'd left school, to those who'd claimed he'd never amount to anything, to those who'd said he'd no talent for painting. Fuck the lot of them.

He watches a plane curve an arc in the clear sky as it begins its landing. Below, the Bay of Angels sparkles and glints in wide stripes of aquamarine, viridian and turquoise.

Paddy Skellion will go a long way to ensure no one gets the better of him. Not then, not now, not ever.

SEVEN

Richie pulled the treehouse down the day Karl died. Found a rusty claw hammer and hacked at it like a madman. And as he'd flung the splintered planks to the ground one by one, he'd told Laura he was going to use them to make their father's coffin. Crazy. But typical of Richie. Anyone outside looking in would have told him to get a grip and stop being so fucking stupid, but Laura knew there was no point in trying to reason with him. And, anyway, he would've been forgiven anything by his family that day. It was his eighteenth birthday. Laura often thinks of how he looked when he was done. Standing on what was left of the treehouse floor, wearing only a pair of orange gym shorts, his eyes dirty thumb-smudges in his paper-white face and his heaving torso shiny from all the exertion. Her baby brother. Officially an adult. What a way to celebrate.

Karl had built the treehouse not long after they'd moved into The Haven. Knocked it up in the sturdy branches of the sycamore one Easter weekend after weeks of planning and designing and agonising over what timber to use and how best to construct it. Laura believes they were all glad Richie took it down, though none of them actually said so. If Angela had thought it a bad idea, she would have stopped him, even in her near-catatonic state. And Amy wouldn't have been slow in letting them know if she'd been against it. As for Laura . . . her father was gone. It seemed perfect that the treehouse would go too. It was like it shouldn't exist without him. She thinks a lot about what Richie did. About how we often have to go with what we feel is right and not worry about the consequences. To Laura, it's the only real way to survive.

'Isn't it, Frank?' she asks. It's evening now and they're lounging on the terrace, having finished the huge salad Niçoise that Frank had prepared for dinner. She'd spent the meal describing the outline of her plan while Frank had listened, one eyebrow raised in disparagement.

'I wish you wouldn't do that,' he says, uncorking a fresh bottle of local plonk. 'A question must have *some* context, surely. I'm not a mind-reader.'

'I was thinking about the day Dad died. And Richie pulling the treehouse down. How it seemed like the right thing to do.'

He stretches over, sloshes three inches into her glass, pours himself a refill. 'As a way of convincing yourself that you're doing the right thing now, no doubt.'

'And what's wrong with that? Going with your gut is the key to survival.'

He cocks his head, frowns. 'Really? I'm not sure what kind of world we'd have if we all thought that way.'

'Look, you clearly don't approve. You've made that fairly obvious.'

'I haven't said a thing.'

'Exactly.' Frank's wariness hasn't been a total surprise. But she hates when he uses silence to convey it.

'I need time to process it. That's allowed, surely.'

'Take all the time you need,' she says. 'But don't think I'm waiting for your approval.' She takes a sip from her glass. 'And this wine is shit, just so you know.'

'Which is why we're on our third bottle, I presume.'

'I was being polite.'

'Well, then, I shall make it my business to inform Bruno. I'm sure his uncle would want to know you're not impressed with his award-winning rosé.'

'Good. Because I'm not.'

'Oh, Laura,' he says, grinning now, 'it's not that bad and well you know it.'

Laura sighs as she scans the view. The landscape far beyond the villa slopes down to the coast, crammed with terracotta-roofed houses and oblong apartment blocks. Any available space between is filled with green: rocket-shaped cypress trees and tall, wavy palms. The sky is pink. The city lights are coming on. Soon it'll be dark. It's beautiful, but looking at it causes Laura only heartache. Her father loved it here. The family spent many summer holidays at the villa when Laura, Amy and Richie were kids, and in the evenings they'd sit out on the tiled terrace, watching the sun set over the bay. Laura and Karl would talk about nature and space travel and alien life forms – conversations Amy found boring and Richie was too young to comprehend. That was enough for Laura until she became a teenager and the extent of her father's knowledge wasn't enough to hold her attention. She'd wanted to be 'down there' instead of 'up here'. The bright lights of night-time Nice were all she could see, and when Karl realised it, it was as if he'd turned to stone. Together, he and Angela had become one huge boulder blocking Laura's path to freedom. At least, that was the way it had seemed.

'Shove up,' Frank says. 'I think we need a cuddle.' Laura makes space for him on her sun-lounger. He settles beside her, his arm circling her shoulders. 'Meant to comment earlier,' he says. 'The new hair. Suits you short like that. The colour too. Blonde looks good on you.'

'Mum prefers my natural black.'

'Of course she does. She's your mother.'

She elbows him softly in the ribs and he pulls her closer. The scent is faint. But unmistakable. 'I thought you'd quit?' she says.

'So did I.'

'Does that mean there's the possibility of a smoke?'

'It does indeed,' he answers, easing himself up. 'I'll fetch some.'

He's back in a minute with a pack of Marlboro Lights. 'I know, I know,' he says, seeing her expression. 'The healthy option.' She laughs, takes one, uses the citronella candle flickering on the patio table to light it. Frank walks over to the stone balustrade that borders the terrace. It's only now, looking at him from behind, that Laura notices he has lost weight since she last saw him. The trousers he's wearing – a favourite pair, petrol-blue linen – seem decidedly looser around the arse.

'Mum talks to Dad, you know,' she says, after a pause. 'I've heard her. I don't know if she really believes he's dead.'

'Of course she believes it,' Frank replies. 'She just can't accept it.'

She shakes her head and exhales. 'I don't agree. I'd almost say part of her brain is missing.'

'Oh, Laura.'

'What? I mean it. It's like . . . I don't know . . . half her sense went when Dad died.'

'Well, that's what happens. We describe a partner as our other half and it's true. I felt half of me was gone when Lee died.'

'You don't still feel like that, though? Not after four years?'

'Sometimes.' He taps ash to the ground.

Trudy appears, searching for warmth now that the sun has disappeared. She slinks around Laura's legs, then jumps into her lap, treading with her paws until she's made herself comfortable. At least she has the decency not to knead so heavily that her claws prick Laura's thighs. That was the speciality of her predecessor, Chilli – a mean-eyed marmalade tom that Lee had found down in the Old Town one night. A mangy kitten circling a heap of bin bags outside a Mexican restaurant, crying like a baby. Frank had showered him with affection right from day one but it had never been returned. That had annoyed Laura. Made her mad. A creature that clearly took pleasure from inflicting pain didn't deserve to be loved.

The family had been holidaying in the villa the summer Chilli disappeared. Everyone was tetchy because of the heat – not just eleven-year-old Laura. Frank was in a flap but he assumed Chilli had most likely found a shady place to hide and would emerge as soon as the temperature dropped. When Lee found the stinking body in the boot of his car two days later, he and Frank had the mother of all rows over who was responsible. In the end, it was accepted that Chilli must have slipped in after their last trip to the market and gone unnoticed when they'd closed the boot. And that, because the car was parked on the gravel at the end of the path, no one had heard his cries. It was plausible. In fact, it was exactly what had happened.

Laura had witnessed it. But she hadn't said anything. She'd skipped past the car several times to listen to the miaowing. And then, the second day, she couldn't hear it any more.

They'd buried him in the garden, down where the fig trees grow. Laura had done her best to look really sad.

Trudy looks up now with her sapphire-blue eyes. Laura holds them with her own. 'Had any successful hook-ups lately?' she asks Frank.

'Ah, I see. Your love life is a topic out of bounds but mine is open season. That's hardly fair.'

'That'll be a no, then, I take it.'

'I didn't say that.'

'You didn't have to. What happened to that Moroccan guy? Wally, or whatever.'

'Walid. And he's Algerian. I don't know. As you would say, it was all a bit bubble-gum. If love happens to seek me out, well and good. But I won't be holding my breath. It's not as if I've a huge amount of time left.'

'Oh, boo-hoo.'

'Well, I won't be here for ever.'

'None of us will, Frank,' she says, idly running her fingers through the soft fur on Trudy's neck. 'Look at poor Dad. Gone before he was fifty.'

She thinks about the treehouse again. How, after he'd pulled it down, Richie had taken his duvet out to the back garden and fallen into a deep sleep under the stars. Laura had sat on the deck for the whole night, watching him. At sunrise, she'd tiptoed over the dewy grass to where he lay, kissed her fingertips and touched them to his clammy forehead. 'Happy birthday, Rich,' she'd whispered. She hadn't been able to say it the day before.

She watches Frank turn around and sit back down on his recliner. The sun has gone now and the air is cooling. He pulls a fleece blanket from under his body, wraps it around his legs.

'I'm doing all this for them, Frank,' she says. 'You know that, don't you? For Richie and Amy and Mum.' She feels Trudy's body stiffen, her tail thumping from side to side. Something small and vulnerable is surely scurrying through the dead leaves in the garden below. 'And for Dad.'

'I know that, my dear,' Frank says, twisting the butt of his cigarette into the brass plate he uses as an ashtray. 'But this revised plan of yours, it's all a little *fanciful*, isn't it?'

'That bastard Skellion gave Dad a V sign when he left the court room that day. Have you forgotten that?'

'Of course I haven't. Maybe you should've gone along yourself. You could've decked him there and then. Saved yourself a lot of bother.'

'I thought it was best if I didn't go. Exactly because I was afraid of what I might do. I told you that at the time. Anyway, I'm glad I didn't go now. This wouldn't work if Skellion had seen me before.'

'Laura.' Frank sits up straight. 'You know your father was the brother I never had. And that your family became mine when the one that raised me didn't want to know. I love you all dearly. And I'm all for doing right by you. But I'm not sure you need to go this far.'

'Well, I do.' Trudy leaps from Laura's lap, slips through the balustrade and disappears to stalk her prey. 'Mum seems to think that getting them to apologise is going to make her feel a whole lot better. Is she deluded? Probably. But it's what she wants. I'm going along with it for her sake. But I'm not going to make it easy for Skellion. A nice little chat in the comfort of his own home? Not a chance.'

'I'm not sure he's the type that does embarrassment, if that's what you're hoping for.'

'Look, I can think of a lot more satisfying ways to make him pay. But I have to work with what I've got.'

'How can you be sure he'll fall for it?'

Her eyes narrow. 'Come on, Frank. I bet he has an ego as big as a fucking mountain. I'll have him eating out of my hand.'

Frank shifts in his seat, as though he's sitting on something sharp. He makes a face. 'You've never met him. How can you be so certain?'

'He's a man, isn't he?'

'But why not target his snake of a son? He's the one who did the damage. And what about the rest of the gang? He wasn't the only one who got away with it.'

Laura sucks the last bit of life from her cigarette. She watches the dark shape that is Trudy down below on the grass, still as stone as she waits to pounce. Frank sets his glass on the tiles and the cat's head spins round at the noise, her eyes two fiery gems in the grainy dusk. 'I know that, Frank. One step at a time.'

'He's a force to be reckoned with, Skellion. It wasn't for nothing that he gave the fingers to your father outside the court.'

Laura gives him a sidelong glance. 'What do you mean?'

'Nothing. I . . .' Frank looks down, brushes invisible dust

from his trousers. 'Look, he's . . . he's obviously a piece of work. Someone who doesn't take things lying down. You need to be careful. It's a risk. Is it one you're sure you want to take? That's all I'm saying.' He scratches at his beard, rubs his palms over his face. 'I think I might retire. I'm exhausted. You don't mind, do you?' Laura watches her godfather wince as he pushes himself out of his seat and shuffles towards her. He bends, takes her upturned face in his hands, kisses her swiftly on the forehead. 'Goodnight, my dear,' he whispers. 'You know how to lock up. Sleep well.'

When he's gone, she takes another cigarette, stands, leans down to the candle. A chill breeze skates over her skin as she blows a stream of smoke out into the night and watches Trudy's lithe form moving across the grass. Well, that wasn't obvious, was it? Frank's clearly trying to put her off with his ominous remarks. *You need to be careful. It's a risk.* She smiles to herself.

Trudy leaps up onto the terrace, opens her jaws and deposits the limp body of a field mouse on the tiles. Laura steps closer to it, lines up her right foot, and swipes it through the balustrade with a swift kick. 'Oh, Frank,' she says to herself, pausing to hear the soft, satisfying thud on the ground below, 'if you think that's going to put me off, I'm afraid you don't know me at all.'

EIGHT

In the seconds before Karl died, a liquid imagery floated beneath the surface of his sweat-stippled skin. Coagulating with the tissues of his organs, it seeped into the sweet marrow of his bones and formed an infusion with the thick, dark blood in his veins. The sum of the life he had led, rushing and sweeping through the remnants of his survival, a pictorial shot of his time on earth. It was an experience that, had he lived, he would've been unable to describe.

And he'd thought he *would* live.

Hadn't he? Before he'd lost what Angela understands as consciousness, before he'd entered the void between here and wherever, split-second flashes of lucidity must have told him so. The lights can't have just . . . gone out.

Surely he spent those last few seconds recalling what had been and looking forward to the years ahead. She can't bear to think that Karl knew it was the end.

She wants to believe it was pain-free, serene, open-ended. Filled with colour, with feeling, with life. A death filled with life. How ridiculous is that? Stop your stupid fantasising and accept it for what it was: acute myocardial infarction.

A heart attack. Violent. Quick. Over in a moment.

And all while she'd been sleeping. Dreaming. Yes, she remembered weeks later that she'd woken that morning with the clear intention of relating her dream to Karl. What the dream was, she can't recall, just that it was vivid and noteworthy. She'd lain beside him, listening as always for the in-out of his breathing, placing a palm flat on his chest, holding her breath in order to detect his, the thump of her own heartbeat loud in her head. How instant the pain had been when she'd realised there was no sound . . . no movement . . . no life.

Angela is in the kitchen, her body pressed hard against the counter edge. She looks at the vegetables arranged on the wooden board, wondering for a moment what she'd been planning when she'd put them there: one red onion, one avocado; one, two, three . . . six cherry tomatoes, a bag of spinach leaves. She hears the front door opening, the jangle of keys being set on the hall table. Of course. A salad for Amy. She'll be ravenous after her dance class but, as usual, mindful of her *carbs*. Her daughter is twenty-two years old, fully capable of making her own meals, of sorting herself out when she comes in, but Karl's death has brought a realignment of Angela's focus. She doesn't care that they're technically adults, her children's needs are centre stage once more.

She turns to see her daughter drift in from the hall, slide a silky scarf from her neck, drape it over the back of a chair. 'Hello, love,' Angela says, remembering to smile. 'How was your class?'

'Okay,' Amy replies. 'Two didn't turn up, for some reason.

That Brazilian girl I was telling you about and a guy who couldn't take his eyes off her last week.'

Since graduating from college, Amy has been teaching dance in the city centre, several classes a week. She's glad of the work, and gives it her all, but her sights are on bigger things – theatre, the West End, Broadway. Laura seems not to have any such ambition at the moment. After school, she'd been talented enough to gain a place at art college. It had lasted all of six months before she'd packed it in, giving no clear reason for her decision. Since ditching it, she's worked in several cafés, a music shop, and now front-of-house at a posh new restaurant on Dawson Street.

Growing up, there'd been little to suggest that Amy would go on to study performing arts. Reserved, thoughtful, some would even have said shy, she didn't seem to fit the bill. If either of the girls was suited to the stage, Angela would've said it was Laura with her brash, self-assured, couldn't-give-a-shit attitude. Laura demanded attention while Amy earned it through pleasing people, by being who they wanted her to be. By *acting*, Angela has come to realise. After starting college, Amy's confidence grew. She came out from behind her sister's shadow a stronger, more resilient girl. But then, after what happened, she'd changed. She'd begun spending more time at home and had ended her relationship with Mark, her boyfriend of two years. Her commitment to her job and her determination to find her 'big break' remain undimmed but she copes only by being someone she's not, disguising her sorrow with a cheery, I'm-so-happy persona. Angela can see right through it but she plays along. Like now. Engaging in small talk about absent class members.

'Sounds more than coincidental if you ask me,' Angela says, turning to the counter and beginning to slice the onion. 'I suppose they've better things to be doing together than listening to you barking orders.'

Amy takes the comment the way it was intended. 'I don't *bark*,' she says, laughing. 'My classes are a collaborative experience between students and tutor. At least, that's what it says on the studio's website. Oh, and I don't want salad this evening, if that's okay. I need protein. Have we any chicken?'

Angela opens the fridge. 'A couple of Kievs,' she answers. 'I'll pop them in the oven. Won't take long.'

'No, I meant actual *real* chicken. Not that coated stuff.'

Angela lifts out the pack and begins reading the ingredients. 'I can't see anything too bad in them, love.'

Amy gives her a look. 'Oh, Mum. Don't try and convince me. It's okay, salad will be great. Thanks.'

'I'll do them for Richie,' her mother says. 'Maybe you'd bring them up to him.'

Amy tries to hide it, but Angela detects the slight slump in her square shoulders and the way the brightness fades from her crystal-blue eyes.

'Sure,' her daughter says, nodding. 'It's not a problem.'

Which is what Amy always says when it is.

Angela opens the oven, releasing the burned-on memory of years of family meals. She stares into the dark, empty cube for a long moment, thinking it might be nice simply to crawl into it and bake herself away. Sometimes it's all too much. This . . . avoidance. It's suffocating. Pretending that everything is normal. Afraid to talk for fear of upsetting one another; of opening the box they prefer to keep firmly shut. Amy knows where Laura has gone, and why. She's fully aware that Angela drove her to the airport this morning. It's not a secret but, still, they behave as though it is. Talk about the elephant in the room. She slides the pack of Kievs onto the top shelf. As she closes the oven door, panic returns, zips up through her body, into her throat, catapulting her thoughts into the air: 'I'm only doing what I think is right.' She turns her head, as if the sentence was spoken by someone on the other side of the room and, seeing no one but a blank-faced Amy, realises the utterance was her own.

Silence beats between them, eight, nine, ten seconds, while Amy chews the inside of her cheek and Angela wonders whether to acknowledge or ignore the words that are still ringing in her ears. In the end, it's Amy who makes the decision. 'I think I'll hard-boil a couple of eggs,' she says, 'get the protein into me that way.'

Angela reaches for the kettle. 'I'll look after it.' She swallows hard. Amy is against it, the idea of approaching the Skellions. 'Dad wouldn't like it,' she'd said, when Angela had run it by her. 'He'd say leave well enough alone.' She'd said it was crazy, stupid, ridiculous ... even dangerous. Angela agreed with her assumptions. And yet not one of them was enough to make her change her mind.

Not even all of them put together.

She suspects the chances of this idea making any difference are slim. But fear of failure should never be a reason not to act. And if something is already broken, what is there to lose by trying to fix it, however dubious the means? Yes, it sounds naïve. And Amy is right, Karl wouldn't have given his consent. But Karl isn't here any more.

Angela carefully places two eggs into a pot, pours in boiling water and sets it on the hob. Amy sits on a high-back stool, tucks one slender leg around the other, twirls a spiral of hair around her finger and watches, exactly how she used to when she was a little girl. There has always been a composure about her, a calm breeze to her older sister's tropical storm. It has been so right from the beginning. Unlike Laura, Amy was born the day she was due, giving her mother plenty of notice – four hours of perfectly paced contractions, which brought bare ripples of pain. And when she slid out – easily, it seemed to Angela – her eyes were wide and knowing, as though she was already fully familiar with her surroundings and nothing, to her, was new. An undemanding baby, requiring little or no attention save for feeding and changing (at exact intervals, naturally), Amy was adept at amusing herself and capable of falling asleep without being glued to one of her parents. Laura had been jealous of her baby sister. Angela had caught her once, standing over the sleeping newborn with a kitchen knife concealed in her sleeve. Karl had brushed it off, had said it was understandable in a three-year-old. But Angela had kept the cutlery on the highest shelf for a long time after that.

She peels the avocado, slides out the stone, chops the slippery flesh into chunks and drops them into a bowl. She adds some spinach leaves, the sliced onion, the tomatoes. Should she have stuck to the original plan and gone over to speak to the Skellions herself? She'd had it all worked out but then Richie had fallen into another depressive episode and she'd had second thoughts about leaving him. She'd discussed it with the girls, voicing her concerns, and Laura had volunteered. Angela had been relieved. She has no reservations about Laura's ability to carry out her wishes but she's concerned about her focus. The timing is off: it coincides with the party Frank is having for his seventieth. She'd suggested Laura postpone for a while – not just because she'd prefer her to have zero distractions but because it's also only fair that Frank has his goddaughter's undivided attention for his special occasion. But since when did Laura consider practicalities? 'It's perfect timing,' she'd told her mother. 'Kill two birds, et cetera.'

'Couldn't Richie come down for dinner?' Amy asks. 'Just this once. And do you still think it's a good idea not to tell him?'

They've kept Richie in the dark. Is that the right thing to do? Angela can't be sure. She can't be sure of anything where her son is concerned. He might be fine with the plan, he might have a meltdown; he might be indifferent, he might want to be involved. There's just no telling. Being hit across the back of your head with a baseball bat is one thing, but add the sudden death of your father on the day of your eighteenth birthday to the mix and see what transpires.

Coming up to Tory Skellion's court hearing, there'd been signs that Richie was beginning to learn to deal with what happened. Not physically – he was still suffering from blinding migraines and short lapses of memory – but he'd seemed to be in a better place mentally. The prospect of justice had given him hope. The dashing of that hope had swept him right back to square one. Then Karl's death had pushed him over the line, to about minus five. It was like Richie burst the day his father died. Every feeling he'd ever had, every thought and emotion flew out and escaped from his grasp. And now, no matter how hard he tries, he can't manage to gather them all up again. Bits of Richie are out there, everywhere, scattered in places he doesn't go to any more. Angela encourages him, of course she does, suggesting he spend less time on his own in his room and more time being the person he once was, meeting friends, revisiting old haunts, collecting the pieces and putting himself back together again. If only he'd give counselling a chance. But try telling an eighteen-year-old they know less than you do.

'I don't have the answer to either of those questions, love,' Angela says. 'You could try asking him to come down but I doubt you'll get anywhere.'

'And telling him? Do you not think we should?'

Angela gathers the vegetable waste into her hands and tosses it into the bin. 'Haven't we been through this enough already?'

'He's not a child, Mum.'

Something inside Angela tightens. Whatever it is that tethers her to her role as mother . . . widow. Reinforcing the awful reality that Karl is no longer here for her, that she must deal with all of this alone. 'Look, love,' she says, placing a table mat on the kitchen island, lining its sides with a knife and fork. 'I'll think about it. But for the moment let's leave it as it is.'

'What's that smell?'

Angela looks up, her heart seizing for a second at the sound of Richie's voice. He stands in the doorway, neither in nor out of the room, his pallid, puffy face framed with flattened hanks of unwashed, straw-coloured hair. Between his upper half, encased in a too-tight maroon T-shirt, and his legs, enveloped by low-slung grey tracksuit bottoms, juts a milk-pale step of recently formed belly fat, which reminds her of the little boy he used to be.

'It's your dinner,' she says, as softly as she can manage. 'I'm sure you're hungry. And now that you've come down, maybe you'll have it here with Amy.'

He looks at her, then around the room, scratching the visible portion of his stomach. 'What is it?' he asks.

'A couple of chicken Kievs,' Angela answers. 'You like them, don't you?'

He nods, squints, wrinkles his nose. 'Smells like burning plastic.'

Angela realises as soon as he says it. She yanks open the oven door and stares at the melted mess that greets her. Some kind of enormity spirals up from her stomach like a cyclone. It's not panic this time. It's rage.

Not at the wasted food. Not at her stupid mistake.

At every bloody thing that has brought her to this point.

She grabs the molten lump, not caring how it burns her fingers, flings it hard across the room. It zips past Amy's face, hits the wall with a muffled *clack*, sending globs of sticky green goo in every direction.

Angela's chest heaves. Her face is aflame. The air in the room seems solid, devoid of any lightness, like it's congealing on her skin.

Richie stares into space for a moment, eyes cold and vacant, before he turns and walks away.

Amy sits, not moving, a single tear trickling down her cheek.

NINE

It's almost two a.m., and Paddy's still awake. He's been in bed since midnight but sleep has so far evaded him. He has mentioned it to Marie numerous times: how the light from their nearest neighbour's security lamp spills into the room around the edges of the ill-fitting curtains but, to date, she has done nothing about it. She breathes deeply to his right, her back to him, her hair spread out across the pillow. The draughtsman in him is teased by the urge to reach for a pencil, a sketchpad, and trace the serpentine lines of her body, the tentacles of her hair. But the feeling disappears before its grip takes hold. Once, these hours of wakefulness would have seen him produce several sketches of her by now.

He's been thinking about earlier times. The past seems more real to him now, at this minute, than the present. Colours more vibrant. Sounds stronger. Tastes sharper. He wouldn't go back there – to his back-breaking labouring days, to his bleak, hungry childhood. He's not looking through rose-tinted glasses or anything. But there must be more out there for Paddy Skellion. This is hardly the be-all and end-all. He sits up in the bed, resigned to his sleeplessness, kicks his legs out from under the duvet. He used to dream about the life he has now: making a good living from his painting, buying a house in the sun, being at a stage where he can take things a bit easier. Isn't that what everyone works towards? He checks his phone again: 2.02 a.m. Marie rolls onto her back as he closes the bedroom door.

After he's used the bathroom, he slips into the studio. He flicks on the floor lamp, stands before his easel, crosses his arms as he surveys the canvas he started yesterday. He can't find fault with it. There's not a stroke out of place. Every single fleck and dot contributes. There'll be moaning from all of them when he puts up his prices. It'll be *overheads* this and *staff expenses* that. Pity about them. As it is, the retail price they charge means they make as much from each painting as he does. One hundred per cent mark-up? How the fuck can that be fair?

Downstairs in the kitchen, he takes a glass tumbler from an overhead cupboard, then makes his way into the tiny back room they use as an office. He sits down in the dark, turns on the laptop and opens the bottom right-hand desk drawer. He pushes his hand to the back, his fingers finding what they're searching for. It's not exactly a hiding place. Marie knows he enjoys a brandy. It's just less hassle if he keeps it out of her sight. Having her give him a look every time she notices the level has gone down . . . no, thanks.

The screen provides enough light for him to unscrew the bottle and pour two inches into the glass, though he could doubtless do it with his eyes closed if he had to. The liquid is both honeyish and citrusy in his throat, the sensation instantly allowing his shoulders to relax and his head to feel less weighty on his neck. It would make sense to turn on the desk lamp to illuminate the keyboard but some things are better done in darkness.

Marie knows about this too. It's not a secret. Why should it be? True, he wouldn't look at the stuff in front of her, but that doesn't mean he's ashamed. Christ, there's a lot worse he could be doing on a starry night on the Côte d'Azur. He could be down in Nice right now. In one of those buzzing bars in the Old Town, dressed to impress, minus his wedding ring. Then on to a club or a casino with a young thing hanging off each arm. That's not wishful thinking. He's seen it. All over the place here. Bald fuckers with far bigger bellies than his trailing a couple of six-foot babes. All you need is cash. And Paddy has enough of that. A man like him, an artist, a – what is it they call them nowadays? – *creative*: over here they understand. They get the need for renewal and reinvention, the need to surround yourself with youth and inspiration. None of your Catholic guilt in this place. Not that Paddy has ever allowed that to stop him in the past. He carries remnants of it – point out an Irishman who doesn't. He might have left school at fourteen but ten years with the Christian Brothers is more than enough to convince anyone that they have a conscience.

The ones Marie knows about are the ones she'd suspected and Paddy had owned up to. And neither of those had lasted long. Fiona. He'd met her at some arts-festival shindig. Still single in her mid-thirties and up for anything. A chubby redhead, five-foot nothing. Fancied herself as a poet; worked behind a post-office counter in real life. That had lasted about two months. And Lillian, the married sister-in-law of Trevor, owner of the Gorlan, the London gallery that buys Paddy's work. A classy bird, but nervy. Obsessed with her weight, smoked like a bloody chimney. Paddy had invented reasons to fly over and back four or five times during the six months it had lasted and, in the end, Marie had smelt a fairly large rodent. Then there are the ones she doesn't know about: Hannah, Dee, and that wild Croatian bit whose name he could never get right. He's saving those up, an insurance policy in his back pocket, a get-out clause should he ever require it. And it's seeming like more of a possibility, these days.

How had he done it? The few pals he has often quiz him. How is it that he's managed to hang on to Marie, even after admitting to those two affairs? It's more her hanging on to him, really. It's her *understanding*, isn't it? Jesus, she blew her top at first. Weeks, it was. But she'd never threatened to leave, never asked Paddy to go. It was the silent treatment and not allowing him to go near her in bed, that sort of thing. Then it was endless talking, analysing, searching for reasons. Imagines herself as something of a muse, Marie. Likes to think Paddy would be nothing without her, that she provides the inspiration for his work, guff like that. In a way, it's not far from the truth. She's been very useful over the years, right from the start, if he's honest.

They'd met not long after Paddy had come back from working the sites in London. At a session in O'Donoghue's. A summer evening, pints out on the pavement and there she was, with her good teeth and her arts degree and her South Dublin accent. She'd been fascinated by Paddy. Partly, he'd figured, because her parents wouldn't approve. A long-haired, uneducated, inner-city good-for-nothing carrying dreams of artistic success on his back. What was not to love? It had been her younger, more attractive sister whom Paddy

had really fancied, but Roisin has a rock-hard shell that he
has never been able to crack. That night they'd all ended up
at a party in Blackrock. Free booze and plenty of weed. Paddy
remembers little except waking up on a pile of coats next
morning with Marie curled up, like a pet dog, beside him.
That was basically it. She latched herself on and he didn't
object. Then she got pregnant. Paddy suggested she get rid of
it – just a suggestion, mind – but she wouldn't hear of it.

They'd got married, of course, mostly to keep her parents
onside. Her old man was keeping them afloat, paying half
their rent, topping up Marie's bank account with a nice lump
sum every now and then. Paddy wasn't about to chuck all
that away. He was still labouring on the sites but the work
wasn't regular, and though Marie was teaching English in a
community college on the northside, it was only part time.
The pregnancy was difficult. Marie was vomiting night, noon
and morning. He'd thought about bailing, many's the time.
But then she'd left the job, not being able for it, and started
to take more of an interest in his work, orchestrating things
behind the scenes for him, pulling strings here and there
with arty types she knew. She encouraged him to change his
style, got him his first one-man show. He wouldn't be where
he is today without her. He has to acknowledge that much.

When Tory arrived, Paddy got caught up in the whole
fatherhood thing. Not so much the responsibility of it, more
the ego-enhancing boost that having a son gave him, a replica
being to mould and guide whatever way he chose. And as
Marie became preoccupied with all the baby-and-toddler
stuff, Paddy began to find other arms to turn to, ones that
didn't need to be wiped of drool.

Another mouthful of brandy traces a fiery path down into his stomach. His eyes are fixed to the screen, his face bathed in the icy-white light. It's only mild stuff. Nothing violent, no kids or anything. Just flesh, really. And they look like they're enjoying it so it's pleasure all round. Outside, a dog barks, the sharp yap-yap of that ball of white fluff that snaps at his ankles every time he walks down the street. Fucking mutt. Once it starts it keeps at it for hours. He feels around the desk, finds his sound-isolating headphones, settles them over his ears. Much better. This requires concentration. He slides his right hand over his thigh. Any minute now.

It happens, eventually. He finishes off the brandy. What he'd really like is a smoke but Marie put paid to his habit years ago. Must be a decade now and he still hankers. Removing the headphones, he senses something behind him, a movement rather than a noise. A twist of his head and she's gone, but the shape of her is still outlined in the empty doorway, like a watching ghost. He's not rattled. She won't say anything. And neither will he.

Time to call it a night. He closes down the laptop and makes his way out to the hall and up the stairs. She's seconds in front of him, the drift of her dressing gown the only bit of her he sees as she turns down the landing and heads for their room.

It will end one day. Of that he is certain. How, when, he can't be sure. But one thing Paddy knows is that there's more to his life than this. There's a whole world out there. And he'll be fucked if he doesn't get out and enjoy it. The sooner the better. Tory's old enough now. Paddy has done his duty. And if this New York thing proves to be a runner, who knows where it could lead?

The more he thinks about it, the more he realises that it wouldn't be easy. Leaving her, a separation, a divorce . . . She'd want her share, would be pulling and dragging out of him for years. God knows how much he'd end up having to give her.

No. If he's serious about moving on, he'll have to think of something far more cut and dried.

TEN

Laura wakes to the sound of Frank downstairs in the kitchen, the rise and fall of his voice as he chats to Trudy. An understandable habit to acquire, she supposes, talking to a pet when you live alone. She throws back the duvet, swings her feet to the floor, checks her phone. It's late. After ten. Opening the shutters, she squints hard against the brilliant morning sunshine – that amount of light needs time to come to terms with.

The shower is cold. The villa's plumbing has always been temperamental. She towel-dries her hair, throws on the scarlet robe she finds hanging from a hook on the bedroom door and makes her way downstairs. Frank's face, before he sees her, is drooping and grey. It tightens when he catches her eye, as though invisible fishing hooks have pulled his features skywards. So much for his early night.

'You look like shit,' Laura says, shoving her feet into the pair of well-worn velvet slippers she finds sitting just outside the kitchen door.

Frank, hands on hips, sticks out his chest. 'And a very good morning to you too, young lady.' Trudy, curled in a square of warm sunshine by the open back door, lifts her head in mild interest, then gets up and pads over to Frank, twining herself around his legs. 'I didn't sleep well, if you must know.' He runs a palm over his crown of thick white hair. 'It's an age thing.'

'Creaking bones keeping you awake?'

Frank grabs a tea-cloth and whips out at her, catching her on the forearm. 'Cheeky.'

Laura grins. 'What's for breakfast?'

'*Pain au chocolat*. Croissants,' comes the answer from the other side of the room. Bruno's walking in, head bowed under the limited height of the back door. He shakes a white paper bag in the air. 'This is okay? I am hoping you like?'

Frank spins round. 'Dear man! You're early.' He takes the bag. 'No matter. Sit, sit. Coffee's made.'

Bruno pulls out a chair, bends his body into its shape.

Laura is instantly aware of her damp, stringy hair, the oversized bathrobe, the strong scent of the rich lavender shower cream she'd used. Not because she's embarrassed. Quite the opposite. The way Bruno looks at her, she can tell he knows that underneath the robe she's naked. That, only moments ago, her hands had moved over every inch of her skin, soaping every curve. Every indent. That if Frank weren't here . . .

'Early?' she asks.

Frank tips the contents of the bag onto a plate. 'I presume you still want to go shopping?'

She raises an eyebrow. 'You've changed your tune.'

'It doesn't mean you have my approval.'

'Who says I need it?'

'Well, there's one thing you *will* need,' he says, slapping a credit card onto the table.

'You're not coming?' Laura asks, selecting a pastry and ripping it apart. 'That was going to be half the fun.'

He pats her shoulder. 'I'm not feeling it today. Besides, I've a mountain of calls to make. And Bruno will keep you company. Won't you, Bruno?'

Bruno shrugs, makes a face.

'You want me to pick anything up for Saturday?' she asks, before stuffing half a croissant into her mouth.

'Everything's in train, don't worry,' Frank replies. 'Catering, entertainment. Going to sort out some security as well.'

Laura talks through her food. '*Security?* What the hell do you need that for?'

'You can't be too careful. Especially when you're intent on adding to the guest list.'

'Security, though. Come on. It's a seventieth birthday party!'

'Just taking precautions.'

Laura rolls her eyes. Jesus. Paddy Skellion's hardly some gangland crime boss. Frank can be such a drama queen. She presses a finger into the pastry flakes on her plate. 'Unnecessary ones, if you ask me.'

'You look after your end of things,' Frank says, sitting down at the table, 'and I'll look after mine. Deal?' He lifts the cafetière. His grip is shaky, his wrist trembles. He dribbles coffee over the sides of the cups and fills one to overflowing. Laura pretends not to notice. So, it seems, does Frank. She takes a *pain au chocolat* and disassembles it while Frank cheerfully chats his way through a mental checklist of arrangements for Saturday night. His enthusiasm is touching.

He has thought of everything: canapés, a mobile cocktail bar, Chinese lanterns, a jazz band, even a mini firework display.

Laura tunes out. God. Does she really have the right to hijack his celebration? It's his night, after all. Birthdays have always been a big deal for him. All the fuss, the attention. And this one is extra-special. The majority of guests will be local creative types to whom Frank has endeared himself over the years: artists, interior designers, gallery owners, art critics. But a similar crowd will be over from Dublin too. People who will know the name Paddy Skellion.

People Skellion will recognise.

People he won't relish being called out in front of.

And it's not going to take long. Half an hour should do it, all going to plan. So, when she thinks about it, there's nothing she should feel guilty about. Who knows? Despite his misgivings, Frank might end up thanking her for the extra entertainment.

She feels the buzz of her phone and reaches into her pocket. A text. From Mollie. *Hey, you:) Everything okay? Still on track for tomorrow?* Laura smiles to herself.

'What's so amusing?' Frank asks.

'Oh, just something,' she says. 'Fill you in later.'

As she taps out a reply, she glances up to see Bruno's gaze firmly fixed to the part of her chest not covered by the robe.

Yep, she texts, *all good. Looking forward:)*

A chill wind spirals down the chimney and whistles into the bedroom where it joins the breeze slicing up through the gaps in the floorboards. Angela lies still. She hears Amy rising: the soft thud of her feet, the harsh snap of the bathroom lock, the shower's dull drone. No need to check: it's seven thirty. Amy's a creature of habit. And even if she weren't, Angela would know the precise time from the quality of the light round the edges of the curtains and the shadow-shapes on the ceiling.

Laura. What will be ahead of her today? Frank will be up long before her, that much is certain. Always an early riser, when Frank was at the top of his game he was at his desk by eight thirty every workday, having already enjoyed a run out to Sandymount strand and back and a leisurely soak in his roll-top bath. Long before the whole world became obsessed with diet and nutrition and regular exercise, Frank was looking after himself. Possibly more out of vanity than any real concern for his health but, whatever the reason, he has never really seemed his age. The last time she'd seen him, though – at Karl's funeral – she'd noticed a certain slowing of movements, as if he'd had to think for a second or two before doing anything. But, then, that was probably as much to do with his grief as it was with the process of ageing.

Frank loves life. Growing up gay in 1960s rural (feral, he's been known to describe it) Tipperary, he'd spent his teenage years attempting to fix the problem he'd been led to believe that he was. The feeling of profound relief he'd experienced when, in his twenties, he finally realised there was no wrong to right has never left him. It colours almost everything he does. Very little appears to thwart Frank's cheerful nature. Even at the funeral, he'd resolutely refused to give in. He'd worn the flower of joy and friendship – a yellow rose – in the lapel of his crimson velvet overcoat, smiling despite his tears when he took his place among the pallbearers.

From the very first time she'd met him, Angela had been

assured of Frank's goodness and loyalty. Karl had introduced them just a few short weeks after he and she had met. They'd called to Frank's Dickensian-like offices on Fitzwilliam Square where, though it was New Year's Eve, he was busy cataloguing the entries that had already been consigned for his next fine-art auction. On top of that, he was holding a masked ball that night in the stripped-out rooms of the townhouse and had asked Karl to help with the organisation. Angela remembers how he'd gripped her cold hands; how he'd welcomed her as though she were an old and very dear friend; and how he'd smiled while telling her that, though he was delighted she and Karl had met, he was sorry that Karl was now unavailable. Angela hadn't been offended. She'd laughed – as they all had – sensing immediately that a need for true friendship was behind his little joke. The friendship of a brother, a father, an uncle – relationships that had, and continue to be, sadly denied him.

Frank had been in business about five years by that time. At the beginning, it had been just himself. Selling a handful of houses a year, managing several small apartment blocks, conducting lettings on behalf of landlords, he was able to handle it. But Frank was ambitious. He'd wanted more. It had been as much about proving he could reach personal goals as it had been about the accumulation of wealth. The auction side of his business came about almost by accident. A Georgian manor house he'd sold in North Wicklow had been crammed with antiques that the vendors had no room for at their new home, so he'd suggested a sale on the premises. It turned out to be an enormous success. In one afternoon, he'd made more in commissions than he'd earned from the sale of the property. He'd instantly seen the potential and had begun holding fine-art auctions at his offices, which netted him good returns for little outlay. This had allowed him to begin investing in property, the Leeson Street townhouse being the third place he'd added to his portfolio.

By that time, Frank Butler was a very busy man. He'd taken Karl on to fulfil a particular role but, in the office, things had begun to pile up. That afternoon, while he still had hold of Angela's hands, he'd asked her, straight out, if she'd like to join what he termed 'the team'. He was offering considerably more than the meagre amount her boss – dry-lipped, swivel-eyed Mr Canning – reluctantly paid her. That would've been enough in itself, but there was also the idea that working for Frank would allow her to see more of Karl. She didn't have to think about it. She'd handed in her notice at the art-supplies shop the following Monday and was working for Frank a week later.

She'd loved the job. She misses it still. It was everything the previous one was not: varied, interesting, satisfying, and well paid. Frank had been fully accommodating when she'd had each of the children, allowing her as much time off as she'd needed. But she'd always been eager to return. She'd learned so much there over the years, had handled so many rare and beautiful things. And had met so many people.

One of them being Paddy Skellion.

It was just the once, probably twenty years ago now, but she remembers the encounter. He'd sauntered in one summer afternoon with a couple of his own paintings tucked under his arm, arrogantly assuming that Frank would be falling over himself to have them included in the contemporary-art auction he was planning for that coming October. They were crude works: clumsy, inexpert oils of weird, winged creatures flying across a night sky. Frank had turned them down when Angela had taken them into his office to show him. When she'd conveyed the answer to Skellion, it had taken several attempts before he'd fully accepted her refusal. Those primitive attempts bear little resemblance to the work for which Skellion is now known today: slick, panoramic seascapes dotted with deft squiggle-figures under huge, polychromatic skies. The ones he paints in his sun-drenched bolt-hole in pretty Villefranche-sur-Mer. Moving away from those early compositions, Skellion had hit on his winning formula several years later. Angela sees no special merit in it. His success hasn't come from any real talent. Skellion got a lucky break and milked it for all it was worth. Word got round that a Hollywood actor had bought some of his pieces on a trip to Dublin and, whether it's true or not, it was enough to see queues forming hours before opening nights and, within minutes, a red dot on every piece. Nothing like a celebrity endorsement. By the time the Celtic Tiger was in full roar, anyone who was anyone had to have a Skellion on their wall. Or two, or three. Even in the current economic conditions, Skellion survives, his work still selling for four-figure sums. Unsurprisingly, for a man of his character, he's made the classic mistake of believing the money he has can buy him anything he desires.

What Angela wants will cost him nothing.

In the car, a loaded silence balloons between Laura and Bruno. Though he's wearing aviators, she knows he's sneaking glances at her in the rear-view mirror. Arsehole. Admittedly, the kind of arsehole she wouldn't shove out of bed but . . . would she give him the satisfaction of getting him there in the first place? The car smells. Sweetly. Of cherries, warm leather, vanilla. The sun's rays shoot through the sentries of trees that line the road, flickering, strobe-like, the slender trunks momentarily blocking the light as the car speeds past. Laura leans back her head, closes her eyes, savours the heat on her face.

Reaching the city, it appears grubby and brutal after the restful greenery of the hills. Traffic, noise, crowds. And it always seems so much hotter here than back at the villa. Laura can't blame Frank for not coming, for choosing silence pierced by birdsong over slick-haired rich boys roaring their targa tops along the Basse Corniche. Is she getting old, understanding stuff like that? And thinking about Frank? Being concerned? Time was, it would've been him worrying about her. When did the switch-over happen? And since when did Frank pass on a few hours of retail therapy?

Bruno drives into a carpark somewhere near place Masséna. He slides into a space, stops, leans his arm across the passenger seat and turns around. He grins, shows a row of even teeth, which could, Laura thinks, be whiter. 'How long I should wait?' he asks.

She cocks her head. 'Eh, until I get back?'

It's mid-afternoon and Richie still hasn't surfaced. Angela climbs the stairs. Her head aches. She hasn't eaten since yesterday. Hunger is rarely present so she forgets. Pushing Richie's door open a crack, she sees him sleeping, his body an almost-naked X upon the bed. Among the tangle of twisted towels and clothes on the floor lies a tube of Pringles spewing its contents, a half-empty two-litre bottle of Coke and the confettied remains of chocolate-bar wrappers, newspaper pages, toilet-tissue squares. Richie likes to shred paper. Pieces into strips, strips into bits, bits into tiny specks that he rolls between finger and thumb and flicks to the floor. Angela suspects it's to do with control. Finding something over which he has power.

'Richie, love,' she whispers, tiptoeing over to the bed. She touches his back. His skin is warm, buttered with sweat. 'Just checking you're okay.'

A grunt of acknowledgement sounds at the back of his throat.

Her eyes linger on the length of him and, not for the first time, the wonderment of his creation causes a burst of pain that's as sharp as any she has ever borne. What is birth without promise? And Richie had had it all. Such an active kid. Climbing at six months, walking at ten. Sitting still was not something he was capable of. Everything that required compliance or restraint was a challenge – meal times, bath times, changing nappies, strapping him into his buggy or high-chair, putting him to bed – which meant that, almost all the time, one or other of them was in conflict with him. But with his cheery nature, it never seemed like a struggle. Rather, it became a family game – waiting to see which obstacle Richie would overcome next.

And look at him now.

Before Angela turns away, she sees Karl, tall and proud in the family photo Richie keeps pinned to his headboard. Her eyes burn with threatened tears. No. It's not your fault, love. Your leaving wasn't the first hurdle Richie couldn't get over. The race was lost several laps before that.

ELEVEN

Frank is sitting on the terrace in the afternoon sun, peeling the skin from a tangerine. He dangles an orange spiral for Trudy to paw at but doesn't tease, lets her take it from his hand without a fight. He must know Laura has arrived back, would have heard her approaching and Bruno turning the car on the gravel. Still, he keeps his eyes averted, gazing out at the hazy view beyond the garden, chewing now on a segment of his fruit. Laura stands to his right, holds up and shakes her shopping bags. 'Hello? I'm back.'

A second passes . . . two . . . three, as he flicks pips out over the balustrade and Trudy, losing interest in the plaything that was too easily won, stretches out on the warm tiles to lick her paws. Laura brings her arms down by her sides, keeping her eyes on her godfather's profile, watching as his head, eventually, turns. 'God,' she says. 'Thought you'd gone deaf there for a minute.'

His mouth makes some movement she supposes is meant to resemble a smile. 'Sorry,' he says. 'I . . .' and leaves the sentence to dangle in mid-air.

She sets the bags down by her feet. Distracted Frank is not the one she'd imagined she'd be coming back to. Fully attentive Frank was whom she'd expected. All eyes and ears. But she can try to bring him round. 'Shame you didn't come,' she says. 'It was like *Pretty Woman*.'

'Uh-huh,' he replies, his expression unchanged.

'Yeah. For rue Paradis read Rodeo Drive. You'd have loved it.' No reaction. Still, she perseveres, attempting to rouse him from whatever black hole he appears to be floating in. 'The looks on their faces when they realised I was actually buying. Jesus . . .' she flops into the recliner beside him '. . . as if everyone spending five-figure sums has to be dressed like they can afford it.'

Frank is no tightwad, demonstrated by the ease with which he'd handed her his credit card. He has done it before and Laura, despite herself, has rarely abused it. At least, not since her seventeenth birthday. He'd said, 'Treat yourself'; she'd taken him at his word. A pair of spike-heeled Galliano boots, a sapphire-studded skull ring, and a chameleon tattoo on the back of her neck. His annoyance had been sharp but short. He'd ended up blaming himself for allowing her free rein. 'Happened in every shop,' she continues, reaching into the pocket of her jeans. 'Here,' she stretches out her arm, 'look after Mr Visa. He's going to need mouth-to-mouth.'

Frank takes the card, turns it round and round in his fingers. Laura waits. The tangible feel of the hard plastic will surely do the trick. Clarity shows, at last, in his eyes. 'How much damage did you actually do?'

'Jesus. I didn't realise there were *restrictions*.'

He shifts his body up straighter in his chair. 'I didn't say there were but . . .' he frowns '. . . *five* figures?'

She could keep it up but she's tired and hot. And there's no real point in stringing him along any further: he's back in the land of the living now. 'I'm joking, Frank, you idiot. Of course I didn't spend five figures. Not even four.'

'Well, thank goodness for that. Though I don't know which is worse – you trying to bamboozle me or me believing you.'

'"Bamboozle". You use such quaint terms sometimes.' She riffles her fingers through the woody sprigs of the potted rosemary bush to her left, releasing the lemony-pine scent into the air. 'Anyway, I had to think of something to get your attention. You were definitely on another wavelength there. Thought you'd be all over me wanting to see what I'd bought.'

'Of course, my dear.' He rubs his eyes with his knuckles. 'How did it go?'

'Well, it wasn't like *Pretty Woman* at all. The opposite, actually. Falling over themselves to help in every shop.'

'Disappointing,' he says, entering into the spirit, though with no real enthusiasm.

'I know. Would've livened things up a bit. And I wouldn't have been as compliant as Julia Roberts.'

He smiles, just about, then falls into silence. Trudy's claws scratch at a creeping insect on the ground, her tail flipping hard from side to side, like a skipping rope.

'You okay, Frank?' Laura asks, concern getting the better of irritation. 'You're not still trying to put me off, are you? Like, it's a bit late now.' She nods at the shopping bags. 'I won't wear that stuff any other time. It's only for Skellion.' She reaches out, grabs the ribboned handle of one bag, drags it close. 'What do you think?' she asks, pulling out one of her purchases. She holds it up – an ivory silk blouse.

Frank gives it a glance. 'Very nice.'

'*Nice?* Two hundred and twenty euro makes it more than nice.'

'Beautiful. Stunning. Sublime. What more do you want me to say?' He reaches for another tangerine from the bowl on the patio table. 'Your mother called me.'

'Oh.'

'Said she'd tried to call you this morning.'

'Yeah. Saw that. Didn't get a chance to call her back.'

He doesn't try Trudy with the peel this time. Instead he places it carefully, as if it matters, on the table. 'I don't like having to be deceitful.'

'Jesus. You make it sound like you're covering for a serial killer.'

'Deceit is deceit, whatever way you look at it. Your father is gone, Laura. This is exactly the kind of thing he would've expected me to advise you against.'

'I'm not sure the godfather tag is supposed to last a lifetime, Frank. I'm twenty-five, in case you hadn't noticed.'

'Well, why not start acting like it, then?'

That stings. But not for long. Only in a needle-prick kind of way. Laura bites at a thumbnail as she contemplates his barb. Frank doesn't normally say stuff like that. Why's he being so bloody moralistic? It's only a bit of fun. Nothing more. Christ, after all they've been through because of the Skellions, aren't they entitled to some of that? 'You didn't say anything, did you? To Mum. You didn't tell her?'

'Thanks for your trust.'

'You're not exactly coming across as a loyal friend.'

'I've never betrayed you, Laura. I've always had your back. You know that. No matter how bad your behaviour in the past.'

'How *bad?* What, like I'm a career criminal?'

Frank expels a long, slow breath. 'I'm only thinking about your mother here, that's all. She sounded so . . . conflicted. Despondent about everything, of course. But hopeful too. Hopeful you might come home with something for her to hold on to. It's not too much to ask.'

'I'll get the apology she wants. Once I have him where I want him.'

'Well, don't make the mistake of thinking it'll be easy.' He rolls the peeled tangerine from hand to hand. 'Playing games with a man like him . . . He'll give as good as he gets. Believe me.'

She sighs. 'Try all you like to put me off. It won't work.'

'I don't want anything coming back on you. Calling him out in public like that, it could be a recipe for disaster.'

'I'm not expecting him to thank me for it.'

Frank's lips make silent word shapes. He inhales, as if ready to speak, then stops before repeating the action.

'What is it?' Laura asks. 'Just spit it out.'

Frank throws a glance over each shoulder in turn, as if someone may be skulking around the potted plants, listening in on their conversation. 'I . . . Well, I promised your father I wouldn't say anything. Gave him my word.'

'Say anything about what? And it hardly matters now, does it? It's not as if he's around to be pissed off at you.'

He gives Laura his best stern face. 'I'm only telling you because I think it's the correct thing to do.'

'Well, tell me, then. Don't dangle it like a bloody carrot.'

'They had history,' Frank says, squirming a little in his seat. 'Your father and Skellion. Or have. Whichever's the correct way to say it.'

'History?' A cloud moves over the sun. Laura watches her godfather's features soften in the duller light.

Frank sinks back further in his chair. 'Skellion worked on one of your father's projects. Probably, I don't know, fourteen, fifteen years ago. Before he was painting full time. He was a bricklayer back in the day. Anyway, he and your father fell out. Karl reckoned he wasn't up to par, accused him of shoddy workmanship. Skellion was cutting corners, not paying enough attention to detail. Something like that. There was a shouting match. Skellion threw a punch, just missed your father's eye, apparently. Needless to say, he was ordered off site. So what did Skellion do? Got a friend of his to fake an accident the following week – a fall from a scaffold – and make a claim. Got a tidy pay-out eventually. Probably shared it. No real proof it was staged, of course, but your father always reckoned it was too much of a coincidence and I was inclined to agree.' Laura listens in silence, her mind computing the information. 'And that wasn't all,' Frank continues, still tossing the tangerine from palm to palm. 'Skellion contacted the authorities, made allegations that the site was unsafe. Word was, he knew someone high up in the council. A brother-in-law, I believe. Got the job halted. Workers walked off site. The bank got scared, called in the loans your father had. It was a dark time for him. Very dark. He had almost everything riding on that job. For a time, he thought he might go under.' His hands settle in his lap. 'He never told your mother. Didn't want to worry her. They'd only just bought The Haven. He thought they might lose it.'

A flood of heat surrounds Laura's heart. 'But why didn't he say anything when he found out Skellion's son was part of that gang of scumbags? And after that day in court, why was he still keeping it to himself?'

Frank shakes his head. 'I don't know. Didn't want to rake it all up, I suppose. What happened to you all, the break-in, the aftermath . . . You were already going through such a terrible time. You know how he was. He probably felt containing it was better. Perhaps he would've changed his mind later on and told you but, well, we'll never know, will we?'

Laura grits her teeth. What makes people think rage should be suppressed? That anger is a bad thing? 'That's what killed him,' she says. 'He kept everything inside and he basically exploded.'

'We don't know that for sure,' Frank says.

'I think the evidence is pretty compelling. You won't convince me it was anything different.' She chews at her lip. 'Jesus. It must've been such a kick in the teeth when he found out Skellion's son was involved. Jesus, it . . . I mean, it couldn't have been *deliberate*, could it? Skellion wouldn't have—'

'No, no, nothing like that. Naturally the suspicion was there when your father discovered the connection. But there was nothing to suggest it was anything other than coincidence. Anyway, Skellion had already exacted his revenge on your father. He'd hardly have risked his son getting involved all those years later. But, of course, he took the opportunity to gloat when the little toad got off scot free.'

'So that's what you meant when you said it wasn't for nothing that he gave Dad the fingers outside the court. Talk about rubbing it in. Bastard.'

'Well, if you're intent on going through with it, it's probably better that you know what you're up against.' He leaves it at that, changing the subject to ask if she's hungry.

'I'm fine. Bruno wandered off to the market while I was shopping,' she tells him. 'Bought me some *socca.*'

'You hate *socca.*'

'Hadn't the heart to disappoint him.' She stands, gathers her bags, noticing the look of mild shock on Frank's face. 'I know. I must be getting all considerate in my old age.'

Upstairs, she dumps the bags on the floor, flops onto the bed to make the call. She taps loudspeaker and sets her phone on her chest. After a minute the ring tone cuts to voicemail, the familiar drawl that amuses and irritates in equal measure: 'Hey. This is Mollie. I guess I'm busy. Tell me what's up after the tone.' Laura sighs as she lifts the phone and taps *end call.*

She stares at the ceiling, her eyes dazzled by the expanse of brilliant white, and thinks about what Frank told her. He's on the brink. She knows it. Her mother might be conflicted but so, in his own way, is he: holding out one hand, keeping the other behind his back; whining about her plan but booking Bruno to take her into the city and handing over his credit card. And now telling her this. It's not like he *had* to let her know . . . Frank is torn between what he sees as his duty and what he feels is Laura's right. But she's pretty certain he'd be fully onside if he knew some of the snippets she has discovered. Like how Skellion pulled strings to make sure his golden boy didn't get a sentence, how he gave his solicitor a hefty wad of cash and a few paintings in exchange for a word in the judge's ear. Oh, yes. And more. But she won't be revealing any of that to Frank at the moment. If she did, she'd have to explain her source. And that's something she's not quite ready to do.

TWELVE

Breakfast is the usual: scrambled eggs and fried tomatoes followed by toasted baguette and apricot jam. Nothing wrong with that but, today, Paddy feels like something different. What, exactly, he can't say. But definitely not more of the same.

Marie sits opposite him, her hair still damp about her shoulders after her shower. She leafs through a newspaper travel supplement, forking flecks of egg through her dry lips. She glances up as he pushes back his chair but says nothing; she hasn't said anything to him this morning at all. The unspoken – that's what she's getting off on. Trying to express her displeasure through silence. It's always her first line of defence. Paddy won't fall for it. She knows that by now. Still, that doesn't stop her trying. Neither of them will break. At least, not where last night is concerned. If Paddy was to falter, she'd launch into a measured lecture about how disappointed she was to catch him at it but, if he declines to comment on her silence, it'll all blow over by lunchtime. *Disappointed.* That's the word she'd use. Not disgusted or repulsed or furious. Disappointed. A word employed to try to make him feel guilty as opposed to defensive. There was a time when he might have felt guilt, when he first started looking at that stuff, before she found out. But not any more.

He opens cupboards, drawers, picks a speckled banana from the fruit bowl on the windowsill, examines it against the light. From the fridge, he takes a tub of yogurt, groaning when he sees it's one of those organic ones containing 'botanicals', whatever the fuck they are. It'll do. As he plops the yogurt into a bowl – thick and smooth, like correctly mixed cement – he hears a voice, like his father's, in his head: *'Tis a long way from botanicals you were raised*. He peels the banana, slices it into the bowl, sits back at the table. He reads the article's title upside-down: 'The Best Secret Places in Berlin'. It seems like Marie is actually interested, not just using it as a distraction. She feeds herself without looking at her plate, dropping blobs of scrambled egg onto the page. She eyes his alternative breakfast fleetingly, then returns to her reading, sipping her coffee with a sound that sets his teeth on edge.

He never expected he'd be staying with her for ever. Even getting married – he'd gone through that on autopilot, just rolled with it, let her take the controls. Promises can't last indefinitely. Especially when you weren't that sure when you made them. Things change. People change. Life turns out different than you thought it would.

There's that meeting at eleven. He'll finish his breakfast, have a shower, then start painting so that when Laura Karlson arrives he can show her the master at work in his studio. They love that, these adviser types. Makes them feel privileged. Gives them the authentic experience. And whether it turns out to be a heap of bullshit or, actually, genuine, at least he'll have made a good first impression. He scrapes the bowl, licks his spoon, runs his tongue over his front teeth. Marie flicks the page. 'Tips for the Lone Traveller'.

One day, he thinks, as he stands and rubs a hand over his stomach. *One day.*

He soaps himself well, more vigorously than usual, washes his hair using one of Marie's fancy shampoos. Mandarin and Mint with Botanical Extracts. Botanicals. Are they taking over the bloody world? It smells okay. Not too flowery. He squeezes a good blob onto his palm. He needs it. He *has* hair. Plenty of it. Growing thick and long over his collar. He's the exception in the family. Of the five brothers, he's the only one who hasn't lost his hair. Eddie was bald as a billiard ball. The rest were heading there the last time he saw them. Eddie's funeral, it was. He hasn't had contact with any of them since then. Must be five, six years ago now.

If he'd laid a bet on which of them would go first, it would never have been Eddie. Forty-two, thin as a string bean, teetotal, non-smoker. Ran a marathon every year. Climbed Kilimanjaro, for fuck's sake. Twice. Brain haemorrhage in Dublin airport on his way to Amsterdam. Out like a light. Bernie hadn't hung around. A year after she'd been widowed, she'd shacked up with some East European bodybuilder. They had twin girls now, apparently, to add to the two boys she'd had with Eddie. Marie had found all that out on Facebook. By accident, she'd said, though she must've been snooping around. Paddy has never bothered with Facebook, Twitter, that kind of thing. But lately he's been thinking about it, feels he might be missing out.

Dressed, shaved, hair brushed back from his face, he heads down to the studio. Ten thirty. He'll get back to the piece he started yesterday. Better to be in the middle of something when she arrives. Makes it seem more . . . profound, enables more discussion about technique and media and inspiration. The beginning and the end are the more worldly elements of the process, the points at which reality encroaches. Anywhere in between is the artist's alone, when he's fully immersed in the practice and his personal creativity is at its deepest level. Or some such waffle. They love that kind of guff. You have to let them think it's more than it is. That it's not something anyone can do, that it takes an infinitely special talent.

For *fuck's* sake.

He stops dead just inside the studio door. Not *again.* Jesus Christ.

He knows what she's at. This is her way to piss him off for catching him at it last night. Not for her a shouting match, a common-or-garden argument. No, that'd be far too simple. Jesus, he'd prefer a fucking fist fight to this. Sneaking in here at the crack of dawn. Using his paints, his brushes, his canvas. Adding her own touches to his work-in-progress. Basically finishing it off. And, as if that wasn't enough, painting one of her own! With *his* colours, *his* strokes. His entire method, for Christ's sake! He'd warned her the first time, told her it was absolutely not on. Now, she's gone and done it again.

And the worst thing, the absolute kick in the balls, is that even he would be hard-pressed to tell her work from his.

He barrels downstairs. She's clearing the table now, loading the breakfast things into the dishwasher. His voice, when he speaks, is reedy with rage. 'What the hell, Marie? What the *bloody* hell?'

She looks at him as she's picking up the plates, her face calm, her brown eyes steadfast. 'What?'

'You know right well what,' he says. 'I told you before. It's not on. I'm not sure it's even legal.'

'Come on, Paddy. For Jesus' sake, would you listen to yourself?'

'I'm serious! You can't just go around finishing off my work. And painting in exactly my style! On what planet would that be okay? Huh? What fucking planet?'

Marie takes a deep breath, exhales slowly. 'Get a grip. I'm not some fly-by-night out to fool the art-buying public with forgeries. I'm your wife, for God's sake.'

'A fake is a fake, Marie. You know that as well as I do.' He's speaking from experience. In the early days, he wasn't averse to a bit of faking himself. Minor stuff. Percy French watercolours were his speciality. He'd throw one into an auction along with a load of prints as a job lot. Some sucker always took the bait. Two hundred here, four hundred there. A grand, once. 'And it's what happens to it in the future that's the real problem,' he continues. 'Years from now. Lines get muddied. Your work might be passed off as mine.'

'I presume you're talking about when we're dead and gone? It'll hardly matter then, will it?'

'Of course it'll matter! My work is my legacy. I'd like to make sure that anything I leave behind is actually *mine*.'

She stops what she's doing, puts the pot of jam she's holding back on the table. 'Look. If it means that much to you, I won't do it any more, all right? I didn't think it was that big of a deal.'

Paddy bristles, words quivering on his lips. He'd been gunning for a fight and now, as usual, there she is, waving a bloody olive branch in his face, making him feel like a fool for getting worked up. He looks around the room, tries to think of something to say but, simply, nods. She's probably expecting a *thanks* but he's not in any mood to offer one. As he turns to leave she looks him up and down. 'And you should take off that waistcoat,' she says. 'It's far too small. Hasn't fitted you properly in years.'

He storms back up to the studio, his face burning, feeling like he could explode. Feeling like he *needs* to explode. Pressure pulses inside his head, and his chest – it must have expanded, ballooned, it feels so tight. Or maybe it's the bloody waistcoat ... Is it really too small? He'd wanted to wear it for the meeting. It makes him look *aesthetic*. Is that the right word? With its hand-embroidered pockets and mother-of-pearl buttons, it says something about him before he even opens his mouth. And that's important for a first impression, isn't it? He tugs at it, smooths it down, opens the buttons, does them up again. It's no use. He'll have to take another look.

He returns to the bedroom, stands in front of the mirror that's propped up against the wall – a huge, ugly art-deco yoke that Marie insisted on buying at the Monday antiques market on the Cours Saleya down in Nice a few weeks back. He turns to the right to examine his profile. Antique, my arse. They had a mirror the very same hanging in the parlour when he was a kid. Ended up in a skip after his mother died. She'd break her shite laughing at the price Marie forked out for this one. Now he turns to the left, sucks in his stomach, pulls back his shoulders. Not exactly streamlined, he'll admit. A tiny bulge here and there, a slight strain on the buttons. But it's grand, isn't it?

He exhales. Ah, fuck it. She's made him all self-conscious. He peels off the waistcoat and tosses it onto the bed. The white shirt he's wearing, is it okay? Without the waistcoat, will it give the right impression? He surveys himself again. No. He needs colour. He rifles through his wardrobe. His salmon pink shirt. Perfect. Real men wear pink. He's definitely heard that somewhere.

Marie has no idea. It's all right for her. She's not the one who'll be on show. A bit of support – that's what he needs. Not snappy remarks about how he's dressed. As if *she*'s the queen of style. The day has barely begun and already she's managed to piss him off twice. Remarks about his clothes are one thing. But copying his work – that's a different matter. That's something he won't stand for at all.

Her phone, plugged in and charging on her nightstand, buzzes and lights up. Paddy leans down to take a look at the box that's displayed on the screen. Message from Serena: *Of course, Marie. A common-sense approach always works best. I don't have any concerns. I'll see to it today.*

Serena? The only Serena Marie knows, as far as Paddy can remember, is an old school friend, a solicitor with her own practice somewhere in Meath. Or is it Louth? Not someone she keeps in regular touch with anyway. Why the hell are they texting each other? And what about? If she has some legal question, why wouldn't she just ask Vincent, their own solicitor? Hasn't he looked after them for years? If Paddy could, he'd take a look at the message history but, fuck it, he doesn't know Marie's passcode. Whatever. Like he cares.

He takes another look at his reflection, rolls up his sleeves, rolls them down again, fiddles with the buttons on his cuffs.

THIRTEEN

The night they came, it was cold. Freezing. Angela often wonders about that. How it hadn't put them off. A plan is a plan, she supposes. You're not going to abandon an idea like that on account of the temperature. It was February. Spring, supposedly. But that time of year has always felt most like winter to Angela. Colder than December. Biting winds. More chance of snow. And the nights, still so long.

That one had been the longest.

Angela sits at the kitchen table. She has made a pot of weak tea and toasted a slice of bread, which she pulls pieces from now and eats dry. Laura never called her back yesterday. It's no big deal. Frank had said she'd gone into the city, shopping for last-minute party items that he'd forgotten to pick up. She was probably tired when she got back. And now, this morning, she'll be getting ready to visit the Skellions. Leave her to it, Angela thinks. Let her get on with what she's gone over there to do.

The house is silent. Amy left over an hour ago, leaving evidence of her rushed breakfast littered across the countertop: the empty half shells of two eggs, a small puddle of milk, a generous scattering of coffee grounds. Angela hasn't heard any stirrings from Richie, though she rarely does before lunchtime. She'll look in on him in a while. Teenagers need a lot of sleep. She'd read that somewhere recently. And, on the face of it, Richie seems to require almost twenty-four hours a day.

She finishes her toast, sips her tea, looks around the kitchen. The stain from the melted pack of chicken Kievs still marks the wall. Her efforts to wash it off were unsuccessful. And half-hearted. What's the point? Though they'd redecorated after what happened, the room still feels tainted. Marble flooring, sleek, glossy cupboards, stainless-steel splashbacks, designer lights . . . None of those things can cover up or alter the memory that still occupies the space.

It was a Friday. Family night. Karl had come home earlier than usual. Angela remembers the tall, dark block of him coming through the front door, bringing with him the smell of frost and smoky air. They'd sat together in front of the fire in the living room, the dry logs crackling and spitting as they each shared the stories that had shaped their day. Silence had played a part too, long pauses punctuating their chat, neither awkward nor loaded, just comfortable chasms of shared reflection.

Amy had already arrived; she was always there for their end-of-the-week get-together, sacrificing a couple of hours away from her college friends, but happy to do so. They hadn't expected Laura. She hadn't been home for over a week. She'd breezed in, out of the blue, ten minutes after Karl but, Angela suspected, her arrival and the fact that it was family night were coincidental. She was different then: her hair long and black, her cheeks fuller, her body carrying more weight than it does now. When she'd gifted her parents a swift, nonchalant greeting before heading upstairs to her room, Angela had voiced concerns to Karl about their daughter's indifference. He had nodded and changed the subject – not disinterested but resigned to the futility of any reprimand where Laura was concerned. He was simply happy that she was there, regardless of her attitude, and hopeful that they might all be able to sit down to dinner together. Karl, at that point in his working life, had begun to relax a little, to appreciate the comforts the previous years of toil had brought. His property investments had given him a yield that many aspire to but only the astute achieve and, as he was fond of telling Angela, he was looking forward to a time when the children would be fully self-sufficient and they could begin putting themselves first. They'd already discussed their options: perhaps they'd start a new business together; Angela might go to college, study art history or psychology; or – that old cliché – they'd buy a boat and sail around the world. Once their children had found their feet, a whole vista of opportunity would open up. For Angela and Karl, it would be like starting again.

One hour later, that all changed.

Chicken burritos. That was what they'd eaten that night. A favourite of Karl's, he'd helped Angela make them. Amy had put together the salad and the yogurt-and-lime dressing, which Richie said tasted like sour milk. Laura joined them but she'd gobbled her food and excused herself as soon as she'd finished. Behind the family chatter, Angela could hear her upstairs: the floorboards creaking under her feet, the ancient pipes banging and clunking as she took a shower. Or does she only imagine that now? She's not sure. Perhaps what she thinks was Laura was really the sound of them. Breaking their way in.

Splintering timber.

Smashing glass.

Screams and roars and scuffles.

Dark, masked figures around the table. Jittering, swearing, shouting. Arms wrenching Amy from her chair, knocking her to the floor, feet kicking her in the back; Richie lunging across the table, desperate to reach his sister lying foetal on the tiles; Karl, on his feet, arms flailing, winded by a heavy punch, bent double, yelling at his wife to Run! Run! But Angela was rooted, watching the scene unfold, not knowing she was part of it, unaware that it was real. Hands shoving Karl into a chair, tying his arms behind his back. Other hands holding down a struggling Richie, binding him too, while Amy is yanked up, ordered to stand, a flash of metal at her throat. Then Laura bursts in. Unafraid but powerless. Defiant in submission, spitting in the face of her aggressor, her upturned chin taking the full force of the resultant blow. Angela is bundled over beside her, told to *fucking stand still* when she stumbles and almost falls. They want the jewellery she's wearing. She hands it over without a thought.

More shouting, more punching. Voices outside in the garden. How many? Are there more? Two stand guard in the kitchen, baseball bats at shoulder level. Another runs through the house, calling out when he finds the safe, returning to demand the code. Karl's second of hesitation earns Richie a brutal belt across the back of his head. Angela's knees buckle at the sound her son tries to suppress. She grabs hold of Laura but her daughter lets her fall, and she slides to the floor in a crumpled heap. As she lies there, arms around her head, she can hear them running around the kitchen, up and down the stairs, the sound of their feet like thunder in her ears.

Freezing air moves in through the broken-down door. Icy needles prick her skin. She starts to shiver. Gently at first and then violently. She doesn't stop. Not when they are gone.

Not for hours after.

Not until the next day.

The gardaí had been thorough and painstaking. She couldn't fault their tenacity, the manner in which they'd gathered evidence, taken statements, kept the family informed at all times. They'd had their suspicions about who the perpetrators might be. Local CCTV footage, eye-witness reports and on-the-ground investigations had led them to question several suspects but, the lead detective had explained, there was no clear-cut evidence. Nothing that would stand up in court. Except in the case of Tory Skellion. He was the only one who admitted actually being there and 'throwing a punch', which, inexplicably to Angela, they seemed to be suggesting was something that would be looked upon favourably in court. How? Angela hadn't been able to understand. It's okay to break into a house and commit violence as long as you own up to it? How on earth can that be right? When she'd seen him in court, she'd been sure he'd been the one who'd belted Richie across the head. Not that what she thought mattered. Her opinions, and those of her family, counted for nothing.

Despite their hope that someone was finally going to pay for what had happened, the only people who've ended up with a sentence are the victims of the crime.

Karl and Angela had celebrated their twenty-third anniversary a week before that night. A registry-office wedding a month after Laura's birth, Angela had carried their sleeping baby daughter throughout the ceremony, despite her own mother's disapproval. It was bad enough, Rita had wailed, marrying *after* the event, without displaying the child like a bloody bouquet. It was quick, fuss-free, the way they'd wanted it, in the presence of Angela's parents, her brother, Brian, and her godmother, Great-aunt Dodie, who'd thought she was at a funeral and kept asking when they were going to the cemetery.

Karl had had no family present. His parents were no longer living and his only sibling – his older-by-ten-years brother Liam – had left for Australia two years before. (Weeks after Karl had died, a card from Liam had arrived, via the funeral directors. He was sorry, he'd said, to hear the sad news, expressing no surprise that he hadn't been contacted. Angela had felt guilty – she'd forgotten he even existed.) For Karl and Angela, their wedding day held only mild excitement. As far as they were concerned, they'd made their commitment to each other almost as soon as they'd met. The formalities over, afternoon tea in the Shelbourne followed, courtesy of Pat and Rita. It had been stiff, uncomfortable, something to be got through rather than enjoyed and, at four o'clock, when Angela began breastfeeding Laura in a quiet corner, the guests had taken it as their cue to leave. Angela has just a single photograph of the day: an awkward group portrait taken in the hotel lobby by one of the staff. In it, her parents look older than their years. They hadn't known it then, but the eight-year battle her mother would fight with cancer had probably already begun somewhere inside her. When she died, Pat had disintegrated, following her sixteen months later.

It was February of this year when Angela saw the TV programme, the night before what would have been her and Karl's twenty-fifth wedding anniversary, the first she'd spent without him. He'd been planning a surprise trip to Vienna to celebrate; she'd discovered that in the weeks after he'd died. There she'd been, googling Vienna on her phone, scrolling through images of the places they might have visited, when she'd looked up at the TV screen, her cheeks wet with tears, and she'd seen them. Paddy Skellion and his wife, Marie. Being interviewed on some arts programme. Relaxed, smiling, chatting in the sunny garden of their home in the South of France. She'd recognised them immediately and, when the camera panned out across the view, she'd recognised that too: she and Karl had marvelled at its beauty whenever they'd holidayed with Frank.

The Skellions. Living in Paradise. A couple. Husband and wife.

How could that be fair? How was it that they still had each other? That their family was intact? She'd switched the TV off, unable to bear looking at them for more than a moment.

It was later that night, as she'd lain in bed waiting for sleep, that the idea of approaching them had come to her. She had to do something productive. Anger could destroy them all, just as it had destroyed Karl. She couldn't allow that to happen. Reconciliation. That was the key. She'd read about restorative justice and how it seemed to help victims of crime to move on with their lives, how it helped criminals to understand the human cost of their actions. She didn't want to go down any official routes, to have to contact the guards or anything like that. The case was over anyway; they had no more involvement. No, if she wanted a meeting, a conversation of some sort, she'd have to arrange it herself. The Skellions themselves weren't criminals but . . . they were parents. Despite their lack of understanding that day in court, perhaps they'd react differently if Angela could talk to them. Now that the dust had settled, they might be more open to seeing things from the Pierces' point of view instead of just their own. Angela wanted them to learn about the circumstances, to see the effect the break-in had had. Would they even know Karl had died? Learning that might cause them to reflect, to take a step back and show some compassion. Who knew what good could come from approaching them? It could herald a new beginning; bring about an inner peace to replace the sorrow and rage.

She stands, empties the teapot into the sink, throws the swollen teabag into the bin. Is she being naïve? Is it all just wishful thinking on her part? One giant mistake that will only make things worse?

To pass time, she clears out the under-stairs cupboard. Dusty old shoes; odd, smelly welly boots; anoraks and jackets that have seen better days – they all go into bin bags. But when it comes to it, she can't bring herself to throw them away. She's not ready. Karl was alive when Amy wore those runners, when Laura bought that coat, when that woolly hat used to fit Richie's head. Defeated, she heaps the bags into the cupboard, pushing them right down to the back, out of sight but not out of mind.

Wasted effort.

Her throat is dry, her eyes sting and her breath is short

as she climbs the stairs. She knocks on Richie's door, gently pushes it open, calls softly, as she always does, 'Richie, love. Just checking you're okay?' The usual scene greets her eyes – the tangle of clothes and towels, the unsteady tower of dirty plates and dishes, the snowstorm of tiny screwed-up bits of paper. But the bed is empty.

She walks across the landing, looks into the bathroom, then into each bedroom. She searches the entire house.

Nothing.

No other sound but her voice, calling his name.

FOURTEEN

Laura surveys herself in the wardrobe mirror. The silk blouse clings where it's supposed to and the grey suede skirt stretches tight across her angular hips and peachy bum. Now, which way to wear her hair? She tries different styles: piled on top of her head; pulled back tight from her face; left to its own devices – tousled and feathery around her cheekbones. She chooses the last option in the end; there's such a thing as trying too hard. Leaning closer, she examines her face, wipes away a slight smudge of eyeliner, makes sure both cheekbones are similarly accentuated with highlighter. Now, to complete the look: shoes, soft leather tote bag, thin gold chain around her neck. Perfect. Wow, even.

She finds Frank on the terrace, seated on his recliner, blanket draped over his legs. 'Morning,' she says, approaching him with a catwalk strut. 'What does one think?'

He smiles approvingly, stretching his arms out towards her. She leans in for a tight embrace. 'You're wearing Lee's cologne,' she says, as she pulls away. 'Thought you'd given that up ages ago.' She can smell the cheap, pungent stuff Lee used to douse himself with whatever the occasion. A scent that could be favourable or foul, depending on the temperature or the direction of the wind. Like cat's piss sprayed with Chanel No 5.

Frank frowns. 'So what if I am,' he snaps, turning his head away. 'It's hardly a crime.'

Laura straightens her back, squares her shoulders. 'God, someone's tetchy this morning.'

He lifts the glass that sits on the table beside him. 'Not feeling the best. Didn't sleep again, if you must know.'

'Then why are you up? Go back to bed.'

'I might, once you're gone,' he says, and takes a long gulp of water. 'I wanted to see you off.'

'Well, I'm all set, as you can see,' Laura says, twirling around in an exaggerated movement and finishing with a deliberately awkward curtsy in an attempt to dispel Frank's bad humour.

It has the desired effect. His wrinkled brow relaxes. 'Have to say, I'm liking the new look. You bought well yesterday.'

'Don't get used to it. It's definitely not permanent.'

'What a shame. You look spectacular.'

'Not bad, am I? But my feet are killing me.'

'There was no requirement for five-inch heels. That was your own choice. But no doubt Skellion will appreciate the look.'

'That's the plan.' She walks across the terrace to stand at the balustrade, looking out all the way to the sea. The morning air is dry and clear, carrying only the faintest chill with the scent of pine and lavender. Behind her, Frank coughs; weak and tentative, as though he's afraid to fully unblock his throat. The sound makes Laura's teeth grate.

'Wretched spring cold,' he says. 'Always catch it this time of year.'

She turns to face him. 'Shouldn't you be inside, then?'

'Makes no difference either way, my dear. Temperature's much the same inside as out. And nothing beats this view in the morning. Sets me up for the day.'

'Have you eaten?'

'I'll sort myself out when you're gone, thanks. You had something yourself, I hope?'

'Yeah,' she lies. 'I'm fine.'

He sips from his glass again, narrows his eyes at the sound of an approaching car. 'That'll be Bruno,' he says. 'You're ready?'

She runs her palms over her hips. 'As I'll ever be.'

He moves to push himself up, winces, swallows a half-suppressed grunt.

'Stay,' Laura commands. 'You don't have to see me off.' She leans down, tucks the blanket tight around his body. Trudy appears from the shadows and Laura picks her up, placing her on Frank's lap. 'There. Trudy'll keep you warm. You can both nod off in the sunshine.' She kisses the top of Frank's head, strokes his cheek. Under her touch, his skin feels thin and cold, as though there's nothing beneath it but frozen bone.

'There's nothing I can say to make you reconsider?' he says croakily.

'I can't be sure you actually want me to.'

He doesn't reply. Instead, he turns his attention to Trudy, rubbing her back with one hand, stroking under her chin with the other.

'And make sure you go back to bed,' she tells him. 'You want to be better for tomorrow.'

Bruno is waiting for her, holding open the car door. He's clearly impressed with how she looks but she doesn't return his annoying smile. She hands him Skellion's address on a scrap of paper before attempting the complicated procedure of sliding into the back seat while wearing a skin-tight skirt and sky-high heels. She just about manages it without making a complete tit of herself. As they drive away, she settles her Ray-Bans on her face, keeping her eyes trained on the villa until it disappears behind the trees. Frank is not himself. In fact, he's all over the place. He's never got over Lee, still misses him a lot. He probably feels his absence even more acutely than normal this week, believing that Lee should be there to help him celebrate his milestone birthday. Wearing his cologne is Frank's way of keeping his memory alive, she supposes. How fucking sad is that?

The drive becomes smoother as they leave the forest track and turn out onto the road.

'This is . . . work?' Bruno asks, eyeing her in the mirror. 'Something important?'

She gives him a swift mind-your-own-fucking-business smile and fishes her notes out of her bag: some printed pages from Skellion's website and other helpful information she'd found online. She's already read and memorised it but she flicks through it anyway, to give Bruno the impression she's occupied. He seems to get the message and leaves her to it, concentrating on the road as the kilometres speed by.

Villefranche is soon visible below: the curved stripe of white sand; the dark clots of seaweed beneath the clear turquoise water; the harbour dotted with yachts and, further out, a huge white cruise liner docked in the bay. But they won't be going that far. She'd known from the address that the Skellions live further back from the bay, not in the prettier Old Town but on the northern side of the busy Moyenne Corniche.

Her phone, resting on her thigh, buzzes.

Text from Amy: *Have you heard from Richie?*

She taps out a reply: *No. Why?*

After a few seconds, Amy calls.

'We don't know where he is,' she says when Laura answers. 'Mum's worried.'

'You've tried calling him?' Laura asks.

'No answer.' Amy is sounding brittle. 'It's all my fault.'

'What is?'

'I . . . I told him.'

'About?'

'What you're doing over there. Apart from going to Frank's party, I mean.'

'Why?'

'I don't know, he . . . I heard him up in the night and I – I went in to him and we – we just started talking.' She sniffs back tears. 'I didn't mean to. I just thought it might . . . help. Make him feel better.'

Laura smooths her palm over and back across her skirt, watching how the suede changes colour from light grey to lighter grey as she does. 'And did it?'

'He was pissed we hadn't told him already. Said it wasn't fair and all that. I said we hadn't wanted to upset him but, of course, he didn't see it like that.'

'And he just left?'

'He was in his room when I went back to bed. He seemed okay, calmer at that stage. I left early this morning. Mum called to tell me he wasn't there when she went up to his room around half ten. She told me not to tell you.'

'Making a habit of this, aren't you?'

'It's not a joke, Laura.'

'And does Mum know you told him?'

'No.'

'Well, it's not like I can do anything about it. I'm a thousand miles away.' Bruno pricks up his ears, throws a glance in the mirror. Laura removes her shades, gives him a wide stare. She doesn't wait for Amy to answer. 'Look, I'm not really in a position to have a private conversation,' she tells her. 'I'll call you later.'

'Where are you?' Amy's sounding a little desperate now.

'In a taxi. En route to the Skellions.'

'Don't go,' Amy says, clearly on the verge of tears. 'Just leave it.'

Laura rolls her eyes. 'Jesus, Amy. I'm nearly there.'

'I have a bad feeling.'

'Don't worry. I can handle it.'

'Not just about that. About Richie.'

'Look, I'm sure he's fine. He hasn't been out of the house in weeks. It's probably a good thing.' She knows that will hardly make Amy feel any better but what else is she supposed to say? 'You deal with stuff your end, I'll deal with things here.'

'I'm scared. He might do something . . . stupid.'

Laura sees Bruno check the GPS, then swing a right down a street bordered by high, cut-stone walls. Every few yards, through wrought-iron gates, she glimpses the coloured flash of a pretty garden, the gleaming chrome of an expensive car. 'This is the very reason we decided not to say anything. Because we weren't sure how he'd react.'

Bruno turns down a short lane, pulls up in a small paved courtyard not much bigger than the car. On a wooden door to the left hangs a metal oval with hand-painted letters reading 'La Maison Bleue'. The Blue House. This is it. This is where Skellion lives. Laura has no time for Amy's concerns. Not that she isn't a little worried about Richie herself, but that will have to wait. 'Have to go,' she says. 'And remember what I said. I don't want an interrogation about what happens with the Skellions, if they apologise or whatever. We'll need time to talk about it and I won't have it. I have to help Frank prepare for the party. Once I'm back home, we can have a proper post mortem.' She stuffs her papers back into her bag, pulls out a pair of clear glass sexy-secretary specs and sits them on her face.

'Are you really sure you want to go ahead?' Amy asks.

'Everything's already in train, Amy. Even if I wanted to, I couldn't stop now.'

Panic is trying to get the better of Angela again. She sits on Richie's cold, empty bed, clutching her phone, having an argument with herself. Rational Angela says not to worry, he's fine, he just needs some time to himself, it's no big deal he left without saying anything. Panicked Angela says he's not fine at all, says he needs watching, says she should report him missing. Perhaps Amy has news. She taps her number. The line is busy; she's on another call. To Richie? Could it be? Her heart quickens as she tries again. She holds her breath when Amy answers. Panicked Angela blurts: 'Was that Richie you were on to?'

'No, no,' Amy replies. 'It was just something to do with work. You haven't heard anything?'

'Nothing. I've texted and called I don't know how many times. We should start ringing round, see if anyone he knows has heard from him.'

'Mum, I've had time to think and maybe leave it a little while, yeah? I mean, he's eighteen. He's not a kid any more. He won't thank us for going mental just because he decided to head off somewhere for a while.'

'But for how long? And where? All I want is to *know*, so I can stop worrying. Is that too much to ask?'

'No, of course not. But let's not go over the top.'

Rational Angela weighs up her daughter's advice. Is Amy right? Should they take a step back? 'You think we're worrying unnecessarily?' she asks.

'I don't know, Mum. Maybe. He can't be gone more than a few hours so let's just wait a while, okay?'

Can Angela be sure Amy hasn't spoken to him? She sounds . . . hesitant, too *reasonable*. Like she's holding back. 'Could someone have said something?' she asks. 'Something that upset him? Why would he just suddenly take off after sitting in his room for weeks?'

'Let me know if you hear anything,' is how Amy answers. 'I have to go. My next class starts in five minutes.'

When she hangs up, Panicked Angela returns, shoving sense and reason out of the way. She falls sideways onto Richie's bed, draws her knees up and lies still, clutching her phone tightly to her chest.

'It's okay,' Laura tells Bruno, as he opens his door. 'I can let myself out.' She unclips her seatbelt, angles one long leg, then the other out of the car and sets her feet on the ground. 'You're going to wait, yeah?' she says, through his open window.

'How many minutes?' he asks, his palms tapping a beat on the steering wheel.

She screws up her face. 'Thirty? That all right?'

He shrugs his shoulders, obviously thinking he looks cool but his affected nonchalance just makes him appear rude. He knows very well that Frank will cover the cost, however long the wait, so he has little need even to ask. She walks off without waiting for a reply.

An intercom is positioned at head-height on the frame of the wooden door. She presses the buzzer, waits, fluffs her hair with outstretched fingers.

'Hello? Can I help you?' A female voice crackles through the speaker.

Laura tightens her muscles, ready for action. 'Good morning. This is Laura Karlson,' she says, adding a slight, plummy tone to her accent. 'I have an appointment to see Patrick Skellion.'

FIFTEEN

Voices in the hall. She must be here. A few minutes early. Paddy examines his reflection one more time, sucks in his stomach, tosses a lock of hair back from his face. Marie has already put paid to his plan to be in the middle of a piece when Laura Karlson arrives so there's no point in hurrying down to the studio to be there before her. No. He'll walk in on her, make a grand entrance. That might be a better idea anyway. He hangs back at the bedroom door, listens to Marie bringing her upstairs, showing her into the studio and, now, striding briskly along the landing.

'Paddy?' She pushes open the door. 'She's here.' She sounds terse. And cranky. 'Don't keep her waiting.' She gives him the once-over. 'And for goodness' sake, pull down your sleeves. You look like a bloody farmer.'

He follows her, doing what he's been told but then, fuck it, he rolls his sleeves up again. He took off the waistcoat, didn't he? He doesn't have to do everything she says. But when Marie heads downstairs and he steps into the studio, the first thing he does when he sees Laura Karlson is pull them down again.

She's standing at the easel, peering at his latest piece, the one with Marie's finishing touches. Blonde, expensively dressed, with legs up to her armpits and a neat little arse. And her face, when she turns, is about as perfect as they come. Even the fact that she's wearing glasses doesn't detract. Christ. No wonder Marie seemed ratty – any woman would be in the presence of this creature.

She steps towards him, her movement bringing with it the exotic musky scent of her perfume. She extends a slim, graceful arm, and Paddy manages to finish fastening his cuffs just in time to accept her firm, confident handshake. 'Paddy,' she says, smiling, showing a row of Hollywood-quality teeth behind her full lips. 'You don't mind me calling you Paddy, do you? I'm not a fan of formality.'

'No, no,' Paddy replies. 'Not at all.' He clears his throat but the dry, gritty sensation he feels there remains.

'Thanks for agreeing to meet me,' she says, her eyes flashing bright like a tiger's. What are they? A sort of ochre? Amber, perhaps. 'Nice place you have here. Amazing view. Incredibly inspiring, I'm sure.'

'Oh, yes. Absolutely. And the light, the light. So different from back home.'

'Oh, I agree,' she says. 'Ireland's wonderful and all that but we love to escape to the sun now and again. And your move here, Paddy? Is it permanent?'

'Um, semi,' Paddy says. 'But . . . you're *Irish*? Sorry, I hadn't thought . . . your name . . . and you don't sound—'

'Half,' she replies. 'My mother's Irish. My father was Scandinavian. Swedish. I lived in the UK for a while too, which might explain my un-Irish accent.'

Paddy nods. 'Interesting, interesting. And you work for?'

'Myself,' she replies, pulling her eyebrows close together in a half-frown.

Paddy swallows. 'Um, I see. Unusual, no?'

'How so?'

'Oh, it's just that you're so . . .'

'Female?'

Jesus, that's the end of that line of enquiry. He's not falling into the feminist trap. He laughs loudly. 'Not at all, not at all. I was going to say, um, young.' Was he? He's not even sure. He clears his throat again, shows her to the low-backed armchairs in front of the slate fireplace. 'Make yourself comfortable,' he says, changing direction. 'Coffee? Something stronger?'

She declines, chooses the seat facing away from the window, smooths the back of her skirt before she sits. Paddy settles himself opposite, aware that, as she crosses her long legs, one high-heeled foot points straight at his crotch. And she's leaning forward a little now, enough so that the silky folds of her blouse gape to reveal the smooth curve of her breasts. Paddy relaxes into his chair. Her foot, her blouse . . . It's hardly an accident. She's doing it on purpose. She has to be. 'So,' he says, images from last night's session in front of the laptop flashing through his mind, 'this client of yours? Would you like to give me some background information?'

'Well, Paddy,' she answers, 'I would. But I can't. Not yet. I'm sure you understand. He's a very private man. A bit sticky about confidentiality. But, suffice to say, his word is gospel in Manhattan. The art-buying elite trust him implicitly. If he says, "Buy Paddy Skellion", they'll buy. I've seen it countless times. I can give you details, names, et cetera, later, if we decide to proceed.' She rolls her eyes exaggeratedly. 'My job here today is to check you out, if you can believe that. Make sure you're serious about moving forward with your career.' She looks around the studio. 'Obviously, there's no question about that. And once I report back to him after I'm finished here, we can move on to the next stage.'

Paddy purses his lips, tries to make sense of everything she has said. 'But I'm going to get to meet him?'

'Absolutely. He's expecting you tomorrow night. He only has a small window. He's flying back to the States on Sunday.'

Paddy nods. 'Of course.'

'Wonderful. We've arranged an event. A *soirée*, you might say. My client has invited some friends, like-minded people, to his villa here in the hills. A cultural gathering. He'd very much like you to come along and bring some of your work. Slightly unorthodox, perhaps, but that's the way he operates.'

'Takes all sorts.'

'Indeed. I'm glad you understand. Some artists can be a little . . . guarded. You don't have that problem, I see.' Her eyes wander over his face, his chest . . . his groin.

He gulps down the suffocating mass that seems to be lodged in his throat. 'Me? What? No. Broad-minded I am, in that regard. I mean . . . in relation to my work. Open to, you know, possibilities.'

'Great! Exactly what I like to hear. I can see this leading to amazing things for you, Paddy. My client only does this if he's really serious. I've been keeping an eye on you and your work for some time now, had a look at some in London. The Gorlan Gallery, isn't it? Some amazing pieces of yours there. When I showed my client the work on your website, he was incredibly excited.' She leans even closer. 'I'm not supposed to say this but, well, it's just that I'm excited too. Basically, he has an open slot in his space next spring and . . .' she lowers her voice to a husky whisper, raises an arched eyebrow '. . . there was the suggestion of a one-man show.'

A vista opens up in Paddy's head. He sees himself wandering around a vast Manhattan space with a goblet of red wine in his hand, an exquisitely produced, tastefully designed catalogue tucked under his arm. A crowd of moneyed attendees hang on his every word as he explains his motivation and describes his technique. Every piece on the white-painted, perfectly lit walls has a five-figure price tag. And every piece boasts a red dot on its bottom right-hand corner. Sell-out success.

'Don't quote me on that, of course,' Laura Karlson continues, tapping the side of her nose. 'I can't make any promises. But what I *can* guarantee is that, if my client takes you on, you can be assured of his utmost attention. He can be demanding, I won't sugar-coat it, but the pay-off, when it comes, will be absolutely worth it.'

'And what would the terms be?' It's Marie. Paddy swings round to see her standing in the doorway. God, the state of her. Her hair is still damp and stringy, the striped shirt she's wearing is badly creased, and her feet are bare, showing her yellowing toenails.

'Terms?' Laura asks, lifting her chin.

Marie places her hands on her hips. 'What commission does this guy take?'

Paddy's insides shrivel. What the fuck is she doing? This is not the time for all that, and well she knows it. 'We can iron out the details at a later date,' he says, trying not to sound too snappy in front of Laura Karlson. 'There's no agreement yet. We're just talking at this stage.'

'But we don't want you wasting your time, Paddy,' Marie says. 'We've had this kind of thing before, when everything's grand until we find out you'll be paying sixty or seventy per cent commission. That's why we've operated the system where galleries just buy your work outright. I'm presuming that wouldn't be the case in this situation.'

Could she be any more embarrassing? Paddy feels a fiery band of heat around his neck. She's doing it deliberately. To disconcert Laura Karlson. Because she's jealous of how she looks. Because she can see that Laura obviously finds her artist-husband interesting, promising . . . attractive. If she ends up ruining this for him he'll bloody well . . .

'As Paddy said, let's not worry about that side of things for the moment,' Laura says. 'Nothing is set in stone. There's absolutely no obligation. If you're not happy with whatever terms may be offered then we can either negotiate or you can walk away.'

Marie's not letting up yet. 'But you didn't come here for the good of your health,' she says.

'Excuse me?'

'You have a vested interest. Get Paddy on board and you get a nice piece of commission for yourself.'

Laura takes a moment, runs the tip of her tongue over her lips. She's irritated, Paddy can tell. He could fucking well strangle Marie. 'My job,' Laura says, 'is to root out talent for my clients. But I'm not running a charity. Of course I'll get something out of it. And a lot more when Paddy achieves the success we're hoping for in the States. It'll be a win-win for all of us.'

Marie relaxes her stance slightly and that fierce, confrontational look in her eyes fades. 'Look, I'm not trying to come across as hostile or ungrateful. I'm just looking out for my husband.'

Dear Lord. Paddy closes his eyes in mortification. *My husband.* Like she bloody well owns him. Fair enough, she looks after the paperwork, the correspondence, the stuff he hasn't got time for, but she's not in fucking control.

'And that's very admirable of you, I'm sure,' Laura says. 'Your husband is a lucky man.'

Paddy squirms. She doesn't really mean that, does she? She's being sarcastic, surely? He searches her face; she's giving nothing away. She's good. Smart. Easy to see how she's got to where she is at such a young age. But now she's telling Marie about the *soirée* tomorrow and saying she has to come. 'My client would expect it,' she says. 'He'd want to meet you both.'

Shit. Paddy shakes his head. 'Oh, I – I'm not sure it'd be Marie's thing, really.'

Marie makes a grunt of indignation. 'I'll decide that.'

'Good for you,' Laura says, smiling. 'Tell him who's boss.' She's being all pleasant now that Marie's down off her high horse, making sure she has her onside. 'You absolutely must come. You'll enjoy it.'

'Well, Paddy's right. Usually I'd decline, leave that sort of thing to him. But,' she laughs, 'someone's got to make sure he doesn't sign his life away.'

There goes Paddy's chance. And he's certain he would've had one. He'd already thought it out: play hard to get with the client, pretend he's not interested, make it clear to Laura he'll only agree to a deal if she gives him some . . . How would he put it? Satisfaction. See how badly she wants her cut when it's in jeopardy. Fat chance of that now, with Marie hovering around keeping tabs on him.

'Trust me,' Laura says, 'you'll enjoy it. And it could turn out to be quite a momentous occasion.'

The intercom buzzer sounds and Marie excuses herself. Paddy leans back in his chair again. Fuck it, she's probably right to be cautious, to question Laura Karlson, who, let's face it, they know nothing about. Still, even if the whole thing turns out to be a waste of time, he would've fancied his chances.

And what's going on with Marie? She can be a pain in the neck but she's not normally so stroppy. Could it be to do with that text he saw? Is it something she hasn't got around to discussing with him yet, or something she doesn't want him to know?

As he listens to her padding downstairs, he pictures her losing her footing, sliding, tumbling head first onto the flagstones in the hall . . .

Laura continues talking, enthusing about the pieces Paddy has in the studio. 'I particularly admire that one,' she's saying. 'It has a depth that's incredibly alluring, almost as though you could fall into it and find yourself in another world, another dimension.' Paddy puffs out his chest and turns, only to see she's pointing to the piece leaning against the leg of the easel. Marie's. He'd meant to hide it behind his stack of finished works but, with Marie making him go and change and Laura being early, he hadn't had a chance.

'Oh, that one,' he says, trying to sound offhand. 'I wasn't sure about it myself. Not one of my favourites.' He can't tell her the truth. How would that make him look? Hardly unique, if his work is so easily duplicated.

'Oh, you don't really think that, now do you, Paddy?' she says, batting her long eyelashes. 'An artist of your ability. You've no reason to doubt yourself.' She uncrosses her legs, places her feet flat on the floor, leaves a gap between her knees. 'And tomorrow evening, everything's going to sky-rocket. Your life, your career, your happiness. It's as good as done. Believe me. I'm in control.' Paddy feels a stirring between his legs. She's displaying all the right signals. But he can't come across as over-eager, as much as she's clearly giving him the come-on. He smiles, just about, enough to let her know he understands. 'I'm really looking forward to introducing you,' she says. 'You and your . . .' she grins '. . . lovely wife.'

How's that going to work out, if Marie's there? Why the hell did she have to invite her?

As if she can read his mind, Laura says, 'It's important that she comes along, Paddy. There's no one better placed to talk you up. While you and I slip away to a quiet corner to discuss . . . arrangements, she can keep my client engaged, make sure you're still the topic of conversation even when you're not in the room.'

Paddy nods. Of course. She has it all worked out. This is no amateur he's dealing with here. In every sense.

He listens as she tells him she can't disclose the location but that she'll send a driver to pick them up at seven p.m. No need to dress up, she says. Her client likes his artists to appear . . . authentic. And no gifts, she adds, their presence is all that's required. Along with the examples of Paddy's work. 'And don't worry about presentation,' she says. 'We have plenty of easels we can use for display purposes.' She leans into her bag, checks her phone, replaces it. Cocking her head, she says, 'Sounds like you have visitors.'

Paddy had been aware of a conversational hum coming up from the hall and it's only now, as Laura has mentioned it, that it fully registers.

'I really must be going,' she says, standing up.

Paddy gets to his feet. He contemplates moving in and kissing her cheeks in the French way that everyone seems to use nowadays, but he's not quick enough and she thrusts her hand out before he can make up his mind. But the touch of her fingers is enough to excite.

A squeeze like that means so much more than a handshake.

As he follows her downstairs, he sees Marie in the hall, her hands waving about to add emphasis to her exclamations. On the floor lie two bags – a beat-up sports hold-all and a fraying khaki rucksack. Marie looks up at Paddy over the top of Laura's head. 'I thought they weren't coming till Sunday!' she says. 'They wanted to surprise us!'

Paddy hasn't forgotten about Tory's arrival, but he's shoved it to the back of his mind. Seeing his son now, the pale, stringy length of him stepping out from behind his mother, the most he can admit to feeling is satisfaction. Not happiness or delight or pride. He's merely *satisfied* that Tory is here and not locked up in St Patrick's or God-knows-where. Even if he had received a sentence, the likelihood is that it'd be over now, but Paddy would've been standing here on the stairs, looking down at his son, knowing he'd served time. He never needs much to convince himself that he did the right thing.

But . . . *they?*

There's a girl. With tattooed arms and a head full of those twisted ropes, whatever they're called. She's small and thin, almost elfin, but looks older than Tory, probably by several years, and his eyes don't leave her, like he's afraid she might disappear.

'Well, this much isn't a surprise,' Marie says. 'I knew Tory wasn't coming alone.' She beams at Paddy, well aware that he won't say anything about her keeping that from him, not in front of Laura Karlson. But what does it matter anyway? Leave them to their little secrets. Paddy doesn't care.

'Oh, you must both come tomorrow,' Laura says. 'I insist.'

Marie briefly explains about 'tomorrow' with exaggerated enthusiasm, trying to make the *soirée* sound attractive. Good luck with that, Paddy thinks.

But the girl's already wide eyes widen further. 'We'd love to. Yeah, Tory?' she says. 'Sounds awesome.' Paddy can tell, from her drawl, that she's American.

Tory smiles. A big gormless grin. Clearly, he'd walk over hot coals for the girl if she asked him to.

'I'm sorry,' Marie says. 'Forgive my manners. Let me introduce you. This is our son, Tory. He's just flown in from Dublin.'

'Pleased to meet you,' Laura says, shaking his hand.

Marie steps aside, and Paddy can see the girl in more light now. She's wearing those skinny-type jeans, a sleeveless leopard-print thing and a pair of clunky black boots with a silver chain across the heel. Her face is attractive – heart-shaped, with high cheekbones and clear, yellowish skin – but might be more so without the piercings in her eyebrow and lower lip. It's difficult to say. But, then, there aren't many who could stand up to scrutiny beside the likes of Laura Karlson. For some reason, the girl reminds Paddy of Marie when he first met her. There's no resemblance. Maybe it's just that he sees himself in Tory, can sense his delusion, his blind attachment to someone he's temporarily mistaken for a goddess.

'And now,' Marie says to Paddy and Laura, as though she's announcing a circus act, 'hailing originally from Annapolis,

Maryland, but living in Ireland for the past . . . four years, is it?'

'Five,' the girl says, directing her focus to Laura. 'Five and a half, if you wanna be exact.'

'Long enough to call yourself Irish, I'm sure.' Marie laughs, as if she's said something amusing. She places a hand on the girl's lower back, gently pushing her into the middle of the hall. 'This is Tory's girlfriend,' she says. 'This is Mollie.'

SIXTEEN

'**M**ollie?' Frank wears a puzzled face. 'Sorry, Laura, I don't understand. What are you saying? What does all this mean?'

Laura drops her bag on the floor, plonks herself heavily on the bed. 'Jesus, Frank, what part of it don't you understand? It's fairly simple.'

'For you, perhaps. But not for me. It's all so . . .' he waves a hand around '. . . Machiavellian.'

'It's just a means to an end. All the better if Tory Skellion is here too.' She lifts each leg in turn and prises her shoes off her feet. 'And it's given me some interesting bits of info about his father.'

Frank shuts his eyes, raises a forefinger in the air. 'So, let me get this straight. You got the American psycho to inveigle her way into young Skellion's social circle and use her, um, charms, to win his heart?'

'Yes. That. More or less.'

'And he fell for it?'

'Seems so. Why wouldn't he? Mollie's very . . . What's the word? Charismatic?'

Frank surveys her through half-open lids. 'Not a word I'd have used.'

Laura makes herself more comfortable, tucks her legs up. She'd arrived back at the villa to find Frank in bed but not asleep. Propped up on the pillows, last week's *Sunday Times* on the duvet and his reading glasses balanced on the tip of his nose. She'd filled him in on how the meeting had gone and he'd listened without comment until she'd mentioned Mollie.

'Keeping me in the dark about her being part of your plan?' he asks. 'Now, why was that, I wonder? Because you knew I wouldn't approve. Isn't that it? Am I right, or am I right?'

'Partly. And because I wasn't sure it was going to happen. Like, Mammy Skellion had booked flights for them and stuff but apparently Tory was a bit freaked. Never brought a girl home before, apparently.'

Frank reaches for a Milky Mint from the bag on his bedside locker, twists one out of its wrapper, pushes it into his mouth. He thinks for a moment as he works it round, clacking it against his teeth. 'But surely,' he says, tonguing it into his cheek, 'Tory Skellion would've recognised you today? From that night? The break-in? Or even from around?'

Laura sits up straight, holds out her arms. 'Come on, Frank. I don't look anything like I did back then. I'm more than a stone lighter for one. And I've cut my hair and dyed it blonde, don't forget. Not to mention the way I was dressed and that I toned down the eyeliner *and* was wearing glasses. Oh, and I put on an accent too. Said I'd lived in the UK for a while.'

'I see. I'm not sure I'd have been fooled.'

'Tory Skellion's a fucking dope. I doubt I even registered

with him that night. He was off his head. I mean, he might've thought I reminded him of someone today but that'd be it. He was staring at Mollie the entire time anyway. She has him on a lead.'

'So he thinks it's the real thing? True love?'

'Course he does. Mollie's an expert.'

'You've no qualms? No pricking of conscience?'

'If you're asking do I feel guilty, then, no.' She yawns, stretches. 'It was all her idea to pretend to be his girlfriend anyway. And I have to say it was a good one.'

'Why am I not surprised?' Frank says. 'I just hope you can keep a rein on everything. That it all doesn't start spinning out of control. I'm not going to pick up the pieces.'

'Thanks for the support. Much appreciated.'

Frank chews, swallows, welcomes Trudy as she curls her fluffy body around the door and leaps onto the bed. 'Why was she so eager to do it?' he asks. 'What's in it for her? I mean, does she actually *like* the chap?'

'That's totally not relevant. She's doing me a good turn. That's all.'

'And how did she go about it? How did she find her way in?'

'Jesus, stop quizzing me, Frank. It wasn't difficult. She found out his haunts, made a point of being there, chatted him up, blah-blah-blah.'

'And he actually fell for it?'

'Well, obviously. Why is that so hard to believe?'

'Bit of an age gap, isn't there?'

'Exactly. Older woman and all that. Couldn't believe his luck.'

'If you say so.'

Frank has made his point. Hammered it home. Any attempt to change his opinion would be futile. Laura reaches out, finds Trudy's tail and plays with the long, soft hairs. Mollie has done well. They're two of a kind, she and her – it's why they get along. Sure, there was all that bitching when they fell out but, even then, Laura had enjoyed the edge-of-your-seat thrill. It's illogical, she knows, but it almost seems as though it's Mollie's unpredictability that's dependable. The plan to fly over with Tory – she'd had to trust her on it, never truly certain that Mollie would get it over the line. Laura had texted her on the way back to the villa – *I love it when a plan comes together :)* – but had received no reply. That's not unusual for Mollie but it's possible she couldn't have texted even if she'd wanted to. Poor bitch is more than likely under interrogation. Marie had been welcoming and hospitable, but that had been in front of 'Laura Karlson'. Mollie looking like she does, on top of being older than Tory by five years, would surely result in her being given the third degree. Laura shudders. God, she'd only had to shake Tory's hand. Mollie's had to go a lot further than that.

She turns her face, speaks into the duvet. 'Richie's gone AWOL.'

Despite the muffled words, Frank hears her correctly. 'Oh, God. When?'

She comes up for air. 'Sometime in the night. Maybe early this morning. Amy called me. I'm not supposed to know.'

'Never a dull moment. It's only a few hours, though. Nothing to get too worked up about.'

'That's what I said. But Amy's in a bit of a state, thinks she's to blame. She let the cat out of the bag about me coming over to talk to the Skellions.'

'I see.' Frank takes a moment to think. 'I'm sure there's nothing to worry about,' he says, not altogether convincingly. He finds Laura's hand, grasps it tightly. 'But I'm also sure your mother will want to speak to you soon enough. Have you thought about what you'll say about the, um, meeting?'

'I'm not saying anything until I get home. That was the condition I made when I agreed to talk to Skellion.'

Frank balks. 'And she was okay with that? To be patient for that long?'

'She'd no choice. I'll tell her the truth once it's all over but I'd prefer not to do it on the phone. If she goes ape-shit it's easier to calm her down if I'm actually there. And it's only a couple of days, anyway. I did tell you I'm flying back on Monday.'

Franks picks at a loose thread on his sheet. 'You did. I just wish it wasn't so soon. I'll still only be semi-conscious after the party at that stage.'

'If you even make it that far,' she jokes. She pushes herself up. 'Come on, up you get. That's enough lazing in bed. I'll go and get changed. Can't wait to get back into some normal shit.' She walks to the door, stops, turns. 'Lunch? On the terrace? I'll sort something out. We can go over the order for tomorrow night.'

A weak smile plays on his lips. 'Lovely, my dear. No need to go to too much trouble. Just something light. Not feeling very hungry.'

When she reaches her room, she takes her phone from her bag. Fuck. Missed call from Richie. She calls back immediately but he doesn't pick up. She tries Amy – same thing. Probably in a class. She texts: *Had a missed call from Richie. Didn't answer when I called back. At least we know he's alive.*

'Why Laura?' Angela asks Amy, when she calls. She's puzzled. 'Why didn't he call you? Or me?' Laura's not even in the country. Richie knows that. Though he thinks the sole purpose of her trip is to attend Frank's party.

'I don't know, Mum,' Amy replies. 'Laura just . . . well, she just thought she'd give me the heads-up. In case there was anything wrong. Contact from Richie is unusual, even when we *know* where he is.'

'You didn't say anything, did you? She doesn't know what's happened?' Angela unlocks the front door, hoping she might see her son walking up the driveway.

'I said I wouldn't, didn't I? Though I don't know why we have to keep it from her.'

'We'll deal with it here. She has enough on her plate. Had she been to the Skellions' place? Did she say?'

'She was on her way.'

Damp, earthy air hits Angela's lungs as she steps outside. 'This is all such a mess. I wish to God he'd called you or me. Or answered when she'd called him back.'

'Look,' Amy says. 'At least we know he's okay, that he's . . .'

'Not really. He could be . . . He could've . . . Someone might've found his phone somewhere. Chosen a random number to call.'

'If that was the case, the first contact they'd look for would be MUM.'

Angela looks up at the threatening grey cloud. 'He could be in some kind of trouble. Could be caught up in something we know nothing about. Maybe he felt he could trust Laura.' The tears she'd only managed to stop a few minutes ago return to prick her eyes. 'More than me or you.'

'Don't be reading too much into it, Mum. Your imagination's going into overdrive. Richie's fine. I know it. Stop worrying. This is just him being himself.'

'If it goes beyond this time tomorrow I'll have to report him missing.'

'Sit tight. We'll keep trying his phone.'

'Why would he just take off when he hasn't been outside the house in weeks? Something must've happened to trigger it.'

'Have to go, Mum,' Amy says, as the heavens open. 'Call you after my class.'

Angela makes her way down the curving, tree-lined driveway. How had Laura got on with the Skellions? Had they even been in when she'd called? Angela had agreed not to discuss the outcome until Laura comes home. She doesn't see the sense of it but Laura had insisted. What with Frank's party and everything, Laura had said, it was logical to wait until they could both sit down together and have a proper talk. Now she's glad she doesn't have to go through any aftermath. Whatever happened can wait. Nothing that went on could be more important than finding Richie. Angela can't concentrate on anything else.

She stands now at the open gate watching the traffic zip by, not caring about the pouring rain.

SEVENTEEN

The buzz of Laura's phone wakes her at 3.11 a.m. She reaches out, holding her breath, instinctively expecting RICHIE to be displayed on the screen. Instead, it's MOLLIE that shines through the darkness and Laura exhales a groggily whispered, 'What's up, girl?' when she answers the call.

'Crazy shit goin' down here,' Mollie says. 'Motherfuckin' crazy.'

Laura pushes herself up on her elbow. 'What?'

'Can't talk long. I'm in the bathroom. I'm guessin' Baby Boy's gonna come lookin' for me any minute.'

'What's happening? What's going on?'

'Big fuckin' fight is all.'

'Between who? You and the kid?'

'Mom and Pop. One of those loud-whisper bust-ups.'

'Not surprised. It's obvious they're operating at different levels. Definite tension there.'

'Heard your name bein' tossed around,' Mollie says. 'Your alias, I should say.'

'Seriously? I had that much of an effect? Are they scrapping about me?'

'Can't tell. Though I'd say you left an impression all right. You looked fuckin' unreal today.'

'Rocked it, didn't I? You should've seen Paddy's face when he saw me. Had him totally onside. Then she came in and started picking holes. That bit was hairy. But I played it cool. Made out like she was the one in charge and she came round easy. Surprise, surprise, he didn't want her to come tomorrow, told her it wasn't her thing, but she basically told him where to get off.'

'When you left, Tory was like "Why the fuck did you say we'd go? It's gonna be shit." And I was like "Trust me. The booze'll be flowin' like water. Always is at these kinda things." That changed his attitude. "It's a big deal for your pop," I said. "Be mature and show your support." He likes it when I take the lead.'

'Taxi's going to pick you all up at seven, okay?'

'Cool. If they don't kill each other first.'

'It's that bad?'

'Well, Baby Boy coughed up a little story when we were lyin' on the sofa listenin' to Mom and Pop havin' their brawl upstairs. Seems Pop was caught up in some kinda trouble in London back in the day.'

'Yeah? Like what?'

'Beat the crap outta some guy in the street, left him for dead.'

'And was he?' Laura sits up straight in the bed. 'Did he kill him?'

'Who knows? He got the hell outta Dodge next morning. Didn't hang around to find out.'

'How does Tory know?'

'Pop was rat-assed one night after one of his shows a coupla years ago. Was givin' Baby Boy the whole arm-around-the-shoulder-speakin'-from-experience-keep-outta-trouble talk. Probably doesn't even remember sayin' it but, point is, keep it in mind.'

'Must be in the blood.'

'Seems so.' Mollie's voice becomes indistinct, like she's under water. Laura almost hangs up but then she's back, clear again. 'Gotta go. Baby Boy's callin' out for me like he's a lost pup. Christ.'

Laura smiles. 'What're the sleeping arrangements?'

'Not sure. But I hope to fuck they're acceptable.'

'And what's acceptable?'

Mollie whispers. 'Now, that'd be tellin'.'

Dawn. Amy snores lightly on the couch, her head lolling awkwardly between two cushions. Angela gets up from her chair, pulls the soft throw over her daughter's shoulders, tucks the edges of it around her long legs. The room smells of ginger, cold chicken and sweet chilli sauce. They'd ordered a takeaway last night. Some local Chinese place Amy had suggested. Foil containers sit on the coffee table, a translucent film glazed over their uneaten contents. The TV screen flickers on the wall. Sky News on mute. Angela has kept it on throughout the night. Unable to sleep, she'd sat watching the hourly repeated reports of worldwide bloodshed, unrest and catastrophe until she knew their order by heart.

No contact from Richie. She opens her phone again, sees

she's called him nine times and sent six texts. Where is he? Why hasn't he answered, replied, called? Is he in trouble? She doesn't mind if he wants to be alone but the least he could do is say he's okay. The only glimmer of hope is his missed call to Laura. But for that, Angela might already have gone out of her mind.

She has told no one else. She can't. Not yet. She has to keep it contained between herself and Amy. Here, within the house, this room, until it's resolved. Once she lets it out, it becomes something more than she hopes it is: nothing.

She wants so much for it to be nothing.

Even if she did tell, what could anyone do? She can't burden Frank with it. Not today. He deserves to have his celebration without worry. And it wouldn't be fair to expect him not to tell Laura. There are no friends who would understand, let alone be able to help. Since Karl died, the couples they used to know seem to have distanced themselves from her. Or has she distanced herself? Perhaps it's a little of both. There's Brian, her brother, but how effective has he ever been during family emergencies? Unmarried and childless, he has no concept of what it's like to be concerned for someone other than himself. After the break-in, his primary emotion was one of relief that he hadn't had to personally experience it.

The only person she wants to tell, she can't.

But that doesn't stop her asking for his help, begging him to give her something to hold on to, some small sign that everything will be all right. She sits back down beside the empty fireplace, staring into the black chasm where no fire has been lit since Karl died. She opens *Photos* on her phone, scrolls to find one she'd taken during a holiday at the villa. Richie's smile . . . Could it be any wider? There he is, sitting on the terrace wall, swinging his legs over the balustrade. And Karl behind him, a protective grip on his son's shoulders, his face a picture of love and pride. You'll look after him, won't you, love? If anything happens, if anything *has* happened, you'll make sure that he's safe? She fights hard against it but sleep finally claims her, dragging her into its depths. And he's there. A beaming Richie. The clear outline of his boy-body. Stark, against the bluest sky.

Frank is at the front door, taking delivery of what looks like the entire contents of a florist's when Laura comes downstairs. She stops on the last step to read Amy's latest text: *Still nothing. Mum's asleep. Think she stayed awake most of the night.*

Laura replies: *You've tried contacting his friends, yeah?*

Amy texts: *As many as we have details for. None had any info. Not sure how much he's in contact with any of them. I know I'm not supposed to ask but . . . Yesterday? Did you talk to them? Did anything good happen?*

Laura thinks carefully. Her reply needs to be enough to keep Amy happy, without being dismissive. She decides on: *It was constructive. I think we can afford to be positive.* Waffle. But it sounds good.

Amy seems satisfied enough: *Can I say that to Mum??*

OK. Be in touch later. Have to help Frank with stuff. Any news, call me x

'What's the problem? Am I invisible?' Frank complains from behind a huge arrangement of thick green stalks topped with clusters of gold and crimson berries. 'This thing weighs a ton.'

Laura stuffs her phone into her back pocket. 'Just texting Amy. Still no word from Richie.' She relieves Frank of his burden.

'Living room,' he orders. 'Sideboard.' He follows a moment later, breathless, carrying a minimalist display of orchids and squiggly twigs. He slaps it down on a side table, exhales and launches into a coughing fit.

'God, Frank,' Laura says. 'Why didn't you ask the delivery guy to bring them in here?'

'Wasn't sure where exactly I wanted them,' he says, after clearing his throat. 'I'm still not.' He nods at the sideboard. 'That one doesn't look right there. Bring it back out to the hall, would you? I think it'll look better on the console.'

Laura raises her eyes behind his back. As if it fucking well matters. Typical Frank – details, details. And to hell with the fact that he's not feeling well: the show must go on, regardless. 'Let me guess,' she says. 'Didn't sleep again?'

'What? No, I . . . Well, not great. Blasted cough.'

'Get it seen to. Ever heard of doctors? I believe they can do amazing things.' She lifts the display. 'What's the story with the lights? I presume you've someone coming to help.'

Frank turns his wrist to look at his watch. 'Should be here soon. Some guy Walid recommended. He's going to come back and look after the fireworks tonight too.'

'Thought Walid was out of the picture.'

'He's still a friend, dear. That's what tonight's all about. Friends.' He gives her a pointed look.

'Okay, okay, I get it.' She walks out to the hall. 'The Skellions won't be here long. I just want to make sure it's a night to remember for them.'

Frank follows. 'And what about repercussions? Have you factored them in?'

'I highly doubt there'll be any. He's going to want to get the hell out of here ASAP. And you'll have security, won't you? If he starts anything, they can take care of him. Escort him off the premises, as they say.'

'Seeing security as a positive now, are we? You made me out to be a complete diva when I mentioned it.'

'I can change my mind, can't I?' Laura places the flowers on the console table. It's not that she's worried about violence. The story Mollie told her about Skellion in London may or may not be true – it's possible he made it up in some skewed attempt to rein Tory in, to get him to behave – but, still, he might get stroppy. He's not a man to take things lying down, his blow-out with Marie last night being proof of that. Having his massive ego dented is not something he's going to take kindly to. 'Bruno will be on standby to whisk him away,' Laura says. 'I've already cleared it with him.'

'As long as the whole thing isn't too disruptive,' Frank says, fiddling with the position of the arrangement, making sure it's centred. 'I want things to run smoothly.'

'And they will. Don't worry. When are the caterers arriving?'

'Around five. So there'll be no pickings till then.' He makes to move away, then stops. His tired, cloudy eyes find hers. 'Don't think I don't understand how you feel. Just remember, nothing you do is ever going to bring your father back.'

The morning passes. Laura and Frank work in bubbles of edgy silence, pierced every so often with the sound of chairs dragging across tiles, the clackety-clack of crockery being unstacked, the chink and clink of glassware and cutlery being laid out on polished tables. The light guy arrives, small and swift, squirrel-like in rust-coloured overalls, watched intently by Trudy as he goes about his work. When he's finished, multi-coloured Chinese lanterns swing from the bushes and ropes of LED lights snake around tree trunks and branches.

Frank gives Laura the job of polishing his silver, laying it out on sheets of newspaper on the dining table in front of the open terrace doors. She sighs as she sits down. How shiny is silver supposed to be? And what does it even matter? Like, who's going to be inspecting it? She unscrews the tub of polish, dabs some on a cloth.

It's not like she doesn't know Frank's right. Of course nothing will bring her father back. Still, hearing it said was like a wet slap on the cheek. Enough to leave an impression. She works polish into the stem of a candlestick, harder and harder until heat seeps through the cloth. Is she being stupid? Thinking that going one further than her mother's feeble idea will be enough? Paddy Skellion will be embarrassed, taken down a peg or two, but then what? When it's all over. Everything just settles back to normal? She holds up the candlestick, lets the light bounce off the shining metal, feels the gratifying heft of it in her hand. No. It'll be worth it. This is a man who's got away with things all his life. Has he ever known what it's like to truly suffer?

She gets up and heads out onto the terrace. Below, in the garden, Frank stoops under the fig trees, tweaking the placement of the lights to his own exacting standards, softly reprimanding Trudy as she paws, frustrated, at the trunks. Then the cat is off, streaking across the grass at some sound or movement, and Frank comes out from the shadows, straightens up, shielding his eyes from the light. His gaze wanders, seems to focus, then finds Laura and he starts walking, beckoning her down. She descends the steps, falling in with his pace, asking, 'What is it?' as they move quickly towards the front of the house. She detects the flash of a car through the trees, turning on the gravel, driving away, and then the lone figure of Richie standing on the path.

EIGHTEEN

Marie is dyeing her hair. 'Colouring my roots', as she describes it. Paddy's eyes water. Whatever she's using, it looks like she's squeezed a tube of burnt sienna on top of her head. The stinging chemical smell follows her as she wanders through the house trying to be inconspicuous – her way of keeping an eye on Tory and Mollie. Though, with that stink, if they're up to anything she's not going to catch them. They'll have plenty of warning. And who cares anyway? Tory's a grown lad. Just because that Mollie one is a few years older, Marie's got herself into a flap. Made them sleep in separate rooms last night, for Jesus' sake. Paddy didn't get involved. Of course, that led to a fierce fucking row. Marie saying Paddy hadn't treated Tory like a grown lad last October at the hearing. That he was all about protecting him back then and how could things be so different after only a few months? Paddy had laughed at her, said she was being ridiculous, that you couldn't compare the possibility of a shag with the possibility of a stint in prison. That had really got her goat.

Fair play to Tory for bagging an older woman. He could've found one a bit more attractive, mind. Not that she's ugly or anything but she's not the most appealing thing Paddy's ever seen. It's the age factor that Marie can't get her head around. As if Mollie's grooming him. Predatory female and all that. Paddy wouldn't have said no, back when he was Tory's age. There was a woman once, when he was seventeen. Not bad-looking, but must've been forty if she was a day. Over from Liverpool for the weekend, she was. Came on to a paralytic Paddy in the Saturday-night chipper queue. It hadn't been his first time, but she'd taught him a thing or two. Got the fright of his life next morning when he woke up beside her in a dingy B&B on Gardiner Street. Couldn't wait to be rid of her. Had walked her all the way to the ferry at North Wall to make sure she definitely got on it. Now, that was what you'd call an age gap. This one – Tory and Mollie – it hardly registers.

Marie had put on the liberal-mother act when they'd arrived yesterday but, when it came down to it, she couldn't keep it up. She's been civil to Mollie – friendly, even – but at the back of it all, she doesn't like her, doesn't *trust* her, apparently. Started spouting on to Paddy last night about something not being right, that Mollie's not the kind of girl Tory normally goes for. How the hell would she know? Has she had conversations with him on the subject? And what does it matter anyway? It won't last. He's nineteen. Let him have his fun. And what does Marie think they get up to back in Dublin, for God's sake? Not separate rooms, that's for sure. She's being bloody ridiculous. 'We have to have house rules,' she'd told Tory. Paddy had considered going to bat for his son but, weighing up the options, whose wrath would cause him the most pain? Tory will be gone in a couple of days. He can't, as yet, say the same about Marie.

The hair dye – that's all to do with tonight. 'Laura advised us to dress down,' Paddy says, nodding at Marie's head as she wafts around the studio, suspicious eyes darting about as if Tory and Mollie might be *in flagrante* in a corner.

'I know,' she replies, 'you told me. That's all very well for her to say – she'd look good in a bin liner.'

'Just reminding you,' he says, flicking through the stack of his recent works, trying to choose which ones to bring tonight. 'No need to be going to any trouble.'

'Colouring my roots doesn't constitute dressing up. It's ongoing maintenance, that's all. Like you having a good shave.' She steps closer, scrutinises his face. 'Which you need, by the way.'

Paddy runs a hand over his jawline. Stubble. It lends a certain, what's the word? *Ruggedness.* 'Thanks for the suggestion but I'll pass, if you don't mind.' Marie can look after her own maintenance; he'll take care of his own.

'You'd look a lot smarter if you got rid of it,' she says. 'But that's just my opinion. You don't have to do what I say.'

'Exactly. I'm glad you recognise that.' And he bares his teeth at her. A forced, rictus smile.

'So, psychology, is it?' Paddy asks Mollie. 'That's what you studied in college?' He's not overly interested but someone has to break the awkward silence. The four of them are having lunch outside, sitting around the table at the end of the small, sunny garden. Marie has made some yoke she's calling a *frittata*, though it looks, to Paddy, no different from an omelette. She has it loaded with ham and melted cheese –

not bad, it is – and keeps asking Mollie is she sure she doesn't want any. It's almost like she's doing it on purpose. Mollie's one of those vegans. No meat, no fish, no eggs. Nothing from an animal at all. Sure what would that leave you with? Fruit and veg? No wonder she looks so pasty.

She stabs at the salad Marie has made for her, loading her fork with spinach leaves. 'Yeah. Gonna set up my own practice one day.'

'And when will that be?' Marie asks.

Mollie pushes the leaves into her mouth. 'When I feel like it.'

Is it meant to be disrespectful? Paddy's not sure. Hard to tell with these Yanks. They speak their minds, don't hold back, have none of the hang-ups us guilt-ridden Irish drag around. Whatever it is, it's difficult not to admire her for it.

'Trinity, was it?' Paddy asks. 'Where you did your degree?'

Mollie grunts, nods.

'What brought you over to Ireland?' Marie wants to know.

'Felt like a good place to go. Someone way back was Irish. Great-grandfather, -mother, not sure.'

'Your family,' Marie says. 'They must miss you. Do you get to go back home often? Or do they visit you in Dublin?'

'Don't have any folks. They're dead.'

'I see. I'm sorry.' Marie lifts the wine bottle, tops up their glasses. 'Brothers? Sisters?'

'A half-brother somewhere,' Mollie says. 'Delaware, last I heard. We hate each other's guts.'

'Oh.' Marie frowns. 'So you're on your own in the world?'

'Pretty much. You get used to it.'

Tory takes a sip from his glass, shooting a sharp glance at Paddy over the rim to indicate his unease at his mother's line

of questioning. Paddy gives him a look of reassurance. 'So!'
he says. 'Where did you two meet?'

Tory rolls his eyes. Paddy ignores him. He wanted the
subject changed, didn't he? Jesus. You can't say anything
right, these days.

'Let Tory answer that one,' Mollie says, picking a cherry
tomato from her plate with her fingers. 'I like the way he
tells it.'

Tory returns her grin with a nervous one of his own and
starts describing their eyes-across-a-crowded-room story.
As Paddy listens, he can't help wondering. Does Mollie know
everything about Tory? Has he told her who he got himself
mixed up with? About being charged? About the court
hearing? Is Mollie the type who'd care about stuff like that?
She's a strange one to make out. Laid-back, self-assured,
couldn't-give-a-shit attitude. There's not much that would
faze her, that's for sure.

'And the age thing,' Marie is saying now, as she heaps
more food onto Tory's plate, 'that didn't, you know, make
any difference?'

'Ah, now, Marie,' Paddy says. 'That's none of our business.'

'It's okay,' Mollie answers. 'We get that from old people a
lot. They seem to find it kinda . . . interestin'.'

Paddy almost laughs out loud. By God, that's put Marie in
her place. *Old people*. Mollie would doubtless put him in the
same group too, but that's not the point. She didn't direct
her comment to him.

Marie says nothing but you could cut the tension with a
knife.

Mollie reaches over to Tory and takes his hand. 'It's not an issue for us, is it? Like, what's a few fuckin' years, right?'

After lunch, Tory and Mollie head out for a walk. Paddy returns to the studio to make a final decision on the pieces he's bringing tonight, leaving Marie in the kitchen to tidy up. She hasn't said much since Mollie's putdown; it obviously left a mark. What did she expect? Paddy might find the age gap a source of amusement – fascination, even – but it's not something he'd go commenting on. Not to Tory and Mollie. If Marie thought she was being smart, it backfired. Big-time.

Three pieces? Four? What would be acceptable? The works are unframed, so they're light, easily transportable. But, still, they have to be taken care of, properly wrapped and handled. Uniformity is a good idea. Balance. He settles on four twenty-by-thirties. It's a good size. Enough to make an impression without being too big to fit into a car boot. Satisfied, he leans them against a chair while he goes looking for wrapping materials.

'I'll do that, if you like.' Marie comes in as Paddy is opening the storage cupboard. 'That's my job.'

'Thought you were busy,' he says. 'Didn't want to be assuming.' It's true, Marie usually looks after any packaging that needs to be done. She's better at it than Paddy, more thorough. Now that everything he paints ends up being sent overseas, it's important that it's done right.

'Will I get a crate?' she wants to know.

'Not necessary. Bubble-wrap and tape will do the job.' Paddy senses a vibe. She wants something, is after something. He pulls out the folding table, unhinges the legs, stands it level on the floor. He unravels a long length of bubble-wrap, bending as he slits it from the roll with a Stanley knife.

'I don't like her.' Marie blurts it out, as if the words have been pushing hard against the back of her teeth.

'So?' Paddy says. 'You'll probably never see her again after tonight. If the client takes me on, her job is done. End of.'

'Not her. Mollie. I don't know what Tory sees in her.'

Paddy straightens up, turns to face her. There's a hard, flinty look in her eyes, and her chin is raised in what seems like defiance. 'You've a very short memory,' he says.

That shakes her. The chin retreats into her chest, the eyebrows come together. 'What's that supposed to mean?'

'Your parents. Back in the day. Shoe's on the other foot now.'

Her breath races noisily in and out of her nose. 'That was different.'

'Really? How so?'

'That was narrow-minded prejudice. It wouldn't have mattered what you were like, they'd made up their minds before they'd even met you.'

'What's wrong with her?'

'I told you. She's not right for him. He's been, I don't know, sucked in or something. I can't explain.'

Paddy waves the Stanley knife in the air. 'You just can't stand the fact that your little boy has found another woman. Isn't that it?'

'Don't be ridiculous. It has nothing to do with that.'

'And not just any woman,' he continues. 'An older one. That's the real crux of it. What had you been expecting? Little Bo Peep in pigtails and ankle socks?' He lays the bubble-wrap on the table, places a painting on top. 'You don't like her. I get it. You've made yourself clear. You don't seem to like anyone much, these days.'

'Meaning?'

'I saw the way you were looking at Laura Karlson.'

'Likewise.'

Paddy stares hard at her. He walked into that one. Gave it to her on a plate. He thinks fast. This can go one of two ways. He can keep it going, dig a bigger hole than the one they're already in. Or he can bail now. There's too much riding on tonight. Whatever about tomorrow, next week, next month, he needs to keep her onside for the time being. He's confident about this guy. More than confident. There's a . . . feeling in the air, a sense that things are about to change for him. Like he's standing on the crest of a wave, waiting for it to crash down on some brand-new undiscovered shore. He stops what he's doing, walks around the table to Marie.

'Look,' he says, as soothingly as he can manage, 'I did what I had to do. Nothing more. You know how these things work. There's always a bit of flirting involved. But that's all it is! I'm not going to say she's not attractive. Of course she is. But that's not my fault.' That seems to do the trick. The iciness in her eyes melts a little and the hard set of her mouth relaxes. He tries to read what might be going on in her head, which way her thoughts are trained. He has to keep it up. 'This could be huge for me. I mean, for us. If I have to play the game, you're not going to hold that against me, are you?' He runs a hand across his head, waiting for her to respond. When she does, it's not how he expects.

'Do you think she knows?' she says. 'Mollie. Do you think she knows what Tory was involved in? What he did?'

'What?' He's genuinely puzzled. Was she listening to

anything he'd just said? 'I don't know, Marie. I haven't a clue. I mean, I wondered myself, to be honest. But does it matter?'

'What if I told her?' Marie says, biting at a fingernail, her gaze directed towards the view beyond the windows. 'Do you think it might put her off?'

Paddy tries to compute the thought processes that might have brought her to this point. He hadn't thought his wife could be that cold-hearted. That devious. But he's going to steer clear. He won't let her drag him into that. And risk an even bigger blow-out? 'Ah, lookit,' he says, attempting to make light of it, 'I don't think we need to go that far.'

'But we're agreed she's not good for him?'

What the hell? Paddy hasn't agreed anything of the sort. He nods anyway, gives her a straight-lipped smile of acquiescence, and returns to finish the wrapping.

Marie's phone rings. She takes it from her pocket, answering it as she hurries from the studio. 'Hi, Serena,' he hears her say. 'Last night? Brilliant. Thanks for taking care of it. Of course, I . . .' Her footsteps are swift along the landing, her words a fading hum that disappears behind the bedroom door.

NINETEEN

'About twenty minutes ago,' Frank says into his phone. A pause and then: 'I know, Angela. I'm sure she will, later. She just asked me to let you know.' Another pause, longer this time. Frank's anxious eyes find Laura's as he paces across the kitchen floor. 'Fine, as far as I can see. Of course we'll try. But at least you know he's safe now. That's the most important thing.' He says his goodbyes.

Laura looks up as Richie returns from the bathroom. His hair is slicked back from his forehead, his face flushed a deep pink. 'Okay?' she asks.

'Yeah,' he says, to the floor.

Frank breathes a large sigh of relief as he slips his phone back into his shirt pocket. 'You've a lot to answer for, young man,' he says. 'Your poor mother. Scared the life out of her, running off like that.' Richie sits down at the table, opposite Laura. 'Well?' Frank asks. 'What have you got to say for yourself?'

Richie lifts his elbows onto the table, rests his chin in his hands. 'Sorry,' he mumbles.

Frank eases himself into a chair. 'And you think that's going to cut it?'

'Why didn't you answer your fucking phone?' Laura asks. 'A text. That's all it would've taken.'

'I called you. You didn't answer.'

'And I called you back! What the fuck, Richie? Why didn't you just contact one of us? And what're you doing here? What's this all about?'

He pushes his hands up over his ears.

'Richie, you might officially be an adult,' she continues, 'but you're acting like a bloody kid. You know how Mum worries. What you did was selfish beyond belief.'

His hands move over his face, fingers rubbing at his bleary, part-bloodshot eyes. 'I said I was sorry, didn't I? I didn't do it on purpose. Not exactly.'

Laura relaxes her shoulders, allows herself to breathe a little easier. 'You want to explain?' she says, her voice calmer now.

Richie blinks hard several times. 'I need a drink.'

Laura gets up, fills a glass at the sink, returns to the table. 'Hungry?'

He shakes his head, gulping the water, then wipes his mouth with his sleeve. 'The party. It's tonight, yeah?'

Laura frowns. 'Is *that* why you're here? Because you wanted to come? Jesus, Richie, if—'

'I don't care about some shitty party. I'm not here because of that.' He sees Frank's face. 'Look, I – I'm not saying . . . I didn't mean . . . '

'Any offence,' Frank says, finishing the sentence. 'None taken. Not exactly your thing, I know.'

'It's not that. Happy birthday and all. But it's not the reason I used all my savings to fly over.'

'Thanks for the wishes,' Frank says, not entirely without sarcasm. 'Though I don't officially hit seven-oh till next week. And if we don't get a move on here, we may not be having the celebration till then.'

Laura checks her phone: 4.36 p.m. The caterers will be arriving soon. And the guests only a few hours after that. 'Frank's right,' she says. 'It's not exactly perfect timing.'

Richie keeps his head bowed. 'I know why you're here. Amy told me.'

'She explained. She was afraid that was the reason you disappeared.' She studies his face. 'Is it?'

'Partly.'

'Partly? What else? Come on, Richie. I haven't got all day.'

'Have you been? To the Skellions' place? Have you done what Mum wanted you to do?'

'I went yesterday. I spoke to them. I . . .' She stops. There's no use pretending to Richie. He's here now. He'll be here tonight when they arrive. 'Look, I didn't do exactly what Mum asked. I want to do something more . . . satisfying, I suppose.' She runs quickly through the details: Laura Karlson and her 'client'; the meeting with Paddy; the plan for this evening.

'Seriously? What's that going to do?' Richie says. 'I don't get it.'

'It's just a bit of fun, Richie. We can't do anything too drastic. But I want to see Skellion squirm.' She reaches over to touch his arm. 'I'm glad you're here. You'll be able to see that smug expression wiped off his face.' Richie's not convinced. She sees it in his eyes. 'Don't worry,' she tells him. 'It'll be worth it.' Richie lifts the glass to his lips, takes a sip, places it carefully back on the table. He almost says something, takes a breath but draws it back in. 'What is it?' Laura asks. 'You said finding out why I'm over here was only part of the reason you came. What else is there?'

He leans back in his chair now. 'Your friend Mollie's hanging round with Tory Skellion, these days.'

Laura gives a grunt of pleasure. 'Oh, yeah. I almost forgot. She's doing me a favour. He thinks it's true love, of course. Fucking idiot. I didn't want to leave him out of the picture. He deserves a piece of payback pie.'

'So you're behind them hooking up?'

'Well, she offered. When I told her what I was planning. Suggested it'd work better if he was over here too. And she's right. It will. Make it a family affair.'

'You know they're here now? That they flew over yesterday?'

'Of course I do. I saw them. They arrived during my meeting with Paddy, exactly as planned. They're coming tonight. But how the hell do you know?'

Frank wriggles in his chair. 'Look, I'm not sure where all this is going but can we please cut to the chase? It's almost five.'

'Yeah, Richie,' Laura says. 'What's going on? And how do you know about Mollie and Tory?'

'Just because I stay inside most of the time doesn't mean I'm not in contact with people.'

'But who? Why? For what?'

'You're not the only one who wants revenge, Laura. Mollie wants hers too.' Before Laura can reply, he continues, 'I never told you this but there was some kind of history between Dad and Paddy Skellion. Bad blood, Dad called it.'

'I know, I know,' she says. 'Frank told me about it. But,' she addresses Frank now, 'you did say Dad hadn't told anyone else?'

'That was my understanding,' Frank says. 'I guess I'm not right about everything.'

'Well, he told me,' Richie says, 'after he found out Tory Skellion was involved in the break-in. Told me what had happened with Tory's father when he'd worked on some site Dad owned. Felt really guilty because for a while he thought this bad blood was behind the break-in.'

'What's that got to do with Mollie wanting revenge?'

'Nothing.'

'You're not making any sense, Richie.'

'Give me a chance. I'm getting there. It wasn't anything to do with Dad and Skellion, like Dad thought it was. It wasn't that bad blood. It was yours and Mollie's. She planned the break-in to get back at you.'

Laura shrinks away from the table, feels the need to put more distance between her body and his. '*What*? No, Richie.' She shakes her head. 'You've got it all wrong. You're mixing things up.'

'I'm not. I trust my source.'

'Trust your *source*?' She pulls a face. 'What are you? An undercover cop? Get a grip. Your fucking source doesn't know what they're talking about.'

Frank interjects: 'Let me attempt to decipher things here.' He addresses Richie: 'What you're trying to say, I believe, is that Mollie was behind the break-in. Do I understand that correctly?'

Richie nods. 'She's a sick, twisted bitch, Laura. You did the dirty on her. She wanted to get you back.'

Laura thinks for a moment, her mind racing. 'Sure we fell out. But we made up. We're friends again. It's all good between us. Why else would she be whoring around with Tory fucking Skellion? She's only doing it to help me. Are you seriously trying to say that they've been plotting against us all this time? That she got him to break into our house because I fell out with her?'

'Not him. Not back then. The others. She has a shitload of cash. You know that. She put the feelers out, found people willing to do the job for the right price. It was pure coincidence Tory Skellion was mixed up with them.'

Laura sits still and quiet, her brain trying to piece together the crazy story Richie is telling. Could Mollie truly be capable of masterminding something so vindictive? So disgusting? Simply because Laura hadn't wanted to be more than just friends?

'This thing now,' Richie continues, 'acting as his girlfriend. My bet is she's doing it just to mess with your mind, to keep you close. To keep you thinking she's on your side.'

What was it Mollie had said when Laura told her about her plan to dupe Paddy? *You gotta be one step ahead, girl. Keep your friends close, your enemies closer.* 'If,' Laura says, 'and I'm saying *if*, all this is true, surely Tory would know she was behind the break-in.'

'The other scumbags wouldn't have told him who was paying them off,' Richie says. 'Wouldn't even have told him they were *being* paid. All he was to them was another baseball bat. He's a clueless sap.'

'But if they saw him with Mollie? Wouldn't they think it's weird that she's hanging around with him?'

'I doubt they go to the same places. And why would they

care if they did see them together? They don't have anything to do with him any more. They wouldn't have given a shit if he'd got a sentence. As long as he didn't rat them out. And he didn't. He made sure not to do that so they'd leave him alone.' Richie's lips curl into a snarl. 'They got paid for the job and they walked away. That's all that matters to the likes of them.'

Laura narrows her eyes. 'Richie. Seriously. Where are you getting all this from?'

'I haven't made it up, if that's what you think.'

'So while we thought you were lying in bed, you were actually conducting a one-man investigation into the criminal underworld, thanks to your iPhone?'

'We're talking small-time here. Not major gangland stuff. And I didn't start an "investigation". The information came to me. I got lucky.'

'But . . . all this to get back at me? Why would Mollie . . .?'

'You want revenge, don't you?' Richie says. 'Why's it so hard to understand she wants some of her own?'

'But going to those lengths? Paying lowlife scum to break into our fucking house? To beat us up? Steal our stuff?'

'Says the person who's come all the way to the South of France for her kicks.'

'I was coming anyway. For the party. It was good timing, that's all.'

Frank stands up from the table. 'I hate to be a killjoy, but I'm pretty sure that's the food arriving.' He opens the back door and looks out. 'I'm right,' he says, turning back to face them. 'You'll have to take the conversation elsewhere. I'll join you once I've given Pierre and his team their bearings.' He heads outside, his words of greeting combined with the crunch of his feet over the gravel sounding, to Laura, oddly comforting, solid and reassuring against the incredible story Richie is trying to convince her is true. How can she believe him? How can he trust the people who told him?

The white-coated 'team' march into the kitchen carrying huge cloth-covered platters, baskets of fruit, crates of champagne flutes, elaborate cakes on silver stands. 'Come on,' Laura says, grabbing Richie's arm. 'Upstairs.'

She brings him to her bedroom. It's still dark and cool. She'd forgotten to open the shutters earlier, so engrossed she'd been in the text conversation with Amy. She pulls them open now and light spreads quickly across the floor, warm sun touching every surface.

'Why didn't you just call me?' she asks, as she sits down on the unmade bed. 'I mean, to tell me this stuff. Why bother coming all the way over?'

Richie joins her, sits cross-legged, his back pushed up against the wooden bed-end. 'It was like . . . I don't know . . . everything just . . . snowballed over the last few days.' He clasps his hands together, starts kneading one against the other. 'Remember Griff? Jack Griffin?'

Laura thinks. 'The name, maybe. Not the face. He was in your class at school, right?'

'Yeah. One of the non-arseholes. I can kind of talk to him, you know? I'd told him about Tory Skellion. About how he got away with it, and about the guards not having enough evidence on the others. He knew the story. Anyway, he trains with this guy in the gym, Marko, says he's dead sound. They got talking one day a while ago about street crime, violence, all that sort of stuff. Griff mentions me, our break-in, and the way only Skellion ended up in court and no one actually got punished and how pissed off we were and about Dad having his heart attack and all. Anyway, one night last week Marko's in his local with his mates and they're sitting beside this scumbag who lives on his road. Some little prick with a pit bull who thinks he's a hard man. Marko knows he's been mixed up in shit, robberies and stuff, but he's smart enough to keep on his good side, says he's not someone you want to fall out with, so he always acts friendly-like when he sees him. Anyhow, this dickhead was there, off his head, bragging about jobs he's done, talking about some big house he and some other blokes had broken into and robbed while the family were there. Marko heard him mention someone called Skellion, saying he'd been the only one thick enough to get himself charged and Marko copped it was the break-in Griff had told him about.'

'Okay if I come in?' Frank is at the door.

'Sure,' Laura says, making room for him on the bed.

'I'll stay standing, if you don't mind, my dear,' he says as he enters. 'I'm already exhausted. If I sit down on the bed I'm not sure I'd be able to get up.'

Laura fills him in on the story Richie has just told her.

'But what about Mollie?' Frank asks. 'Where's the evidence of her involvement?'

'I was just getting to that,' Richie says. 'Marko wants to find out more, so he can give Griff the lowdown, knows he's gonna be interested. So he asks the little toe-rag what he's drinking, gets the beers in and starts talking to him, making jokes about what a bunch of useless arseholes the guards are and stuff. So then he asks him how much he got, was the job worth it. Your man says it was okay, jewellery and some cash, but the sweetest thing was the pay-off they'd got for carrying it out.

Marko's all ears and he's, like, "Ah, go on, you're messing," and your man says, "No, I'm telling you, easiest money I ever earned." And Marko's like, "Who pays someone to do a break-in? How does that make sense?" And your man says he doesn't ask too many questions and a job's a job. Marko says, "You mean you don't know. You were just doing what you were told by one of the big players." The scumbag doesn't like that. He's pissed off cos Marko's making out he's only small-time – which he actually is – and he's like, "What're you talking about? I work for meself. I don't have to do anything I don't want to. And it wasn't what you think," he says. "It was some American bitch who wanted this family roughed up." She didn't care what he took from them as long as he scared the shit out of them. Marko gives him a nudge, says, "Was she good-looking? Did you make a move? Did you get more than a nice few quid from her?" Your man's like, "You must be fucking joking. I'm not into birds who have their life story tattooed all over their arms and hair like a nest of fucking rats' tails." So Marko feeds all this to Griff, and Griff tells me and I know straight away that it's Mollie.'

It seems to Laura that the room has darkened. Like shadows are forming in the corners, swallowing the light. She knows Richie's not lying, knows from the set of his mouth and the clear, steady look in his eyes. Frank crosses his arms, leans his head to one side, draws a breath. 'Don't say it,' she tells him. 'I can do without the I-told-you-so lecture. And take the mock-sympathy off your face. Save it for that bitch. She's the one who's going to need it.'

'I'm sorry,' Richie says. 'I had to tell you. I was going to wait till you got back but that was when I thought you were coming over here just for Frank's party. Then Amy told me you were going to talk to the Skellions and I thought, *Fuck*, cos I'd literally just found out that Mollie was supposed to be going out with Tory and that they were flying over to visit his folks. I didn't know you already knew about them being together.'

'Who told you that?' Laura asks. 'Griff again?'

'No. Jenny Mason. She asked me to her debs last year and I didn't feel able to go and I explained why and she was really decent about it. She's straight up. Anyway, she sends me a picture on Thursday night. Thinks I'll find it interesting. She was in some hole of a place on Pearse Street, her and her mates, just for the crack, like. One of those pubs that looks like your granny's sitting room. Who's in the corner, staring at each other? Only Mollie and Tory. She knows Tory vaguely from when she was a kid. They went to the same after-school club or something. And she knows he was involved in the break-in cos I told her all about it. So I'm like to myself, Jesus, is he going out with Mollie? And I text her back and ask her to find out. So she goes over to talk to them, acts all innocent like, and Tory says, "Oh, yeah, I remember you," blah-blah-blah, "and this is my girlfriend Mollie," and he says it like she's some kind of trophy cos she's clearly older than him. And then he's like "we're heading over to Nice tomorrow to visit my folks – they have a place there," blah-blah-blah. So Jenny lets me know and I'm like, What the hell? And then Amy tells me what you're planning on doing over here and I'm saying to myself, "If Laura's over there and she's heading to the Skellions' place and Mollie turns up with Tory . . . And Mollie was behind the break-in . . ." You needed to know.'

'You didn't have to come all the way out here, Laura says.

Richie sighs. 'I couldn't tell you about her being behind the break-in over the phone. I just couldn't. And, anyway, stuck in the house for weeks, I felt like fucking off somewhere.'

'Without thinking to inform anyone,' Frank says.

'Of course I thought about it. But if I'd told Mum, she'd have tried to stop me. And I didn't want to get Amy into trouble for letting me in on the plan.'

Frank frowns. 'I'd say that ship has sailed.'

'Yeah, well, I'm here now.'

Laura slips from the bed. Her feet carry her to the window, feeling strange, as if they're not properly attached to her legs. Her heart thumps hard and fast. It throbs thick in her chest, her throat, her head.

The bitch.

The absolute fucking bitch.

She turns, picks up her hairbrush from the bedside table and hurls it across the room.

TWENTY

'Calm down,' Frank says. 'I know you're angry but let's try and tease this out. How could she have been sure you'd all be at home that night? They could've been breaking into an empty house for all she knew.'

'Oh, she would've been certain,' Laura says, biting at a fingernail. 'She knew we always ate together on Friday nights.'

'Ah, yes. Of course. But you weren't always there yourself. I remember your father lamenting the fact many times.'

A cynical smile curves Laura's lips. 'I bumped into her that evening. Didn't think anything of it at the time. I was working in that shitty café in Temple Bar. I'd just finished my shift and she was there, passing by, when I left. She must've planned it. Probably knew my every move. It was a bit awkward. We hadn't spoken since I'd broken up with her. I hadn't intended going home but I wanted to get away from her. She'd always been weird when I mentioned family. Jealous, because she didn't have one of her own. She'd told me that even when her parents were alive they'd never had time for her. I said I was on my way to catch a DART home and she was like,

"Oh, I'll walk with you." It was only ten minutes so I didn't object. Now that I think of it, she actually waited till I got on the train.'

'So she knew you'd be at home?'

'I guess that was her cue. Must've called her lowlife pal and told him it was game on.'

Richie, stretched out across the bed, speaks up: 'How the hell were you ever friends with her? Like, we all told you she was a weirdo. Remember that time you brought her home and she'd bought us all expensive presents? Mum and Dad didn't like her.'

'Yeah, okay. So I got it wrong. Like, hindsight is twenty-twenty and all that.'

'We told you at the time! She was so fake but you couldn't see it. Or didn't want to see it.'

'Fuck off, Richie. I didn't see you giving her back the Xbox game she gave you.'

'Like, that would've changed everything, yeah?'

'It might've given you permission to adopt the moral high ground but, seeing as you didn't, you can't talk.'

'One Xbox game and you think you can drag me down along with you? She wasn't *my* friend, Laura. I didn't think the sun shone out of her arse.'

'And you're perfect, yeah? You've put Mum through hell. Refusing to get help, wallowing in your room.'

Richie sits up, scrambles to his feet. 'That cow destroyed our lives. If you hadn't let her in, none of this would've happened. You were warned, Laura. Everyone told you she was bad news.' He turns to Frank. 'You never liked her. You made that plain, as far as I remember.'

Frank holds out his hands, palms facing the floor. 'Take it

easy. None of this is helping. Pitting you against each other is exactly the kind of thing someone like Mollie enjoys. She's already done enough damage. Don't perpetuate it. We should be finding things to bring us together, not searching for ways to tear ourselves apart.' His eyes flit between Laura and Richie. 'Now, in case you've forgotten, I have a party to host and it'll be kicking off in . . .' he glances at his watch '. . . approximately one hour. We can continue the conversation tomorrow, if I have the head for it, that is. I know it's important but, for the moment, we'll have to park it.'

'But what about Skellion?' Richie asks Laura. 'Are you going to go through with it? Is there any point?'

'Any *point*? This doesn't change how I feel about him or his snake of a son.'

'But your plan's dead in the water now. If it was ever even alive. Mollie's double-crossed you. What good will getting one over on Skellion do when she was the one behind it all?' He looks at Frank. 'Am I right?'

Before Frank can answer, they hear his name being called from downstairs, followed by some frenzied words in French. He cocks his ear. 'That's Pierre. Going bananas about not having enough of something. I'll have to investigate.' He looks at Richie, still waiting for an answer, and throws his hands into the air. 'You know, if I'm really honest, I don't care what you do, Laura. It's your call.' He walks across the room, pausing for a moment before he leaves. 'This is your mess. You clean it up.' He shuts the door sharply. Not quite a slam but as good as.

Brother and sister hold each other's gaze for several seconds before Laura says, 'He's under pressure, I guess. And we're not helping.'

'Speak for yourself.'

'Come on, Richie. Lighten up. I don't want us to fight.' She holds out her hands. 'Remember what Dad used to say? Don't let it destroy us. Let it strengthen us. Don't let them win.' Richie moves towards her, folds her in his arms. 'I held Dad's hand in the hospital after he'd gone,' she says, into his neck. 'I told him I'd see to things, that he could count on me.'

'Is this what you had in mind?'

Laura shrugs, in the grip of his arms. 'I'm not sure what I had in mind. I was angry. I guess I just wanted to let him know I'd do *something*.'

'How the fuck did we get into this mess?' He pulls away now, pushes his fingers through his hair, starts pacing the room. 'It feels like we're in some kind of, I don't know, black hole. Sometimes I can hardly breathe, I'm so fucking pissed off.' He rounds on Laura, his deep-set green eyes flashing with rage. 'Have they any idea, any *real* idea, how we feel? I wish to God I could make them suffer. Really suffer. I want them to know what it's like. What you want to do tonight is too good for them. We deserve more than that.'

'Look, I understand how you feel. And if I had my way I'd be planning a whole lot more than this. But we have to be careful. We don't want to make things even worse than they already are.'

'I don't see how they could be.'

'Remember how you wanted to find someone to beat the shit out of whoever was responsible? Imagine if that had happened. If you'd been found out. How would Mum have coped?'

'No one would've found out. I'd have made sure.' He sits back down on the bed now, his head in his hands. 'I wish I'd never mentioned it. I should've just gone ahead with it and said nothing.'

Laura joins him, slips her arm around his shoulders. 'We can't change what happened, Richie. No matter what we do. I know what I'm doing with Skellion isn't going to fix things but I'll make sure he fucking well apologises. And he's going to have to do it in public too.'

He lifts his head now, looks straight ahead. 'What about her?' he says, monotone. 'What price is *she* going to pay?'

Laura stands under the shower, freezing water beating hard on her head. It feels good not to let the temperature get the better of her, to steel herself against the icy pain. She grits her teeth, digs her nails into her palms, can hardly catch her breath it's so cold. Even when she decides she's had enough, she forces herself to count to a hundred before turning it off. Towelling herself dry, she looks at her reflection in the bathroom mirror.

Mollie has always been jealous.

Since the very first time they met.

Attracted and repelled at the same time. Fascinated and repulsed.

Okay, so that last word might be a bit extreme but there'd been an edginess right from the start.

They'd met at some random bitch's twenty-first that Laura had gate-crashed with some fat-walleted dope she'd loosely attached herself to in a Donnybrook pub. To escape his curious paws, she'd gone walkabout, finding her way onto a roof terrace. And there was Mollie, lying flat on the decking, blowing smoke-rings into the air. She'd sensed straight away what Mollie wanted from her. Things that Mollie didn't have.

Family. Security. Love . . . Laura's love. That was what she'd yearned for most. And Laura had given it. Not freely, not at first. She'd made her work for it, had allowed Mollie to think she wasn't interested in anything more than friendship. Okay, so she'd played with her, but the chase had been half the fun. Once that was over, it hadn't taken too long before Laura had grown bored. Sure Mollie hadn't taken it well when Laura had ended it. She'd been seriously pissed. But . . . *this*?

They'd always thought the break-in had been random, opportunistic. That, on any other night, it might never have happened. Knowing now that that wasn't the case makes it even harder to take.

There had been purpose behind it. It hadn't been preventable. It was always going to happen.

Mollie had wanted to cause them harm.

She'd accosted Laura that evening after work for a reason. Had cold-heartedly confirmed she'd be in the house, had made doubly sure by seeing her onto the train. And while Angela had been making dinner, while Karl had been on his way home from work, as Richie had sauntered up the driveway with his school bag on his back, and Amy had practised a new dance routine in her bedroom – all that time Mollie's scumbag had been waiting. Waiting for her to give him the go-ahead.

To tear a family apart.

Back in the bedroom now, she opens the wardrobe. As well as buying the silk blouse and suede skirt on her shopping trip, she'd bought a black bodycon dress, which she slips from its hanger and drapes over the bed-end. Dress code for the party is *formal*, which is why Laura told Paddy to dress down. From the off, he's going to feel uncomfortable.

Her phone lights up. Message from Mollie: *All good?*

Laura bites her tongue as she texts back: *Perfect. You?*

Same. Mom n Pop all starry eyed. Baby Boy's whining but don't worry, he'll be there. See you very soon x

She drops her phone onto the bed. The heartless bitch. *All good?* She has some neck. And, now that she thinks of it, the way Mollie had called in the middle of the night, telling Laura about Paddy and Marie fighting, and that stuff about Paddy beating someone up in London. Laura can't be sure any of it is true but she gets now why Mollie told her – to emphasise how much of a 'friend' she is, to show Laura she's on her side, filling her in with titbits of information that Laura has to thank her for. The scheming, vindictive cow.

Jesus. She should have known. Frank has always been right. Mollie's a fucking psycho. But Laura's the one who put up with her. She'd ditched her when she'd lost her flavour, but she'd taken her back, hadn't she? When Mollie heard Karl had died, she'd texted, asked to meet up, told Laura how sorry she was. *Friends?* she'd asked. *Just friends this time. Nothing more.*

Laura's stomach feels heavy, queasy. A bitterness rises, sits at the back of her throat. Richie's questions spin around her head. *What about her? What price is she going to pay?* Laura's not sure. But they'll have to think of something.

The band has arrived. She can hear them tuning up, the throbbing bass and lazy sax rising up through the floor. She blow-dries her hair in front of the mirror, swiftly and expertly applies her make-up, wriggles into her dress. Towering heels, the clear-glass specs and she's Laura Karlson once more.

She makes her way downstairs. The two security guys Frank's hired hang around the hall chatting, hands in pockets, slit eyes widening as she approaches. She flashes a smile. At another time, in another place, they might regret their lewd stares. Today, her wrath is reserved for other things.

The villa's grounds are all a-glitter as she steps outside, lanterns and fairy lights twinkling in the bushes and trees. Around to the left, she climbs the steps leading to the terrace, standing at the balustrade to gaze out into the evening. In the distance, the lights of the city are beginning to shine and a half-moon hangs, silver-white, in the darkening sky.

Frank appears, smelling strongly of Lee's cologne. He wears a baby-blue suit, expertly tailored to fit his slim frame, daffodil-yellow satin waistcoat, brilliant-white shirt, lilac silk tie. 'Apologies for my snappiness earlier,' he says, taking her hand in his. 'Party planning is not for the faint-hearted.'

'Place looks great,' Laura says, keeping things light. 'You look pretty good too. Kept it toned down, I see.'

He laughs, squeezes her hand. 'Richie not joining us?'

'Later.'

He pulls a cigarette case from his top pocket, flips it open. They each take one and he produces a gold lighter.

'Lee gave you that, didn't he?' Laura asks, as she leans into the flame.

Frank nods, lights up, blows a line of smoke into the air. 'Here in spirit,' he says, 'if not in person.'

Trudy sidles up the steps, tail in the air. Laura bends, gathers the cat up under her arm. 'But we're here,' she says. 'Your two current favourite beings.'

He smiles. 'Of course.'

'Happy birthday. Didn't get to finish your present before I came. I'll send it over.'

'Thank you, my dear,' he says. 'But no need to send it. I'll pick it up myself. I'm planning on going back to Dublin in a week or so.'

'Oh? Something on?'

'Fill you in later,' he says, as one of the dark-eyed, chisel-faced young waiters he'd engaged for the evening slips out from the living room with champagne on a silver tray. 'Perfect,' Frank says. 'All we need now is for the guests to arrive.'

The sound of a car pulling up beyond the trees reaches their ears. 'And here they are,' Laura says. She takes a glass, raises it. 'Let's get this party started.'

TWENTY-ONE

'**W**ouldn't you think she'd change into something else?' Marie says, keeping her voice low, as she and Paddy carry two paintings each down from the studio. 'She's been wearing the same clothes since she got here yesterday. I think she might've even slept in them.'

'Ah, would you give over. What does it matter? We're all different.' Paddy couldn't give a shit what Mollie wears. And he doubts the people attending tonight will either. 'Sure won't they all be arty types there anyway?' he says. 'She might even show some of them up.'

'Don't be ridiculous,' Marie says. 'There's arty and there's downright scruffy.'

'Give her a break. Poor kid has no one. Couldn't you be a bit more, I don't know, maternal or something?'

Marie stops on the bottom stair. '*Kid?* She's a grown woman. Tory's the kid here, not her.'

'All right, all right. Whatever you say.'

She doesn't look too bad, Marie. She's wearing pink lipstick and those dangly silver earrings Tory bought her for

Christmas, a pair of black trousers and some kind of white shirt. The hair, too, is all right, whatever she did with the colour. Thank God for the dress-down thing. If she's not reined in, she can turn herself into a bit of a dog's dinner at times. Paddy has decided to wear his working clothes. Clean ones, mind, but paint-flecked, bearing the marks of his profession. That's what potential clients want to see. Artists who look like artists. A denim shirt, unbuttoned, over a grey T-shirt and a pair of beige cords. He has brushed his hair back and, despite Marie's advice, hasn't shaved. Young ones love the rugged-older-man look. Young ones like Laura Karlson.

The buzzer sounds. 'That'll be the taxi,' Marie says. 'You get these into the boot. I'll go and see where those two have ended up.'

Paddy has something he's been itching to ask. Now could be a good time. 'You look . . . um . . .' he coughs '. . . nice.'

That catches her off-guard. Her lips twitch. One hand reaches for her hair, the other clutches at her throat. 'Oh. Thanks.'

He reaches to take the paintings from her. 'Meant to ask,' he says, as if it's only just crossed his mind. 'Why was Serena whatever-her-name-is calling you earlier? Haven't heard you mentioning her in a long time.'

Marie's face freezes. 'Oh, nothing.'

'Just called you out of the blue?'

'Well, I . . . No, she . . .' she waves her hands about '. . . wanted to tell me something, that's all.'

Paddy purses his lips, nods, as Marie scuttles off towards the kitchen. Jesus, does she think he's that much of an eejit? He could say something about the text he saw from Serena but why bother? Let her have her secrets. Why does he care?

The journey is awkward. Paddy sits up front beside the driver – Bruno, he introduces himself as – one of those broody types who thinks he's God's gift because he's tall and tanned and dressed head to toe in black. Paddy attempts a conversation but the monosyllabic replies he gets in return aren't worth the effort.

The other three sit in total silence in the back. Not a word between them. Mollie's in the middle but must be practically stuck to Tory, there's such a gap between her and Marie. Paddy throws his wife a look over his left shoulder but she ignores him, turning to stare out of the window. As they speed up towards the hills, he does the same. Expensive property up here. The type only the very wealthy can afford. A tingle starts in his groin, runs down his legs. This guy must be a serious player. If he bites – and why wouldn't he? – and it all pans out, Paddy might be searching for a place up here himself in the not-too-distant future. The house they have now is fine – a view of the Med is not to be sniffed at – but this area is the real deal. He can see himself here in the hills, creating an artistic haven, like Monet at Giverny, or Dalí at that place he had in northern Spain. Entertaining the great and the good. And the beautiful, of course. The young and beautiful. Yes. Paddy Skellion is destined for greater things.

They climb higher, where the view over the bay is spectacular and the signs of civilisation become less obvious. It's all about privacy up here: tall gates, high walls, banks of dense growth and trees, all serving to camouflage the homes of the rich and the even richer. An aerial view would, no doubt, show a substantial amount of habitation but, from the ground, most of it is successfully concealed.

This Bruno knows how to drive. He negotiates the twists and turns with just one hand on the wheel, relaxed into his seat as though he's watching a movie rather than the road. He swerves left, through a shady, wooded area and stops on a gravelled space where several cars – classy, exclusive models – are parked. Paddy looks around. Is this it? Bruno hops out, opens Marie's door.

'We're here?' Paddy asks, as he gets out and walks round the back of the car.

Bruno nods. 'I show you. Come.' He clicks open the boot, reaches in to lift a painting.

'It's fine,' Paddy tells him. 'We'll take them.' He's not entrusting his precious work to a taxi driver. Did it once, back in Dublin, and the bastard had his keys clipped to his belt. Scored a whirl of scratches all over an important piece. Never again. Tory can help him, make himself useful. Paddy knocks on the side window. 'You two getting out?'

Jesus Christ. There's a time and a place.

Him and Mollie. Beat into each other, they are. Here. Now. In the back of the taxi. He turns to Marie. 'What the hell are they playing at? Said not one word to us for the whole journey and they're eating the faces off of each other in there.'

Bruno smiles, shrugs, mumbles in French. Marie says nothing but there's a guilty look on her face. 'What?' Paddy asks. 'What is it? Come on, Marie. This is an important day for me. If there's something wrong, I need to know.'

'I . . .' she darts a glance at Bruno who, give him his due, takes the hint and steps out of earshot '. . . I told her. About Tory. What he was involved in. Being charged and all.'

'When? Why?'

Marie lifts her chin, stares hard at her husband. 'Just before we left. I took her aside and mentioned it, said I thought she should know.'

'Well,' Paddy says, 'it had the desired effect, I see. Looks like she wants nothing more to do with him.'

'Less of your bloody sarcasm,' Marie whispers. 'I was only doing what I thought was right.'

'What did she say?'

'That she already knew. That he'd told her. Said it wasn't an issue and he'd explained how he'd got involved.'

'So your little plan didn't work. All it did was turn them against you for meddling and push them closer to each other as a result.'

'How was I supposed to know she already knew?' Marie snaps, turning her head and keeping her voice low. 'I didn't think he'd told her.'

'I'm surprised they still agreed to come, after that. Or maybe they wanted to stick it to you after your act of sabotage. Look at them, they're really rubbing your nose in it.'

'Well, for your information, Tory didn't want to come. I heard her persuading him. Saying he shouldn't let you down and that he owed it to you. After everything you'd done for him.'

'There you go, then,' Paddy says, watching Tory and Mollie climb out of the car. 'She can't be that bad after all, can she?'

'I'll reserve judgement, if you don't mind. I don't trust her. I wouldn't put it past her to have something up her sleeve.'

Paddy rolls his eyes. Let Marie get her knickers in a knot about Mollie if she wants. He's had enough. The least she could've done is leave her nosy-parkering for another time but, no, she had to go and stick her oar in tonight. Is that an indication of how little all this means to her? Surely to

God it's Paddy's imminent success that should be uppermost in her mind. Not her petty and unfounded dislike of Tory's girlfriend.

'Let's help your pop with the paintings,' Mollie says to Tory, as they approach. 'We can take one each.'

Paddy gives Marie a now-there's-one-in-the-eye look, which she returns with an icy glare. She thinks she's so smart, that she's so in control. That she holds all the cards. That's going to change after tonight.

No matter what, things are not going to carry on as before.

They follow Bruno through the trees and along a path that, Paddy sees, leads to a villa. Not huge, but impressive nonetheless. Probably, what, a hundred years old? Or not far off it. Nothing showy, none of your modern minimalist rubbish. Elegant. Refined. Though the Chinese lanterns and fairy lights are a surprise. For a *soirée* of the kind Laura Karlson described, they seem a tad . . . flashy? Still, each to their own. When you have money you can do what you like and to hell with what people think. Or perhaps they're supposed to be ironic. A creative nose-thumb to those less open-minded. Yes. That's more than likely it. On second thoughts, he decides the lights are a nice touch.

There's a good buzz about the place. Music and laughter rise into the air against a background drone of crowd-chatter pierced with the intermittent tinkle of glass. Paddy had envisaged a *soirée* to be a reserved affair. This has definitely more of a party atmosphere.

They approach the open front door, flanked on either side by two brutish types in tuxedos. A little over-the-top, perhaps, but you can't be too careful nowadays, Paddy supposes.

'Um, Laura?' he says, to the less intimidating one. 'I'm here to see Laura Karlson?'

They both look Paddy up and down, eyes steely slashes under heavy brows. 'You have . . . invitation?'

'I go now,' Bruno says, heading back down the path.

'Um, yes, thank you,' Marie says, her head all a-whirl as she looks for someone – anyone – to come out and greet them.

'Laura,' Paddy says to the blockheads again, more bluntly this time. 'Laura Karlson? Is she here? Can you go and get her? We have an appointment.'

'You are on list?' one asks, producing a piece of card from his inside pocket. 'Your name?'

'Skellion. Patrick Skellion.'

'I no see you here,' he says.

'It's an unusual one.' He spells it out for them.

The guy shakes his head, turns down the corners of his mouth.

'Want me to go find her?' Mollie asks.

'What? No, no, it's fine,' Paddy says, trying to cover his embarrassment. 'She ordered the taxi for us at seven, so I presume she knows what time we'd be arriving. We'll wait for a moment. I'm sure she'll be out shortly.'

More guests arrive. A middle-aged couple, the woman in a floor-length glittery gold dress with a fluffy, feathery thing around her shoulders, and the man in a dress suit – white waistcoat and dickie-bow, tails, the lot – a potted orchid nestling in the crook of his arm. And following them comes a guy wearing a dark green velvet three-piece and carrying a small box tied with purple ribbon.

Dress down? No gifts? It's all very odd.

'Should we just head in?' Marie says, a puzzled look on her face. 'Everyone else is. Maybe that's what she's expecting.'

'We have to get past the Kray twins first,' Paddy says.

'We can't stand out here like spare fuckin' wheels,' Tory says, under his breath. 'I need a drink.'

More guests arrive. All wearing what can only be termed formal dress, all bearing gifts of some description. Paddy looks down at his shoes – his seen-better-days moccasins – and a heavy, lumpen feeling tightens his stomach. He's not sure what's going on but . . . what if Laura Karlson's not here? If she's fallen out with this guy, if it's all gone belly-up and she's forgotten to let Paddy know. Or couldn't be bothered, especially if there's nothing in it for her now. Christ, wouldn't that be just his fucking luck? What if—

'Paddy! You made it. Sorry, have you been waiting out here long?' It's her. Thanks be to Jesus. 'Did Bruno not show you in? God, he can be useless at times.' Paddy's insides relax as he watches her step out from the hall in a black dress so tight she must've been poured into it. Her eyes move over the four of them – Paddy, Marie, Tory and, finally, Mollie. 'Welcome,' she says, her gaze fixed hard on Tory's girlfriend. 'Please, come in.'

TWENTY-TWO

All this time Laura's focus has been on Paddy Skellion and, now that the opportunity to humiliate him has arrived, it's Mollie she can't take her eyes off. The bitch winks, an almost imperceptible squint, designed to make Laura feel she has her back. Pathetic. She thinks she's so smart, so cute. She's going to pay a big price for that. A big fucking price.

Dragging her gaze away, Laura detects Paddy's discomfort, his awkwardness. Oh, he tries to disguise it now that she's arrived but he's on the back foot, knocked off kilter. Just as she'd planned. Flashing that smile at the two security buffoons earlier had proved useful. She'd asked them to act cagey if anyone mentioned the name Laura Karlson and they'd obviously obliged.

'Great. You brought some of your pieces,' she says to Paddy. 'Follow me. I'll show you where to put them.' She leads them into the crowded living room, pushing through the throng to the middle of the floor. 'Couldn't find those easels, unfortunately. We'll just prop them against the sideboard.'

Paddy is clearly miffed and opens his mouth, probably to protest, but she cuts him off, raising her voice over the music and chatter. 'Okay if I leave you here for a moment?' she says, moving off without waiting for an answer. But not before Mollie manages to grind herself against her side, hoping, Laura assumes, for a covert conspiratorial squeeze of hands or link of fingers. Laura obliges, brushing her palm quickly over Mollie's forearm before she grabs a Manhattan from the counter of the cocktail bar and leaves the room.

Back in the hall, she sips her drink as guests mill about and a cool breeze floats in through the open front door. She sways along to the jazz band, the cello's deep *dun-dun-dun* sharing its beat with her heart. Leave them to stew in there for a while among the beautiful people. That should enhance their discomfort. Paddy in his repair-man attire and Marie rocking her supermarket-checkout chic. Tory and Mollie – nondescript youth and boho hipster girl – won't care that they're surrounded by style and glamour. They'll revel in being different. But not to worry, their arrogance will be short-lived.

Looking up she sees Richie crouched on the stairs, his hair tousled, his face puffy and grey.

'You okay?' she mouths, as she starts climbing towards him.

He nods, wraps his arms around his knees.

'You sure?' She sits down on the step beside him, notices he's shivering. 'Have you spoken to Mum yet?'

He shakes his head.

'Did you text, even?'

A nod, followed by a sniff. His eyes seem to have sunk further into their sockets and the skin around them is purplish-blue. He looks like he did after he pulled the treehouse down, the day their father died. Exhausted. Mentally and physically spent. He shouldn't have come. There was no need. A phone call would have done. But there's no point in her saying it again. No point in saying anything. Not now. When this is over, when they're back at home . . . She's going to try harder. She owes it to him. Especially now. She places a hand on his knee. He's just a kid. Officially an adult but still, really, just a kid.

'Laura. Can we talk?' It's Frank, at the bottom of the stairs.

She gets up. 'Go to bed, Rich,' she says. 'Seriously. You look wrecked.'

His eyes, glazed and distant, stare past her. 'And miss all the fun?'

'Laura.' Frank sounds more insistent now.

'It's your call,' she tells Richie. 'I'd better head back down. Sounds like I'm being summoned.'

Frank is agitated. 'They're cluttering up the room,' he mutters, as she descends. 'Attracting the wrong kind of attention. Do what you need, then send them on their way.'

'Chill out. All in good time.'

'Ten minutes tops. Then I'll turf them out myself if I have to.'

'Okay, okay. I get the picture.'

'I just want it over and done with. I'm nervous, Laura. I don't want any hassle.'

She kisses his cheek. 'Yes, sir,' she says, as he turns to go back to his guests.

Laura watches from the doorway as Frank moves through the crowd. He makes his way to the open terrace doors and holds court, goblet in one hand, cigarette in the other. He appears happy. But his happiness is tinged. She can see it.

Although he's surrounded by friends, Lee's absence is a gap that will never be filled.

The atmosphere is heightening. Trays of canapés are carried in full and carried out empty; glasses are topped up without request; the cocktail waiter – a tasty type with a handlebar moustache – is on autopilot, such is the queue at the bar. She recognises some friends and acquaintances of Frank's she has met over the years, and sees Skellion giving a nod of recognition to a couple: some old guy in a straw boater – a well-respected dealer from Dublin, if she remembers correctly; and a wrinkly blonde in a black cape, Veronica McSomething-or-other, Laura recollects, a rich bitch who owns a hugely impressive collection of Irish art. Neither looks too interested. They'll possibly recognise him, but Skellion is a painter neither would rate very highly, if at all. Skellion won't consider it inconceivable that there are familiar – important – faces here. He'll be keen to impress. Being on the same guest list will be a huge ego-boost. Laura watches him whisper in Marie's ear, a smile playing about his lips.

She's about to move into the room when Mollie is suddenly there, right before her, with her hard grin and harder grey eyes. 'Hey,' she breathes, in Laura's ear. 'Told them I'm going to the bathroom. Quick word.'

Laura leans back against the wall. 'What's wrong? Lover-boy not giving you enough attention?'

'Too much, more like. A fucking octopus would be easier to fend off.'

Laura clenches her fists, digs her nails into her palms. 'Don't knock it,' she says. 'You might be longing for it one day.'

'What're you tryin' to say? That I'm enjoyin' this?'

'Aren't you? It was your idea, after all. To burrow your way in and get him on board.' Glancing up, she sees Richie still on the stairs, his face half hidden in the shadows. The temptation to tell Mollie that she knows she was behind the break-in is strong. But it's not time. Not yet.

Mollie smiles. 'For you, you crazy cow. To make sure he'd be here. It's not like I'm actually attracted to him.'

'You're playing the cute couple well, then,' Laura says. 'Thought you looked very authentic.'

'Yeah, whatever. Look, what's with after? I'm stayin' here, right? That's the plan?'

That *was* the plan. Before Richie delivered the truth. It's not any more. 'Sure,' Laura lies. 'You should get back inside now. It's time to get this over and done with. I'm kind of bored with it all at this stage.'

'What? Thought you couldn't wait for it.'

'You know how it is. Things change. They never turn out the way we expect them to.'

Mollie's not stupid. Laura's cryptic words cause a wrinkle of suspicion around her eyes. But Laura gives her no time to reply. She puts a hand on Mollie's back, pushes her into the room, guides her towards Tory whose eyes light up when he sees her.

TWENTY-THREE

Standing like a pack of vagrants among this crowd better be worth it. Paddy's not sure what planet Laura Karlson lives on but she's turning out to be a bit of a spacer. Stacking his paintings on the floor like that doesn't look good. Makes him seem like some kind of amateur. And in front of a crowd like this! He's already spotted several big players from back home. Types he wouldn't have suspected would mix in the same circles as Manhattan dealers but then . . . if this guy is into Irish art he's bound to have made some connections. He bets they're all surprised to see him here. Very surprised. It's one in the eye for that snooty Veronica McAnee. On the invitation list of each gallery Paddy shows at but has she ever deigned to attend one of his opening nights? Not once. She might have a different opinion of his work when it's being celebrated in downtown Manhattan. Paddy would lay a bet she'll be clamouring to get her hands on it then.

Laura Karlson should be getting a move on, shouldn't she? Where even is she? Paddy looks around, sees her beside the bar. He makes his way over. 'Laura,' he says. 'Your client? Can

I expect an introduction anytime soon?' Marie catches his eye from across the room. She's still not convinced. He detects a flicker of her I-told-you-so face: one eyebrow higher than the other and a slight pulse at the corners of her mouth.

'Of course, Mr Skellion,' Laura says. 'Just waiting for the right time.'

What's with the *Mr Skellion* business? What happened to *I'm not a fan of formality*?

'Everything okay?' Marie rustles up beside them.

'Fine, fine,' Paddy says. 'We're going to get an introduction shortly. Isn't that right, Laura?'

Laura moves off through the throng without answering. Paddy scratches his chin. He wishes now that he'd listened to Marie and shaved. Fuck looking rugged. It's irritating as hell.

'What's going on?' Marie asks. 'She doesn't look very interested. Is this going to happen or is it all as I suspected at the start? Not worth the trouble.'

'Jesus, Marie. Would you give it a rest?' Paddy pushes his way back to Tory and Mollie. 'Get me another glass of something,' he orders his son. 'Anything will do.'

Tory's on the way back with a champagne flute in each hand when the *clink-clink* of metal on glass rings out.

'Can I have your attention please, ladies and gentlemen? I'd like to say a few words.' It's Laura, standing at open doors that seem to lead out to a terrace where the band is playing. 'We have some distinguished company here this evening. Someone I'd like to introduce.'

Finally. Paddy takes a flute, knocks back a glug. Making the introductions publicly? A little unorthodox, but sure what does Paddy know? Laura Karlson appears to do things her own way. He catches her eye, raises his glass. He's 'misunderstood' everything else about this evening. Why would this part of it be any different?

The music stops. The crowd falls silent. Everyone turns to face her.

'Thank you,' Laura says. At least she looks confident, like she's well used to this kind of thing, is comfortable addressing a gathering. 'For those of you who don't know me, my name is Laura and I'm here tonight, like all of you, to celebrate with Frank.' Paddy looks around the room. Frank? Celebrate? Is Frank the client? 'But before we get into the serious business of partying,' she continues, 'there's one small matter to attend to. Actually, it's not that small, if I'm honest. Not for me, anyway. It's something I've been working on for some time.' She catches Paddy's eye, flashes a wide, warm smile. He puffs out his chest, tosses his head. She's talking about him. Has to be. About signing him up. This is a big coup for her. She has every right to feel proud of herself and announce it to the crowd. *Something I've been working on for some time . . .* Now that he thinks about it, is this what they're celebrating? Is Paddy some kind of guest of honour? Was she being offhand earlier just to unsettle him, deliberately making him feel awkward as some kind of joke? He wouldn't put it past her, could see her being capable of it. He gives Marie a triumphant glance but her expression is one of bewilderment. Clearly, she doesn't get it.

'Now,' Laura continues, 'most of you here are involved in the arts in some way or another. So you will, I'm sure, appreciate the value of authenticity. Of honesty and trust.' A wave of empathy spins around the room: nodding heads and murmured sounds of approval. 'Without those things, where would we be?' She begins to pace a little, all eyes focused on her. 'But sometimes trust is hard to come by. Or it's robbed from us or lost or, perhaps, was never really there in the first place.'

What? Paddy places his glass on a side table, folds his arms over his chest, shifts his weight to his left leg. He's not sure where she's going with this but, from the sound of things, they could be in it for the long haul.

'When trust is broken,' she says, 'sure it can be mended. But it will always carry the marks of repair. Invisible, perhaps, to most, but plain as day to the trained eye.' More murmurs of understanding from the room. Paddy stifles a yawn. 'The art world is built on trust. A handshake, a gentleman's word, a nod at an auction that secures a multi-million-dollar piece of art. But, of course, it's not a world that's immune to dishonesty. Far from it. Fakes, forgeries, copies. Sometimes even the experts are fooled.'

She's right about that. Sure didn't Paddy make a fair few bob himself from painting all those Percy Frenches back in the day? If you can trick an expert they deserve it. That's Paddy's take on it anyway.

'But when authenticity comes along, you just know it straight away. It's a wonderful feeling. It restores your faith in humankind.' She seems to be staring right at Paddy now. Or is it at someone behind him? He glances around, comes back to meet her gaze. 'Yes, Patrick Skellion,' she says, nodding. 'I'm referring to you.'

Every head in the room turns. Paddy flicks his hair back. This is more like it. Again, her approach is a tad strange, but he's becoming used to that. He grins at Marie. Not worth the trouble, eh? Tory appears indifferent – what's new? – though

Mollie smiles, gives Paddy a thumbs-up. She's okay, that girl. Marie has her all wrong.

'Ladies and gentlemen,' Laura announces, 'I'd like to introduce Mr Patrick Skellion, artist. Hailing from Dublin, Ireland, but living here now on the Côte d'Azur.' A hesitant ripple of applause. 'Please, yes, he deserves to be congratulated.' The crowd react, clapping enthusiastically.

Paddy squares his shoulders, straightens his spine, clears his throat. The way this is going, he can see her asking him to give a speech of appreciation. Though he expects – hopes – that will be after she introduces her client. He'd like to know whom he's supposed to be grateful to.

Laura resumes once the applause dies down. 'Mr Skellion is here tonight for a very important reason,' she says. 'Something . . . life-changing, I think it's safe to say. And he's brought his family along with him for the occasion. His wife, Marie, his son, Tory, and Tory's, um, partner, Mollie.'

Marie, pink-faced, shrinks back as heads turn, hand to throat. Tory stiffens, rolls his eyes. Only Mollie's expression remains static – the same teeth-baring smile. Paddy wonders at the necessity of calling each of them out. It's not something they would've been expecting. But, fuck it, it might make them appreciate the significance of the occasion, see what the breadwinner has to go through in order to support them. Well, Marie and Tory anyway – it's not like it really affects Mollie. Though, Jesus, of the three of them, she seems the most enthusiastic.

'While we're fortunate to have Mr Skellion here tonight,' Laura carries on, 'he, in turn, is privileged to be in the company of so many influential members of the creative community. Many of you have contacts all over the world, and Mr Skellion is aware that his presence here this evening could have far-reaching implications for his future career.'

Paddy suppresses a grin. Bring on the big-time. But the contact with the space in Lower Manhattan will do nicely, thanks very much. If she could only get around to actually introducing him.

Laura waves her arms in an arc. 'Let's give you some space, Mr Skellion.' The crowd obliges, moving back so that Paddy is left standing on his own. 'I know this isn't a huge gathering, but its influence is, as I've said, extensive. It takes courage to talk about ourselves, about our past. But that's what we're doing tonight, isn't it, Mr Skellion? So that you can go forward from here with a renewed sense of purpose.'

Past? Paddy shakes his head. Renewed sense of purpose? He can feel all eyes on him, can sense the anticipation of the crowd. What is he supposed to say? What's she talking about? Is this the shape this *soirée* or whatever it is was supposed to take? His gaze flits about the room and he feels a sensation he hasn't had for more than forty years: standing in the headmaster's office, trying to figure out if he could leg it before Brother Ignatius unhooked the bamboo cane.

His heart picks up speed. His skin stretches tight across his body. Christ, he feels he might split.

TWENTY-FOUR

How has she imagined this moment? Laura has to admit that she hasn't really. Not for any protracted length of time. Perhaps for three, four seconds at various points. But not in any real detail. She'd put off the visualisation, perhaps realising that no amount of projecting could conjure up the true nature of the moment. Now that it's here, she tells herself to enjoy it, to savour the look of discomfort on Paddy Skellion's stubbled face. Even just for that, the lead-up was worth it. Contrast this with what her mother had wanted. Private conversation versus public humiliation. There was never any contest.

'You come from humble beginnings, isn't that so, Mr Skellion?' she asks. 'You're proud of your inner-city upbringing?'

He's flustered, unsure of her tack. 'What? Yes. I mean . . . Of course. It's who I am.'

'You've come a long way. You'd agree with that, I'm sure.'

He laughs. 'I'm . . . successful. I make a reasonable living.'

'And lucky to have the support of your family.' Laura

catches Frank's eye. His hand close to his chest, he furtively
holds up three fingers. She has that many minutes. And then?
As if reading her mind, he jerks his head towards the door.
It shouldn't need to be that drastic. Three minutes will be
sufficient. After that, people will get bored anyway. Already,
there's a sense of confusion, an almost palpable atmosphere
of *what-the-fuck?* And who can blame them? They came here
to celebrate with Frank. Not to listen to this shit. Still, at least
it's going as well as she'd hoped. No hiccups so far.

'Of course, of course,' Paddy answers. 'Very lucky.'

'You've brought along some pieces tonight to give us an
idea of what it is that you do. Perhaps you'd like to show
them to us. I'm sure everyone here is very interested.'

'Me? Oh, um, yes.' He takes a step backwards, stumbles a
little, is surprised at being asked to do the honours himself.
He summons Tory, silently imploring his help, but he turns
away, pretending not to notice. Instead it's Mollie who comes
forward to assist. She and Paddy lift the still-bubble-wrapped
canvases and carry them to the cleared floor space with all
the grace of a couple of hawkers at a car-boot sale. Clumsily,
Paddy starts unwrapping one painting, pulling at the tape
with his thick fingers. He gives Laura a glare but she just
throws him a smile. Outside, the band has started up again,
a soft but up-tempo rhythm that lends comedy to the scene,
with Paddy in the lead role.

Laura swallows a laugh. 'Almost done!' Paddy tears away
the wrapping. 'And there we have it. Hold it up for us, if you
don't mind.' Paddy sheepishly does as he's asked. It's a typical
work: a garish seascape – sky streaked pink and magenta,
sea striped in blues and greens, sand a wash of orange and
ochre. She moves her head from side to side. 'Interesting.

I'm sure we all agree.' But the pedestrian nature of the work will not appeal to Frank's guests. Laura is well aware of that. Back home Paddy has achieved, for some reason, a popularity that continues unabated. But over here, there's limited appreciation of his kind of work. In the markets, and spread out on the promenade, you might see similar stuff – intended solely for the tourist trade. Not the kind of thing that's taken seriously by the local creative community. But the guests from back home . . . Influential types from the Irish art scene . . . Paddy won't relish being humiliated in front of them. As much as he's become successful back home, without the respect of well-thought-of connoisseurs, he's not an idiot. 'How would you define your state of mind when you created this piece?' she asks him.

He flicks hair from his forehead. 'State of mind?'

'Were you happy, for instance?'

'Um . . .' he furrows his brow '. . . I'm generally in good form so, yes, I'd say I was happy.'

'Would you say happiness is essential for successful creative expression?'

'Um . . . not particularly. I'd say that some of the greatest works of art were born out of despair.'

'True. But, for Patrick Skellion, happiness is essential?'

Paddy gives her an are-you-serious look. 'I'm not sure I said that but, yes, it helps.'

'So what do you do when tragedy strikes?'

'Tragedy?'

'When bad things happen. Does it affect your output? Or maybe you're one of the few who've managed to escape misfortune so far in life.'

'I'm not sure any of us can do that.'

'Oh, I don't know. Some people seem to be able to sail through life without hitting any speed bumps. Or, at least, successfully managing to avoid them.'

Paddy sets the painting down, leaning it awkwardly against his right leg. He nods, as though he understands. But he looks uncomfortable. 'At times of stress, yes, I do find my work is affected,' he says.

'Interesting. And what sort of times would they have been?'

'What . . . *sort* of times?'

'Yes. Are we talking global or personal?'

Paddy pauses, obviously trying to decide how to reply. Or if he even needs to.

Laura has to get to her point. Frank is agitated. The crowd is losing interest. She fills the gap. 'I'm guessing personal,' she says. 'Though, please, correct me if I'm wrong. It's just that I don't think any of us truly understands tragedy until it hits close to home.'

'Lord almighty, this is all very morbid, isn't it?' Paddy says, with a forced laugh. 'I'm sure no one here wants to listen to this kind of thing.'

'Probably not. When my father died, for example, I found people well-meaning. But only up to a point. After that, they didn't want to know.'

'Right. I see.' Paddy scratches his nose. 'Of course.'

'He died suddenly. No lead-up. No time to come to terms with it. That helps, apparently. So I'm told.'

'I . . . um . . . This is . . .'

'Is your father dead, Mr Skellion?'

'He . . . well . . . yes. Yes, he is. But—'

'Suddenly?'

'What? No. Cancer. But he only had a few months. After he was diagnosed.'

'So you had time to say goodbye? I didn't have that. None of my family did. My mother woke up one morning and there he was, dead in the bed beside her.' Laura looks over at Marie. 'He was only forty-eight.'

'Very sad, I'm sure,' Paddy says. 'What's that they say? We all have our crosses to bear.'

'Do you know why he died, Mr Skellion?' Paddy remains blank-faced. 'Officially, it was a heart attack. But the real cause was stress.'

'Oh. Stress. Yes. It's a killer. Something we all need to try and avoid.'

'He wasn't able to, unfortunately. He'd suffered a major setback just a week or so before. Last October, it was.'

Frank steps forward. 'Maybe we should take this into another room. Come along, Laura. Mr Skellion is right. It's all a bit too morbid for tonight.' Murmurs begin to rise up from the crowd. People are turning away, embarrassed, losing interest, eager to get back to enjoying themselves. This stuff is wrecking the atmosphere. But Laura doesn't care. She gives Frank her best filthy look. He firmly takes her arm, lowers his voice, his tone darkening. 'I'm not trying to stop you continuing. I'm simply suggesting you take it elsewhere. At this pace, it could go on all night. You can't expect me to agree to that.'

'It won't take much longer,' she whispers. 'Jesus. You can allow Dad's memory a few minutes more, surely.'

'The location won't make the slightest difference to your father, Laura. You want your revenge, I understand that. And,

God knows, you're entitled to it. But I don't want this getting out of hand. Let's try and keep things under control.'

Laura sees Paddy gingerly lift his painting and begin to skulk away. 'Hold on, Mr Skellion,' she cries, ignoring Frank's words. 'We're not finished.'

'Oh, I think we are,' Paddy replies over his shoulder.

'Wouldn't you like to know my father's name?'

'I'd prefer the name of this client you were banging on about but I'm beginning to wonder if he even exists.'

'Karl Pierce. My father's name is Karl Pierce.'

Paddy keeps walking.

Laura calls after him. 'Don't pretend it means nothing to you.'

Marie's face is twisted in shock. Tory's mouth drops open. Mollie pulls at a dreadlock, takes another sip of her drink.

A friend of Frank's – a stick-thin woman in emerald green – sidles up to him, kohl-ringed eyes narrowed in curiosity. Before she gets a chance to ask any questions, Frank places his hand on the small of her back, guides her towards the terrace. 'Outside, everyone! *Tout le monde! Maintenant!*' he says, his voice loud and husky as he summons the rest of the throng.

The band ups the volume, increases the beat. The murmurs grow louder and laughter breaks out. Frank clicks his fingers at the young waiters, beckoning them to bring their trays of champagne and canapés out to the terrace. There's a look of sympathy on his face when he catches Laura's eye but she keeps her mouth set in a hard line. Two more minutes. That's all she'd wanted.

Paddy quickly gathers his paintings, shoving them hurriedly under his arm. He ushers Marie and Tory out to the hall.

Mollie hangs back, waits for Laura just inside the door. 'Guess that didn't go like you planned it. Intense, though.'

'Why would you care?' Laura says, pushing past.

'Hey. Hang on.' Mollie grabs Laura's arm, yanks her back. 'What did I do?'

Laura corrects herself. It's too soon for that yet. 'Nothing, nothing,' she says. 'I'm just . . . I'm just so pissed, that's all.'

The Skellions are trying to make their escape. She pulls away from Mollie, shakes her head at the doormen. They understand her signal.

'No,' the burlier one announces, holding up a huge hand. 'No go.'

Paddy tries to push through them but he's no match for their combined bulk. He bundles his paintings into Tory's hands, shakes out his arms, makes loose fists of his hands. 'We want to leave now. You can't stop us.'

'I haven't finished,' Laura says. 'I have more to say.'

'I don't give a shit,' Paddy says. 'We're out of here. Never should've come in the first place. Knew you were fake as soon as I saw you.'

'Really? Funny how that didn't stop you going to all the trouble of coming here. You didn't think I was fake when you were coming on to me in your studio, did you?'

'What the . . .? How dare— Look, I don't know what all this is about but—'

'You know exactly what it's about.'

'But all this? These lengths? For what? What're you trying to prove?'

'My father is dead because of you.' She turns to Tory. 'And you, you piece of scum.'

'What? Like we're murderers?' Paddy says. 'You can't blame that on us. I didn't even know Pierce was dead.'

'Well, he is. A week after your golden boy walked free from court.'

'Tory went through the system. The judge decided. What were we supposed to do? Beg for him to go to jail?'

'My family is *destroyed* because of you. Broken apart. What we had is gone. But you didn't care about that. It was all about you and how you might suffer. Not a single thought for us. None of you. A simple "sorry" would've gone a long way. Some kind of sympathy for what we went through.'

Marie starts to speak, her voice trembly, barely audible: 'B-but—'

'Shut up, Marie,' Paddy tells her. 'Leave this to me.' He points a finger at Laura. 'What happened wasn't Tory's fault. He was dragged into it. It's not us you need to be harassing, it's that shower he got himself mixed up with. If it wasn't for them, we wouldn't be here arguing the toss.'

'What about personal responsibility? Free will?'

'What about undue influence? Peer pressure? He was only seventeen. Things aren't as simple as they seem.'

Laura rolls her eyes. Is Skellion for real? 'Give me a fucking break. It's *very* simple.' She directs her gaze to Tory. 'You knew exactly what you were doing. It's not like you were *forced*.'

Tory squints his piggy eyes, twists his fleshy mouth around his words. 'What the fuck would *you* know?'

'I was there, in case you haven't copped on to that yet. But I guess you weren't first in line when brains were being doled out.' She turns to Paddy. 'And I know about your little arrangement with your solicitor. How you pulled every string to make sure there was no punishment.'

Paddy stares, clearly shocked, his eyes still and glassy. 'I don't have to listen to any more of this. We're leaving now, whether you like it or not. You can't keep us.' He moves to take Marie's arm but her hand shoots to her head.

'I – I don't feel good,' she whispers. 'I think I . . .' and she slumps against Tory, who drops his father's paintings as he tries, but fails, to keep her upright. Her legs buckle under her, the unwrapped canvas breaking her fall, its wooden stretcher snapping under her dead weight.

'Jesus Christ!' Paddy cries but, as he bends down, it's unclear what it is he's most concerned about: Marie prone on the floor or the damaged painting that lies beneath her.

TWENTY-FIVE

'**Y**ou're fine. You're fine. Come on.' Paddy hooks his arm through Marie's, attempts to pull her up.

She moans. 'Stop, Paddy. Give me a minute, for God's sake.'

'You're grand. It was just a dizzy spell.'

'How would you know?' Tory says. 'You're not a doctor.'

Paddy ignores his cheek. It obviously wasn't a stroke. And he doubts it was a heart attack. She's not paralysed or unconscious. She felt faint, that's all. But, Jesus, she could've chosen a better time to collapse. He tries again to lift her but she's not budging. Does she not get that he wants to leave? Can she not see the bigger picture here? And never mind that picture, what about the one she's on top of? With the stretcher broken, the canvas is bound to be torn. Surely she knows Paddy wants to see what can be salvaged.

But no. 'I need to lie down,' she says. 'For a few minutes even.'

Paddy groans. Isn't she already lying down? Typical. Cautious to the bloody last. God knows what could happen if they stay here any longer. Laura Karlson, Pierce, whatever the hell she's called . . . She could be a total psycho for all they know. Look what she's managed so far.

'What's going on? Is everything okay?' Paddy looks up to see the tall, silver-haired bloke he'd noticed back in the room. Sky blue suit; shiny yellow waistcoat. Bats for the other team, obviously. You'd have to, wearing gear like that.

'Everything's fine,' Paddy snaps. 'We want to go home. We were brought here under false pretences. But I'm sure you knew all about that.'

'This lady obviously needs a moment,' the bloke says, ignoring Paddy's question. 'You can bring her to my study. It's quiet in there. You won't object to that, I assume.'

'I've already told you. We're leaving. And who're you anyway?'

'Frank Butler. A family friend.'

'Frank Butler. Well, that's handy to know. I'll need that when I'm suing for false imprisonment. I won't be letting this go, you know. You'll be sorry you ever—'

'I need a . . . drink,' Marie mumbles, trying to push herself up on one elbow. 'I feel really . . . weak.'

'Dad, for fuck's sake, just bring her to sit down somewhere,' Tory says. 'There won't be any problem getting outta here after. I'll see to it.'

Marie pushes her hair off her face. 'And . . . it might be good to . . . talk. It can't hurt.'

Talk? She's not serious, is she? 'Did you hit your head?' Paddy asks. 'Because you're not making any sense.'

'Stop, Paddy,' she says wearily, as Tory helps her up from the floor. 'Listen to yourself. It's that . . . bullheadedness has us here in the first place.'

Paddy watches as she gets to her feet. She seems unsteady all right, but could she have pulled a fast one? Deliberately 'fainted' to delay things? He wouldn't put it past her. Here's an opportunity to stick her oar in, to go against him and start apologising for what Tory did, just like she's always wanted. Hadn't she been about to chip in earlier on there, when Laura was saying stuff about a sorry going a long way? Look at her. With her veiny cheeks and her shiny nose and her hair all over the shop. And what about his painting? He picks it up. He was right. There's a three-inch rip in the canvas at the point where the stretcher snapped. Ruined. Beyond repair.

'Come on, Paddy,' Marie says weakly. 'You can sort that out later.'

He's not going to win this one. 'Five minutes. That's all. Then we're going.'

Frank Butler leads the way along a dim, picture-lined corridor followed first by Tory and Marie. Mollie trails behind, then Laura. Paddy fixes his gaze on her firm arse, her heels clicking louder and louder across the tiles as the party chat fades and the music becomes a muted, muffled hum. Bitch. How the hell does she know about his arrangement to get Tory off? How? Only Tory, Marie, Paddy and Vincent, their solicitor, were in on it. Someone blabbed. That's for certain. Marie. Has to be. Must've let it out to one of her southside lunch set. Might as well have been on Sky News. When this is over and done with, when they get back home, he'll have it out with her. She's banging on about him being bullheaded? What about her not being able to keep her trap shut? Loyalty, how are you?

They bundle into an office-like room that smells of dust and cigarettes and furniture polish. Fancy marble fireplace;

plush sofa and chairs; floor scattered with antique rugs; a fancy gilded desk in front of a window shuttered against the night. All very cosy. But claustrophobic with it.

Marie sinks into a chair, Mollie and Tory sprawl on the sofa. Laura leans against the desk, Paddy stands in the centre of the room. 'Brandy?' Frank asks Marie. She nods, though Paddy has never known her to drink the stuff. Frank lifts a crystal decanter from a side table, pours two fingers into a glass.

'I'll go and check on the guests,' he says. 'I trust you'll be all right here without me for a few moments, Laura.'

'Perfectly fine,' Laura says. She waits until he's gone, then she folds her arms across her chest. 'So, here we are. It all comes down to this.'

'What's that supposed to mean?' Paddy wants to know. 'We're not here for some kind of a showdown.'

Laura tips her head to one side. 'I wouldn't be so sure about that.'

'Marie's having her brandy. Then we'll be off.'

'I didn't go to all this trouble for just a couple of minutes, Mr Skellion. Now, first things first, phones on the desk, please.'

Tory laughs. 'You must be fucking joking.'

Laura fixes her gaze on Paddy for a second, then her eyes slide to Marie, to Mollie, to Tory. She shakes her head, makes some sort of tutting sound with her tongue against her teeth then steps over to the door.

Paddy watches as she turns the key, removes it from the lock, stuffs it into her bra.

He feels heat rising to his face. 'What the hell do you think you're doing? You can't keep us here.'

'Not nice, is it?' she says. 'Believe me, I understand. Now,

I'll say it again. Phones on the desk. No calling anyone for help.'

'Help?' Marie says. 'What do you mean?'

'If you think you're going to get away with this,' Paddy says, 'you're deluded.'

'I'm not giving you my fucking phone,' Tory says. 'No way.'

'Just do what she says,' Mollie tells him. 'It'll be easier if we cooperate.'

'What?' Tory asks. 'Whose side are you on?'

'Interesting question,' Laura answers. 'I'll get to that in a moment.' She holds out her hand. 'There's just the small matter of the phones first.'

Paddy sees the ugly face his son pulls and feels a flash of pure revulsion. This is really Tory's fault, as much as Paddy might defend him. No amount of Marie's reasoning or Paddy turning a blind eye is going to change the bald truth. But this? Laura Pierce? This is just spite. True, Tory didn't have to do what he did, but wasn't he carried along by that gang of shitheads? Laura Pierce, it seems, is acting alone. Butler has to have been in on it but she's the driving force. That much is pretty clear. She has the same streak of defiance her father had. The superior attitude that Paddy had found so fucking annoying. And there she is blaming Paddy for Pierce's death.

That man was an explosion waiting to happen. It was only a matter of time. Even back fifteen years ago it had been obvious. Blowing his top over the slightest thing. Going ballistic, saying Paddy's work was slapdash. Jesus Christ, he wasn't a bloody machine. No one had ever said anything of the sort to him before. It wasn't just offensive to Paddy, it was a slur on his father's memory too. Paddy hadn't gone too far arranging that claim with his work buddy. It was no skin off Pierce's nose. His insurance would've covered it. Paddy was only getting his due. And making the report about site standards was just Paddy making sure Pierce knew he meant business. It worked, didn't it? Never heard a peep from him after that. Never saw him again till the court hearing.

He thinks back to how he'd felt that day last October, the sense of victory when he'd managed to get Tory off without so much as an hour's community service. He'd almost go so far as to say the whole affair had been worth it. But now? Is he having second thoughts? He looks again at his son, is relieved to find that the revulsion has vanished. Replaced by . . . pride? Well, not exactly, but certainly by satisfaction. Big-shots like Pierce regularly need reminding that they're mortal like the rest of us. If what happened ended in his wife becoming a widow, that's not anyone's fault. When it's your time, it's your time. Why should they do what she says? Give her their phones? Who does she think she is? A fucking drug lord or something? Losing the run of herself now. Big-time. 'You tell her, Tory. Stand up for yourself. We don't have to take any of this shit.'

Marie takes another glug of her brandy. 'For God's sake, Paddy. Let's just do as she says. Cooperate. For once in your life.' She reaches into her bag, still looped across her chest. 'Here.' She holds her phone out. Laura takes it, places it on the desk.

If Paddy's face was hot a few moments ago, it's steaming now. Who's in control here? Talk about folding under pressure. He shoots Marie the coldest stare. She can do what she likes. He's not going to capitulate.

Laura turns to him. 'Your phone, Mr Skellion.'

'I don't have it on me,' Paddy lies. 'I left it at home.'

She smiles. 'Pathetic.' Then to Tory and Mollie: 'Come on. You two as well.' Silence. Laura walks around to the front of the desk. She looks at Tory. 'I expect you'd use a baseball bat in this instance, wouldn't you? When you're not getting what you want, I mean.' She pulls open a drawer. 'Unfortunately, we're all out of those. But what I do have . . . is this.'

The glint of metal catches Paddy's eye.

He takes his phone from his pocket and hands it over.

TWENTY-SIX

Funny how things turn out. How one thing leads to another. Laura keeps a firm, tight grip on the gun. The weight of it in her hand is comforting, reassuring. Not that she's worried or anxious in any way but, well, there's something about a weapon, isn't there? It affords power like nothing else.

Perfect. It's not just the sight of the gun that has Skellion rattled, it's the fact that he knows Laura's not afraid to use it. It's a sort of reverse trust. A belief, on his part, that she's crazy enough to pull the trigger. And the look on his face. Priceless.

He's not to know the gun isn't real. That it's an excellent-quality replica Colt something-or-other that Frank has had for years, procured for the murder-mystery parties Lee was so fond of. Skellion might suspect it's fake, of course, but that's all it'll be – a suspicion. He won't have enough certainty to defy her.

Laura has Frank to thank for this turn in direction. All that stuff about her father, she shouldn't have brought him into it until later on. She'd revealed too much too soon. Frank had seen it. Skellion was never going to stand there in front of the crowd listening to her rambling poor-me tale. She'd fucked up, had allowed her emotions get the better of her. Frank had been right to shoo everyone out to the terrace and insist she take it elsewhere. Marie's fainting fit had forced them here into the study and Laura is grateful. She's back in control. She hadn't planned on using the gun, had forgotten all about it until they entered the room. But once she'd locked the door, it had become an essential component. Frank being a neat-freak, she'd known it'd still be in the drawer where he's always kept it. She nods at Tory and Mollie. 'Phones. Hand them over.'

Mollie raises a pierced eyebrow as she does as she's told. 'How do we know that thing's real?'

Brazen cow. Thing is, Mollie knows the gun's fake. Laura remembers mentioning it once and it's not the kind of thing Mollie would forget. But the American psycho can't let on she knows: she's still acting the part of dutiful girlfriend, can't pretend she's acquainted with Laura. That bubble will burst very shortly, though. Playing with fire? She'll soon be in fucking flames.

Laura chooses to ignore her, doesn't let her catch her eye. 'You too,' she says to Tory, pointing the gun at his head. 'I'd move quickly if I were you.'

'Just do it,' Marie says, her voice wobbling. 'You can't call anyone if you're dead.'

'Your mother speaks a lot of sense,' Laura says. 'You'd be wise to listen to her.'

Mollie elbows him in the ribs. 'You wanna get us all *shot*? Do what she fuckin well says.'

With a sigh of reluctance, Tory hands over his phone. 'Nice,' Laura says, as she turns it over in her hand. 'I'll bet that cost Daddy a pretty penny.'

Skellion comes over all bristly. 'Enough of the spiky remarks. You have what you want. What next?'

Before Laura can answer, they hear a knock on the door. Soft at first, then louder, more persistent. 'Laura?'

Richie.

'My wife isn't well,' Skellion says. 'You've no right to keep us here against our will.'

'The concerned husband,' Laura says. 'How sweet. Finally she has a use.'

'Laura! I can hear you,' Richie calls. 'Let me in!'

Laura keeps a steady grip on the gun, aiming it at Marie. 'Don't get any stupid ideas. Any of you. One false move and I'll shoot. I'm not afraid to use this thing. I'm not afraid to kill.'

'Y'all do what you're told,' Mollie says, like she's in charge. 'If y'all wanna get outta here alive.'

There's a silence, just a few seconds, before Tory slowly rounds on her, eyes narrowed to slits. 'What the fuck? Are you in on this or something?'

'That would upset you, would it?' Laura asks.

Mollie pulls at her lip piercing, twists the silver ball between her thumb and forefinger. She rolls her eyes, sighs heavily, speaks without pausing between words: 'Me and Laura are friends I'm not into you Tory I was just helpin' her out.'

Tory pulls his arm from her shoulders. 'Helping her out?'

Laura smiles. 'And there was you thinking you were something special.'

Tory leaps from the sofa. 'Jesus *Christ*! Is this true?'

'You didn't think I actually had a *thing* for you, did you?' Mollie says. 'I mean, come on.'

Paddy flaps his arms about. 'So – so *neither* of you is who you say you are? Is that it? You're both in on this – this fiasco? For Jesus' sake. What sort of— I mean, who in their right mind would—'

'Would what, Mr Skellion?' Laura asks. 'Try and manoeuvre a situation to suit their own ends? Not something entirely alien to you, is it?'

'You.' Paddy looks at Mollie. 'We welcomed you into our home and all the time this was a – a charade? You might think you're clever but you're a dirty tart, that's what you are.'

'Just helpin' out a friend,' Mollie replies, with a flick of her head. 'Nothin' personal.'

'Nothing *personal*? Are you for real?' Tory leans over, takes a swipe, but she's quick, blocks it with her forearm.

'Back off, asshole,' she yells. 'You're only gettin' what you deserve.'

Marie stands up, moves to restrain her son. 'Don't!' she cries, her strength returning. 'You're upset, I understand. But that's not the answer.' Her fiery eyes find her husband's. 'Paddy?'

'What? What do you want me to do?' Paddy says. 'This whole thing has gone beyond a joke. He's every right to feel mad!'

Marie reaches for Tory's arm, pulls him away. She looks at Mollie with disgust. 'You should be ashamed of yourself.'

'Laura?' Richie calls again. 'You okay in there?' He twists the knob. 'If you don't let me in, I'll break down the door.' Then a thud sounds as he attempts to do just that.

'Take it easy,' she calls.

'I mean it,' Richie shouts, and gives the door another shove. As much as she doesn't want to open up, it's probably unfair to keep Richie out. And it doesn't sound like he's about to stop banging the door anytime soon.

Laura reaches down the front of her dress and finds the key while still pointing the gun at Marie. 'Okay, Rich. Just give me a second.' She keeps her gaze on the room, steps backwards towards the door, manages to insert and turn the key. Richie's face peeps through the small crack, his eyes wide and searching. He pushes the gap wider, slides in, followed closely by Frank.

Frank gapes when he sees Laura brandishing the gun but that's as much reaction as he's able to convey before Paddy makes a run for it.

He roughly shoulders Frank aside, grips the knob with his left hand, curls the fingers of his right around the edge and tries to yank open the door. Richie reacts quickly, launching his full weight against it to stop Paddy's escape.

The sound, when it comes, is sickening.

The clear slam of door against frame is muted by four wedges of skin and bone.

Paddy's unrestrained roar expresses not only his physical pain. It goes far beyond that.

He sinks to his knees, rolls onto his side, cradles his limp right hand in his left.

The tool of his trade has been shattered. The reality of it is clear to them all.

As he lies there moaning, Richie locks the door and pushes the key into the pocket of his jeans.

TWENTY-SEVEN

The pain is greater than any Paddy has known. All those words that people use – unbearable, excruciating, agonising – none of those comes close. Indescribable. That might do. Because there are no words to explain it.

Could anyone possibly have experienced worse? In the seconds that follow, a movie reel plays in his head: days, months, years into the future. He knows, is certain, that things will never be the same again.

One finger, two . . . There might have been a chance. But four? He has no doubt they're all shattered. The instrument of his success, his livelihood, his existence: what remains of it is a dangling, mangled mess.

Through the fog of pain, he turns to Marie. His eyes plead with her. For sympathy. For understanding. *What?* How is it that her face is grim, her mouth a fixed, hard line? His voice is strangled with pain as he says her name. 'Marie?'

'You were going to *leave* me here,' she says, with venom. 'With a *gun* being held to my head.'

'What? No! No, Marie. I – I— *Jesus!* I'm in agony, woman. My hand's broken to bits. What do you want me to say?'

'Did you not think about me and Tory? Did you not worry about what would happen if you left us here? I'm sorry about your hand but you brought it on yourself. Where were you going to go?'

'To get help! Where else?'

She looks away. 'You were prepared to risk me having my head blown off.'

'Well, you know what this proves, don't you?' He turns to Laura. 'What happened to "One false move and I'll shoot"? Either you don't have it in you or that thing's not real. Or not loaded.' He struggles into a sitting position on the floor. 'Go on, tell me I'm wrong.'

Laura sniffs, ignores his question. She brings the gun slowly to her side. 'You all know my brother, Richie. He had the pleasure of being on the receiving end of your baseball bat,' she says to Tory. 'And he was the one trying to comfort my mother when she broke down in court. I'm sure you remember that, Marie.'

Marie mumbles. 'I . . . um—'

'That wasn't me!' Tory protests. 'I didn't hit him. I—'

'Your face might've been covered,' Laura interrupts, 'but you weren't able to disguise your height, your body shape. It was clearly you.'

'Jesus, give it up, will you?' Paddy says, groaning. 'What does any of this matter now? It's over. You can't change it. Can you not just move on?' Christ. Can they not see he needs a doctor? His hand is totally banjaxed and they're arguing the toss over who did what. It beggars belief.

'It *was* you,' Laura's brother says to Tory. 'You piece of dog shit.' He stares at Mollie. 'And you needn't look so fucking innocent.'

Mollie's hand flies to her chest. '*Me?*'

'Yeah, you. Tell her, Laura. Tell her what I found out.'

Frank steps forward unsteadily, shooting Paddy a look of disdain. Paddy watches him place a hand on the brother's shoulder, as if the kid might need restraining.

His fingers throb like hell. The pain! 'Jesus!' he pleads. 'Spare us your revelations. I need to get to a hospital. Does no one understand that?'

But there's no reaction. Seems they couldn't care less. God almighty. Well, fuck the lot of them. Even Marie and Tory. *Especially* Marie and Tory. Talk about showing your true colours. What's that they say? You find out who your true friends are in a crisis. Just wait. When this thing is over it's going to be all-change. They won't know what hit them. Maybe he should be grateful this has happened: it's given him a whole new perspective.

'So, Mollie. Dear Mollie,' Laura says. 'Have you anything you'd like to confess?'

Mollie bites at one of her already well-chewed fingernails. 'Like what?'

'Oh, I don't know. Maybe like . . . "I was behind the break-in." Maybe . . .' Laura moves her head from side to side '. . . "I paid some lowlife scum to teach you and your family a lesson. To get my own back after you pissed me off."'

'Don't bother denying it,' the kid brother says. 'I know everything. Friend of mine has a mate who got it straight from the shithead who did the job for you.'

Mollie surveys the nail she's been biting.

'Is this true?' Marie asks, features twisted in shock. 'Tory?'

'Mollie?' Tory asks. 'They're bullshitting, right?' Mollie stares ahead, chewing at the inside of her cheek. It's enough for Tory. 'You bitch!' he shouts into her face. 'I fucking *trusted* you. I thought . . . And all this time you were . . .' He pushes his fingers through his hair. 'Jesus *Christ*.'

She ignores him, pleads only with Laura. 'I was tryin' to help. Seriously. I felt bad for doin' what I did to y'all. It wasn't meant to get so fucked-up that night. I just thought they'd, you know, scare you or something. I've changed since then, Laura. Can't you see that? I wanted to help you with this. I wanted to make sure it'd go right for you. So you could get some, you know, closure.'

Laura laughs. 'You honestly expect me to believe that? You're only admitting it because you've been found out. Stop making out that you give a fuck. Your sick little act doesn't fool me.'

'I knew she was bad news,' Marie says. 'I just knew it. Tory could've gone to jail! Do you realise that?'

'Take it easy,' Laura says. 'Don't use her as the scapegoat. Your darling boy didn't have to do what he did. No one forced him. He's as much to blame as she is.'

Marie sits down again, perches on the edge of the chair. 'So, if what you're saying is that *she* orchestrated the break-in, that the heartache, the worry and the stress were all down to her spite, then why the hell were you pointing that gun at me?'

For once, Paddy agrees with Marie. 'Look,' he says to Laura, 'I don't know what sort of . . . vendetta or whatever is going on between the two of you but it's obvious that we're the innocents here. Do you not see that? If it wasn't for her, none of this would've happened.'

'I was only following orders,' Laura mocks. 'Is that it? You make me sick. All of you.'

Mollie gets up from the sofa. 'Girl, I mean it,' she says, her voice low and coaxing. 'It was wrong. I get that. But I'm sorry. Truly. I tried to tell you but I just couldn't. I felt so . . . ashamed. You're the only real friend I have, Laura. The only person I trust.' She reaches out her hand, whimpers, '*Please.*'

Laura bats her away. 'Save your tears. Not that I can actually see any.'

Mollie shakes her head. 'You're makin' a mistake. I've said I'm sorry. Think about it. I came all the way out here for you. No other reason. Why would I do that if I wasn't bein' honest?'

'Let me see? Oh, yeah. Because you're a scheming, vindictive bitch. Do you honestly expect me to believe a single word you say?'

There's a cold, hard set to Laura's eyes. She's not for turning. Mollie tries again, grovels, begs Laura to yield but it's not happening.

'For the love of God, will you give it a rest?' Paddy says. 'Get it into your thick Yankee skull, will you? She doesn't want anything to do with you. None of us do. You're a waste of fucking space.'

Mollie's lips curl downwards. 'Shut your dirty mouth, you scummy excuse for a man. You've no right to call me out. Like you've always played by the rules? Don't think so. What about that time you beat the shit outta some poor guy in London way back when?'

Paddy forgets about his pain for a few seconds as he tries to figure out how she knows. It doesn't take long. How else? He stares at his son and, for a brief but not inconsiderable flash, wonders how things would've turned out if they hadn't allowed him to be born.

Mollie continues: 'And what about that sting you pulled makin' sure baby boy wouldn't spend time in the slammer? Wouldn't look good for you if that was to get out, would it?'

Tory and his big mouth. Couldn't keep his trap shut. 'Well, I'll be making sure you become familiar with the inside of a prison cell if I have my way,' he tells her. 'Don't think I won't take it further. You'll be sorry you admitted any of it.'

'You think I give a shit?' Mollie folds her arms across her chest. 'You do what you want, Pops, but don't forget, I've plenty of dirt on you too.'

It takes all of Paddy's strength to stay upright. With his good hand, he holds onto the mantelpiece, steadies himself, grits his teeth. The agony. Not just of his fingers but of the situation. Does Tory actively go around seeking out the lowest of the low? Or do they gravitate towards him, regardless, like flies on shite? 'It's all rubbish,' he says. 'Try proving any of it and see how far you get.'

'Ditto,' Mollie says. 'It'll be my word against little Richie's. And his evidence? Hearsay, I think they call it.' She laughs. 'Nobody's gonna shop me. I buy silence same as you buy freedom.'

'Enough of your gangster talk,' Laura tells her. 'It makes you sound even more pathetic than you are.'

'More pathetic than the crazy bitch walkin' round with a fake gun in her hand? Doubt it.'

Paddy's heart takes a jump. Fake? Mollie would hardly claim that unless she knew it to be true. Here's a chance to end this. But it's not something he's able to do. Not now with his hand in bits. He glances over at Tory. Can he depend on the bird-brain to take the initiative? Does he have enough cop?

'You've already proven yourself to be a liar, Mollie,' Laura sneers. 'Who's going to believe a word out of your mouth?'

'Come on,' Mollie says, looking at Paddy. 'She's done nothin' but lie to you herself. Does Frank look like the kinda guy who'd keep a loaded shotgun in his desk? It's just a souvenir.' She turns now to Laura. 'Used it to play detective games with his lover, didn't he? The one you were always jealous of. Remember?'

'I wasn't jealous of Lee.'

'Really? That's not what you told me. You were stoked when he bit the dust.'

'Stop trying to stir even more shit than you already have.'

'I'm only tellin' it like it is. You hated that he grabbed all Frank's attention when he was around. You wanted him gone. You made that clear.'

'Don't be so fucking crazy.'

Paddy tries to catch Tory's eye again but he's turned his attention to his mother, is kneeling beside her, holding her hand. Typical. Here's his father, practically passing out with the pain, clearly in need of emergency treatment, but it's Marie who gets the concern. Can he not see there's an opportunity now? They're distracted, bickering about one of Frank Butler's fancy-men. Tory's big enough to take them both down. But no. What's more important? Asking Mammy if she's okay when there isn't so much as a scratch on her.

'Can we leave Lee out of it, please?' Frank says, irritated. 'I'd rather . . . I'd rather he wasn't dragged into all this. I don't need you badmouthing his memory.'

Mollie laughs. 'Still protecting the loser?'

'Give it up!' Laura shouts. 'Have some respect. The man's dead, for God's sake! He can't defend himself.'

'No, but I can,' Frank says. His voice is wobbling. 'Lee was my partner f-for fourteen years. We had our ups and downs. Who doesn't? He may not have been p-perfect b-but behind it all, he . . . he loved me.'

Mollie's eyes shrink to slits and clusters of veins bulge on her temples. 'I know what it's like to be betrayed, Frank. To find out someone doesn't like you the way you thought they did. You do everythin' to make them happy but it changes nothin'. Lee was a cheatin' deadbeat. You let him walk all over you and you feel like shit cos he's gone now and that's the way it's always gonna be. You can never change what he was and the way he treated you.'

Frank lets go of the kid brother now, steps away from him, keeps his fists tight by his sides. 'No. You're wrong. We were – we were happy. Looking forward to our future. He might've been . . .' he gulps '. . . unfaithful at times but he'd changed.'

'Changed? Gimme a break!' There's a manic look in her eyes and she spits out her words like poison. 'You *still* say that? Even *now*? After he was found wearing nothin' but black rubber shorts and a dog collar? Not exactly the kind of thing you wear on a quiet night in alone, is it?'

That shuts him up. He's still as a statue, except for a twitch that pulses one side of his mouth. He speaks slowly, carefully. 'How . . . do you know . . . what he was wearing?'

Mollie pulls her chin to her chest, shrugs. 'I guess Laura must've told me.'

'I told *nobody*.'

'But . . .' Mollie says, '. . . you must have.'

'Nobody,' he repeats. 'I cut that . . . attire off his body before the paramedics arrived. Better he be found naked than dressed like that.'

'Okay. But you told someone and it got out. It happens. You were, I dunno, confused. Upset. You don't remember.'

Frank speaks through clenched teeth: 'I remember exactly. I kept those details to myself. There's no other way you could know. You must have been there.'

'No. No.' Mollie's head shakes violently. 'How could I? I – I . . . No.'

Laura lifts a hand to her mouth. 'You *were* there. It wasn't . . . He didn't . . . Oh, my *God.*'

'No! You're wrong! He – he just fell. He was outta his head. He—'

'So you *admit* you were there? You knew Frank was away that night. You actually went to his house? Why? What for?'

Paddy watches as Mollie's face contorts and she screams, 'I did it for you, Laura! I did it to make you happy!'

TWENTY-EIGHT

Intermittent wafts of cool, dry air play chase across the smooth curves of Laura's bare legs, competing with the mellow warmth of the sun. She lies on her stomach, still fogged in sleep, savouring the gentle sensations that trace over and back across her skin. It takes a long, slow moment to gather the strength to lift her right eyelid a millimetre: The split-second mascara-lashed view shows blinding sunlight and a flash of fierce blue sky. Jesus. Too much reality. Frank must have been in and thrown open the shutters in an effort to rouse her. She stretches out an arm, fingers blindly searching for her phone. Not on the bedside locker. Or under her pillow. She shifts a little in the bed. Yep. She can feel the hard lines of it pressing into her thigh. Still steeped in sticky drowsiness, she fishes it out, squinting at the screen: 1.27 p.m. What? Like, in the afternoon? She pushes her brain to understand how she has slept so late. What day is it? She can't figure that one out. What was last night? Something special? She thinks hard. Her memory is a sluggish, staccato confusion of colour and sound. Music. People. Laughter. Was it good? A crowd? A party?

Of course.

Frank's party. Jesus, it must've been amazing.

She rolls onto her back just as another drift of cool air breezes in and she realises that she has on only her underwear. She remembers that bit. Pulling off her dress. Struggling with the tightness, tearing it over her head. Falling, ecstatic, onto the bed. Delirious with fatigue. But it had been bright. Everything was visible. Dawn? Or later. That's why the shutters are open: she'd been too exhausted to close them. She rolls again, onto her side this time, drags herself up to sit on the edge of the bed. Her head throbs hard, a dull, aching rhythm that makes her want to fall back down into sleep. But her throat is gritty and sore. She needs a drink. And some painkillers. She pulls the crumpled sheet with her as she stands, wraps it around herself, cape-style. She stretches, yawns, blinks her eyes fully open, despite her lashes' reluctance to separate.

What? There. On the bed. On the bottom sheet. And the pillow.

Smears of . . . dirt? How?

She leans down, looks more closely, rubs at the stains.

Her hands. She lifts them to her face.

Her fingers. Under her nails . . . dirt. Ingrained in the lines of her palms . . . dirt.

Fuck.

Running from the room, flying along the landing, sheet billowing behind her, she swerves left through Frank's door. Empty. Bed neat and tidy. Not slept in.

Richie. She checks his room. Nothing but an eerie silence and squares of yellow sunlight on the floor.

Down the stairs. Into the hall. Remnants of last night's

celebration. Champagne dregs in print-smeared flutes lined up on the console. Lip-sticked butts S-pressed into a silver ashtray. A scarlet satin evening glove, lying on the tiles, like a tidy pool of blood. The door to the living room lies open. Inside, surfaces are towered with plates of half-eaten food, stamped with syrupy bottle-rings, crowded with empty glasses. Several chairs lie overturned at the far end of the room. She doesn't look further than the terrace doors.

She finds them in the kitchen. They sit at the table, white-faced, both, eyes buttoned deep into darkened sockets. Frank is still dressed as last night, minus the jacket, his yellow waistcoat ripped under the arms and missing a button or two. He looks up at Laura for a moment, but nothing like recognition appears on his face. Richie stares hard at some point on the wall, lips tightly squeezed, his T-shirt filthy and pulled out of shape.

Laura waits at the door. But for what? Words of comfort? Of rage? Sorrow? Words are no use. Not now. They used enough words last night, convincing themselves that they were doing the right thing. And it worked, didn't it? Their actions took care of everything. They mobilised, didn't they? Rallied round. Came to a consensus. Common sense prevailed. Laura bites her tongue. It was actually civilised, really. She has to believe that. There's no other way it will work.

'You slept,' Frank says to the table, a statement of fact rather than a query. 'At least one of us did.'

Laura wants to say, 'No' or 'Just an hour or two,' but the truth is, she was in a practical coma for, it must have been, six hours. There's no point pretending otherwise. 'I was exhausted.'

Frank nods slowly. 'Understandable. You did most of the labouring.'

She looks around the room. It's spotless. 'You tidied up.'

'I needed something to occupy myself. I've left the other rooms for the clean-up team. They'll be here soon.'

'Couldn't you put them off? At least until tomorrow? Give us time to . . . you know . . . get our shit together.'

Frank lifts his head. 'Our shit, my dear, had better already be together. There's no time for coming to terms with it or collecting our thoughts. If we start making allowances, then we are, as you might describe it, fucked.'

Laura swallows. 'Carry on as normal?'

'Exactly. Nail on the head.'

'Rich?' she says. 'You're in agreement, yeah? Like, you understand?' Richie's gaze doesn't waver. And, if anything, he seems to become more rigid.

Laura fires Frank a worried glance. He emits a small sigh. 'You've no need to worry,' he says. 'We discussed it last night, didn't we? Richie's in no doubt. We each know how this is going to work. It's in all our best interests.' He stands up from the table, wipes a hand over his weary eyes. 'Now, hadn't you better go and get dressed?'

So, that's that, then. Laura does as Frank asks and heads back upstairs to her room. She supposes he's right. What else is there to do? He'll probably insist that she stick to the plan and fly home tomorrow too. Carry on as normal.

She takes a nail brush into the shower, scrubs hard and long at her fingers, her palms, at every inch of her skin. The water is hot this morning and she's grateful. It's not just that she started to shiver when she dropped the sheet from her shoulders, it's that no amount of cold water could ever wash last night away.

She dresses in jeans and a T-shirt, leaves her face bare of make-up, her hair to dry in the air. She strips the bed, bundles the soiled sheet into a ball without looking at it but then, when it's in a heap on the floor, she unravels it, spreads it out, stares again at the criss-crossed dirty smears. She must have been tossing all night, digging her fingers into the mattress, the pillow.

Digging, digging.

Is it weird that it hadn't been the first thing on her mind when she'd woken up? Maybe her brain had been protecting her, not allowing her to immediately recall what had happened, only gently bringing her round. Will that always be the way? Time will tell. Today is only the first day. It's natural that it'll take her a while to get used to the idea, to understand that it happened and that things have changed. But she won't make it into one of those before-and-after situations, where people measure their lives by what went *before* some event and what came *after*. Because it's not like that. Not really. You reserve that kind of arrangement for stuff that has a significant impact. Laura doesn't intend for this to have any. Why should she? Frank has the right attitude. She's going to get on with things the same as before. True, something's gone that used to be there but, when you think about it, it's no real loss at all.

Richie will be fine. His demeanour now has more to do with lack of sleep than anything else. Poor kid. Guilt can be a terrible thing if you give it permission to invade your soul. Thing about Richie is, he gets hung up on negativity. He's probably sitting there mulling over all the things he shouldn't have done, all the corners he shouldn't have turned. Beating himself up for finding out that stuff about Mollie and coming all the way out here. Blaming himself. He just doesn't see it yet. That he was meant to do what he did, that this was meant to happen. Think about the circumstances. All the minute details that led up to it. No. Laura will simply have to get it into his head that he did the right thing. There's no need for him to be shitting himself over what's after happening. Everything is sweet.

She still needs that drink, those painkillers. She gathers up the sheet, pushes it hurriedly into the laundry basket, heads back downstairs. The kitchen is empty now. She runs the tap, fills a glass, finds a box of paracetamol in a drawer and bursts two pills from their blisters. As she swallows them, eyes closed, it occurs to her how fortunate they were that the earth had been so dry.

So easy to burrow into.

The villa is quiet. Quieter than usual. Or maybe it just seems that way after all the revelry last night. It's as if silence is oozing from the walls like foam, filling the rooms with bloated bubbles of emptiness. She wanders out to the hall and down the corridor.

Reaching the door to the study, she pushes it, standing back until it swings open the whole way. Frank is sitting at his desk, pen in hand. 'Thought you'd gone to bed,' she says. 'Don't you think you should sleep?'

He looks up. His reading glasses magnify his worn-out eyes and the pinkish rims that surround them. He's been crying. Christ.

'Later,' he says, trying his best to sound alert.

'What are you doing? Surely it can wait, whatever it is.'

'Just a few things I need to sort out. Won't take long.'

Trudy lies on the sofa, purring contentedly. Laura steps into the room, sits down beside her. She strokes the soft fur on her back. 'Fully recovered, is she?'

Frank sniffs, rubbing at his nose. 'Never thought to consider how she might react to fireworks. Perhaps we shouldn't have gone ahead with them.'

'What happened to "carry on as normal"? That's all you were doing.'

'I suppose so. Just . . . in hindsight, it seems . . . wrong.'

'You can convince yourself that everything was wrong if you want to. Or you can tell yourself that everything was right. That's what I've decided to do.'

'It's easy for you,' he says. 'Or easier. I . . . Well, I have other things to consider.'

'Like?'

He stares at the sheets of paper on the desk in front of him for a long moment. 'Just business. Nothing you need concern yourself with, my dear.'

'It'll be okay, Frank,' she says, picking at a fingernail, one she's not sure she got completely clean. 'I know you're upset. It's a lot to take in. That part of it . . . I mean, Lee . . . I haven't got my head around it yet.'

Frank sucks at his lower lip. He's swallowing back tears. 'I can't . . . It's not . . .' He sighs, so heavily that Trudy twitches awake. 'I don't know how I'm supposed to feel.'

'She killed Lee, Frank. You should know exactly how you feel. I mean, she basically killed Dad. Indirectly, if you want to put it that way, but still . . . And I'm certain how I feel.'

'I admire your resolve, Laura. It's one of your most enviable traits. Your ability to be so sure that you're right.'

'You're hardly indecisive. You want something, you go for it. Stop doubting everything. Ask yourself, how would you feel if she walked in here now? If she was standing there in front of you. The person who murdered the love of your life.'

Frank inhales sharply, holds the breath high in his chest for a few seconds, then lets it back into the air along with his reply. 'I'd want to strangle her.'

Laura smiles. 'See? Now you have it,' she says, using her hands for more emphasis. 'The more I think about it, the more I realise it couldn't have ended up any *other* way.'

'I suppose there is an element of synchronicity about it.'

'True. So true.' She massages Trudy's silky ears. 'Any smokes to hand? I think we fucking well deserve one.'

TWENTY-NINE

Nothing seems real. Not a single thing. Yesterday, the world was wide open for conquering. He could have done anything. He'd been on the verge of a huge opportunity. Except he hadn't. Not in reality. And now, less than twenty-four hours later, Paddy's world may as well be invisible, it has shrunk so much.

For Christ's sake. It's beyond comprehension.

The more he tries to get his head around it, the more unbelievable it becomes. But he's made up his mind. He's not going to let it get him down. Why should he? It's not his fault. He didn't cause it. He's absolutely no reason to feel guilty about it at all. That's not to say he isn't angry. He's fucking furious. Not just at Tory. At Marie too. Not to mention that devious Pierce bitch. Has it all her own way now, hasn't she? And there's fuck-all he can do about it.

He shakes his head. You see this kind of thing in a film and you look at it, thinking, What the hell? That wouldn't happen in real life. It's too far-fetched. What's the phrase? It *stretches credibility*. You sit there asking yourself, Who writes this stuff? How do they get away with it? How could that possibly reflect reality?

Well, Paddy won't ever take that attitude again. When people are up against it, they do what it takes to survive.

They're in this trap together. It won't hold unless they each hang tight. One lets go, they all fall. That much he understands.

But he's come out of this far worse than the rest of them. What happened last night with . . . Well, that's one thing. But the others can go back to whatever they did before, return to their own normality, if that's what they choose to do. Paddy hasn't got that luxury. His busted hand won't allow him. Do any of them have the slightest idea what he's going through?

The doctor in A&E hadn't believed him. He'd told her the truth but it was obvious she'd thought he was bullshitting.

'How this happen?' she'd asked.

'A door,' Paddy had said. 'I caught it in a door.'

She'd grimaced as she'd looked at him with sceptical eyes. 'Heavy door?'

'Yes . . . yes, it was.'

She'd pursed her lips, then pressed them tight together as though she was trying to stop her thoughts escaping. 'Accident?' was all she allowed out.

'Well, I hardly did it deliberately.' He wasn't sure she'd understood. Her English was good but not perfect. Then there was the matter of the time.

'You come . . . um . . . *immédiatement*?'

'As soon as I was able,' Paddy had said. By that time, the injury had been ten hours old. It was clear from her face that she knew full well he hadn't come in *immédiatement*. Her expression told him she suspected he'd been in an alcohol-induced coma since the brawl that had caused him to shatter the bones of four fingers, and had only made his way into the hospital when the numbing effects of the drink had worn off and he'd realised he was actually in pain. He couldn't blame her. He wouldn't have been the first patient to arrive in the early hours of a Sunday morning, unshaven, covered with dirt and stinking of booze. He'd sent Marie and Tory home in the taxi. By that stage, he couldn't bear the sight of either of them. If his wife and son had been with him, the doctor might have been more inclined to believe his story but, as it was, she had every right to be suspicious. Not that Paddy gave a fuck. What did it matter what she thought? All he was concerned about was when he could get back the use of his fingers. She hadn't exactly been clear on that. And still isn't. After she'd disappeared for the third time with his X-rays he'd felt more than entitled to demand some answers. She'd made what he supposed was a sympathetic face and told him he needed surgery. Surgery, for Jesus' sake. Started babbling on about pins and plates and wires and what-have-you. What the hell happened to plain old plaster of Paris? Gone by the wayside, like everything else that used to work perfectly well, no doubt.

So here he is, lying on a trolley, waiting to be brought into theatre. You couldn't bloody well make it up. He hasn't told Marie. She'll find out soon enough. That'll be a nice wake-up call for her. Regardless of everything that transpired after the door was slammed on his fingers, he still can't forgive her for not even *pretending* she cared. All her whinging about *him* not caring about *her*! It was bloody obvious that gun wasn't real. All he'd been doing was trying to get help. Isn't that what anyone in their right mind would've done? She can tell herself whatever she likes but that's his story and he's sticking to it.

Laura. The scheming witch. And the kid brother. The scumbag. It all went belly-up when she let him into the room. Not that things had been hunky-dory up to then but Paddy wouldn't be here readied up for surgery if she'd left him outside. And the rest of it . . . None of that would've happened.

He watches the strip lights on the ceiling whizz past as they wheel him down the corridor and into the over-bright theatre. Christ almighty. He's actually looking forward to being anaesthetised.

Two hours later they slap his cheeks, rousing him into wakefulness for a second or two. Then he slips back into sleep. And he dreams.

Backwards. In the paint colours he won't be using for some time.

The raw umber of the doctor's doubting eyes; the burnt sienna of the brandy, downed at dawn as a cadmium orange sun had risen over the hills. The fireworks through the window – cobalt, magenta, viridian – great blowsy bursts against the lamp-black sky; the yellow ochre of the crumbly earth when they'd dug deep enough.

And the sticky trail of pure vermilion, all the way down to the trees.

THIRTY

They smoke in silence. Frank takes short, ragged puffs; Laura drags hard and deep, exhaling luxuriantly into the room. She gets it now. It'll be like this for some time, she supposes. An emotional see-saw. As opposed to a rollercoaster. Frank up one minute, Laura the next. And vice versa. It's like juggling. Having the confidence to understand the balls won't fall. Once they find their balance, they'll settle into a regular, rhythmic ride without even having to think about it. It's a subconscious thing. If one wobbles, the other slows, takes a breather, steadies things. It'll be even easier once she gets home. She's sure of it.

'What's the story with you coming back to Dublin?' she asks, leaning forward to tap ash into an empty glass tumbler that sits on the desk. 'Next week, you said?'

'Probably. Haven't booked anything yet.'

'Crap. That reminds me. Richie. I'm not sure if he booked a return.'

'He didn't. But it's sorted. We looked up the flights this morning. Got him onto tomorrow's with you.'

'Great. Thanks.' Then she frowns. 'Wouldn't have thought either of you were in any fit state to be making travel arrangements. You looked brain-dead sitting at the table.'

'He was anxious. You can hardly blame him for wanting to get out of here ASAP.'

'He's gone for a sleep?'

Frank nods, easing himself back from the desk to allow Trudy to climb onto his lap. 'Remains to be seen if he actually does.'

Outside, a wind is whipping up. Through the window, Laura watches a pink Chinese lantern skitter across the gravel. 'It was a good party, though,' she says. 'Leaving aside . . . you know.'

'I'm not sure how I should take that statement,' Frank says. 'It was simply a matter of going through the motions after what happened in here.'

'I know. But still. People enjoyed themselves, didn't they? I mean, no one had any idea. It's weird when you think about it. It was like one of your murder-mystery parties. Except we were playing for real.'

Frank shoots her an uneasy look. He takes a final pull on his cigarette before crushing the butt against the inside of the tumbler. He tidies the desk, gathering the sheets of paper, folding them in half, slipping them into the drawer. He hesitates before closing it, and Laura knows he's looking at the gun, back now in its place, just the way he likes things. His eyes linger on it for a long moment, and when he finally lifts them, they sparkle with tears. 'Did you really feel that way about Lee?'

His face . . . Christ. 'Frank, I—'

'I don't blame you, if that's what you think,' he says. 'It was her decision to do what she did.'

She blows a last stream of smoke from the side of her mouth. 'I might've, you know, mentioned once or twice that . . . well, that I didn't think he was right for you.' Frank jumps forward a little, goes to speak but she cuts him off. 'I'm only being honest, Frank. I always thought you deserved far better. You gave him so much and he treated you like dirt. I wasn't the only one who thought that.'

He sighs. Loud and heavy. His hands move rhythmically along Trudy's back. 'I was blind. I couldn't see it. Well, that's not entirely true. I chose *not* to see it, made excuses, pretended it wasn't happening. But what can I say? I still loved him. I still miss him.'

Laura slowly traces a fingertip around the rim of the tumbler. 'The way you found him. Not just dead but dressed like that. It must've been so shit.'

'It wasn't the best, I'll admit. I knew as soon as I walked into the house that he'd had someone round. Let's face it, it wasn't the first time it had happened.'

Laura shout-whispers what Mollie had yelled last night: '"*I did it for you, Laura! I did it to make you happy!*" She made out she did me a favour. What kind of logic is that?'

'Very much a twisted one. But what she said about Lee taking all my attention. You didn't really think that, did you? You've been at the centre of my world since the day you were born. When your dear father asked me to be your godfather. I was the happiest man alive.'

'You don't have to tell me that. There's no point trying to understand her crazy fucked-up mind. She said that to justify what she did. When you think about it, it's possible she only meant to injure him. She couldn't have been sure pushing him down the stairs would actually kill him.'

'Wouldn't she have said so, if that were the case?'

'Not necessarily. What psycho is going to admit their murder was a mistake?'

'I suppose we can go round the houses all day on the whys of it all.' Frank runs a hand over his head. 'I just wish we knew the truth. At what time did she call to the house? Had she been watching from outside? Waiting until whoever he had over had left? Or were they still there and did a runner when they saw what she'd done, not wanting to be implicated? So many unanswered questions.'

Laura stubs out her cigarette, drops the butt into the glass. 'You know, even if I knew Richie was going to grab that letter-opener, I don't think I'd have stopped him.'

Frank's silence speaks volumes.

And so what? Where's the loss? In what way is any of them worse off? As long as nobody blabs – and that's not going to happen – everything's going to be fine. Skellion can moan all he likes but there's absolutely fuck-all he can do. She has him by the balls and she's not letting go.

His face when Mollie had sunk to the floor. The sly I've-got-you-now smile he'd given Laura. Thought he was so smart. That *he* was the one who'd caught *her*.

It was clear there was no saving Mollie. Richie had aimed right for her heart and, judging by the strength of the thrust, had probably sliced it in two.

She didn't even have time to scream.

Stumbling back from the force of the blow, she'd slammed against Tory, who'd jumped sideways and let her fall.

No one made a sound.

Nothing moved, except the blood. Blooming across her chest like a giant crimson rose. Petals drooping down her sides, spreading across the rug, bordering her body in a scarlet pool.

Together, they watched the stain grow. They watched her cheeks pale, her lips turn a shade of purplish blue.

In the long, wordless moments that followed, no one bent to check her pulse to see if, by some miracle, she was still breathing. They were each, in their silence, content to wait until she was not.

Finally, Richie's eyes – wide and scared – had found Laura's. There was no sorrow in his gaze for what he'd done, only fear at what might happen to him now.

It was Skellion's face that had given Laura the answer. The smug expression that said: Should've left well enough alone. Let's see how you wriggle yourself out of this.

'Police,' he'd said. 'We'll have to call them.' He'd barely been able to contain his glee, despite his injured fingers. 'We're all witnesses. We'll have to make statements.' He looked at Frank. 'You have a number for them?'

Laura had taken a step backwards, leaned against the desk, folded her arms. 'That might prove a little difficult.'

'There'll be no delaying tactics, you hear?' Skellion said, his voice rising. 'This is as serious as it gets. This is fucking murder!'

'I know what it is. And you're right. It's serious. For all of us.'

'Fucking sure it is! He still has the weapon in his hand!'

'Hand it over, Richie,' she said. 'Put it on the desk.'

Richie stepped forward, deposited the letter-opener, stared hard at his empty palm.

'Now, is someone going to call the police?' Skellion moved to reach behind Laura and grab his phone from the desk.

Laura slid to one side. 'By all means, take it. Call them. But I'm not sure how you're going to make yourself understood.'

'Not a problem. They all speak English over here.'

'No, I mean how will you explain things to them when you're not even sure how it happened?'

'What're you talking about? We all saw exactly what happened. The kid plunged that thing into her chest.'

'Really? You sure about that? Because I'm not. From where I was standing, it could've been Tory.' She pressed her forefinger to her cheek. 'In fact, now that I think about it, I'm pretty sure it *was* Tory. More than pretty sure, actually. I'm fucking certain.'

A choking rattle sounded in Marie's throat. She coughed it out, shouting, 'You little bitch!' and threw her arms around her son.

Tory shook his head. 'No. No way. You can't do that. They wouldn't believe you.'

'Let me see,' Laura said. 'Two young men. One with a squeaky clean record, never been in trouble before. The other involved in a violent break-in . . . Who's the more obvious suspect? Which one's version of events is more likely to be believed?'

Skellion's eyes blazed with rage. 'You won't get away with it. Not a hope in hell. I know the truth. I know what I saw.'

'You think they'll accept your truth? A man who has a history of violence? A man who used bribery so that his son wouldn't get a sentence? I don't think so. And then there's the not-so-minor detail about your past history with my father.

A vendetta, I think it might be called. Yes,' she said when she saw the surprise in Skellion's eyes. 'I know all about that too.'

'Good luck trying to prove any of it.'

'I'll take my chances.'

'You lied about who you are,' Skellion said. 'Brought us here under false pretences. They're not going to take kindly to that.'

'Not quite as serious as murder, is it?'

'Look, the kid had a motive, for God's sake! He wanted her dead after finding out what she did!'

'And Tory didn't?' Laura jerked her head, beckoning Frank over. She pulled his handkerchief from his top pocket, used it to lift the letter-opener, wiped the handle thoroughly.

'You think getting rid of his prints leaves him in the clear? It'll be your word against mine. And Marie's and Tory's.'

'And mine, Frank's and Richie's against yours.' She'd shrugged. 'So go ahead. Call the police. But I can be *very* convincing. You of all people should understand that.'

Skellion's breathing deepened. Air raced in and out of his nose as he stood there, rigid, staring into space. 'A girl is lying dead at our feet and you're *still* playing games?'

Laura had narrowed her eyes, pointed a finger. 'Don't pretend you give a fuck about her. She duped us all. No one in this room is sorry she's dead. None of us could care less. I'd even go so far as to say that Richie did us all a favour.' She'd looked at Frank. His face had told her she was right. She couldn't know how any of them might feel a week, a month, years from this night. But right now, they all felt exactly the same.

The volume of the band had increased, along with the beat. The party was hotting up. Through the music came bursts of laughter, alcohol-enhanced shrieks, a persistent, high-spirited hum. Skellion shuffled his feet, swallowed hard several times, let a long moment pass before he spoke. 'So, what are you proposing?'

'Okay. This is how it's going to work. We're all going to stay here in the room, with the exception of Frank, of course. The show must go on. He has to look after his guests. We can't afford to raise any suspicions.'

'But for – for how long?' Marie asked, chin trembling. 'I just want to go home.'

'You will,' Laura answered. 'Once we're done. But we have to take care of this together. We don't have any other choice.'

Marie pulled her son tighter, tucking her head under his armpit. 'Wh-what do we have to do?'

'When the party's over and everyone's gone, we're going to go down to the garden and start digging.'

Marie turned her face. 'We can't do that,' she said, whimpering into Tory's side.

'You have a better idea? One that gets us all off the hook? If you do, please share it. I'm all ears.'

'Laura, I—' Frank began.

'I know it's not an ideal situation, Frank, but it is what it is. The important thing is that we don't panic and that someone stays in control.'

'And that has to be you, does it?' Skellion said. 'You're demanding that we hang around here for hours, then help you with your dirty work?'

'Sorry for the inconvenience,' Laura said, 'but there's no negotiation.'

'But what about my hand? I'm not going to be any use to

you. Just let me go so I can have it seen to. I swear I won't say anything.'

'That's not going to happen. We're going to deal with this together. You've got one good hand, haven't you? As for the pain, you'll just have to suck it up.'

Skellion stepped over Mollie's body and plonked down on the sofa with a heavy sigh. 'Someone pour me a glass of that brandy. I need something strong to get me through this.'

'Jesus Christ, Paddy,' Marie said, turning angry. 'This isn't just about you and how you feel. What about me? What about Tory?' She looked at Laura. 'We can't just . . . I mean, how will we . . . Surely someone will come looking.'

Laura looked down at Mollie's body. 'Mollie Teller won't be missed. I was the only real friend she had. At least, I thought we were friends. She had acquaintances, sure, people she tried to latch on to. And leeches who only wanted her for her money. But nobody who cared. Nobody who'll give a shit that she's not fucking stalking them any more.'

'But won't anyone notice? Neighbours?' She looked up at Tory. 'Where did she live?'

He shrugged. 'Grand Canal Dock. In one of those huge blocks.'

'Where people come and go all the time,' Laura said. 'She owned the place. Bought it out of her inheritance. So it's not like there'll be a pissed-off landlord sniffing around for unpaid rent. If she did know any of her neighbours, they'll be glad to see the back of her. Got more than her share of complaints about her music blaring in the middle of the night and shit like that.'

'But people don't just disappear into thin air without *someone* noticing,' Marie had said. 'At some stage there's bound to be an investigation. They'll check her movements. They'll know she got a flight over here with Tory. And see that she didn't go back.'

'Not if no one is actually asking what happened to her. But, to shut you up, we'll think of a story to tell this *someone* you're talking about if they ever ask us.' Laura had thrown her hands into the air. 'I don't know. She – she had a fight with Tory after you got to the party, we saw her talking to some strange guy Frank didn't know and then she was gone. Fucked off with him somewhere and we haven't seen her since. How does that sound?'

Marie bit her thumbnail and cast a worried glance at Tory. 'Not very convincing.'

'But perfectly plausible. Especially for someone like her.'

Skellion coughed. 'Tory. Brandy. Now. I'm in absolute agony here.'

Tory obeyed, pouring a glass and handing it to his father, but not with any real concern. Skellion raised his arm, waved the tumbler around. 'Cheers,' he said. 'The perfect end to a perfect evening, wouldn't you say? Best party I've ever been to. By a mile.'

While Paddy had knocked back his brandy and Marie had a whispered conversation with Tory, a white-faced Frank had held Laura by the wrist, spoken to her under his breath: 'I hope you know what you're doing. This could go very badly wrong if you're not careful.'

'I'm thinking on my feet here,' she'd said, her voice low and rasping. 'How was I to know what was going to happen? I'm doing the best I can.'

'And what about him?' he'd said, nodding at Richie, who

was still standing, shoulders hunched, staring at the floor. 'I don't think he even knows what he's done. What happens when the realisation hits?'

'Look, right now, we have a situation we need to take care of. And what I've outlined is the best – the only – way forward. You go back out there, be the best life-and-soul Frank you can be and entertain your guests, send them home happy. Think of this as a minor hiccup that'll be done and dusted in a matter of hours.'

Frank had released his grip, run his hands down his cheeks, over his beard. 'I'm not going to wake up and discover this is all just a bad dream, am I?'

'No, unfortunately you're not. But that goes for all of us.'

Laura takes another cigarette, offers one to Frank but he shakes his head. 'I think that might be the cleaning help arriving,' she says, watching a white van pull up outside.

Trudy thumps to the floor as Frank begins shifting himself. He leans heavily on the desk as he rises, grimacing as though he's carrying a gigantic weight on his back.

'Life goes on,' Laura says, stroking the wheel of the lighter.

'So we're led to believe,' Frank replies, walking stiffly out of the room.

THIRTY-ONE

He'd made up his mind to leave. Right after the door had been slammed on his fingers. Definitely. It was too much. Or too little, if you want to look at it that way. The lack of concern. The absolute absence of any compassion. What had Paddy done to deserve that kind of reaction? He'd been the subject of a cruel, cynical hoax; had had to suffer the indignity of a personal interrogation in front of all those people. The least a man can expect from his family is some loyalty. But what had he been given? Barely an acknowledgement. Marie's all in a heap over what happened after – and that's as may be – but Paddy injured his hand *before*, so she needn't think he'll accept that as an excuse for her behaviour. Or Tory, for that matter. He's just as guilty. Fair enough, Marie had fainted, collapsed, whatever it was, but that's a run-of-the-mill thing, isn't it? She was clearly perfectly fine after a few sips of the brandy.

Smashed bones, though – that's a different thing entirely.

He lies in his own bed now. It's Monday morning. They hadn't kept him long after the surgery yesterday. In and out.

He'd thought they might keep him overnight but, no, they let him go after a few hours in recovery. A shame, in a way. He'd been practising his French on one of the nurses once he'd come round. Not a bad-looking little thing; a bit like one of Gauguin's Tahitian girls. She'd spent a lot of time hovering around Paddy's bed, checking this and that. Told her he was an artist. All starry-eyed, she was. And totally sympathetic regarding his injury. Another day and he'd have been in with a clear chance there. No question.

Marie comes into the room, carrying a tray. Easy to see what sort of mood she's in. Mouth on her like a cat's arsehole. But he'll have to put up with it for the moment. He can't start hinting at a separation when he's not able to dress himself without help. Jesus . . . when he thinks about what happened . . . Despite what she did to him, he has a sneaking regard for Laura Pierce. Rock 'n' roll, dig a hole. That's what it was like. Didn't think twice about it. She's the kind you want in an emergency, that's for sure. Keep calm and carry on, what? True, that Mollie bitch had done the dirty on her – on all of them – but, Christ, there was no love lost, was there? He could learn a thing or two from her, by God.

'Scrambled eggs on toast,' Marie says flatly, planting the tray on the bed. 'That okay for you?'

He fancies a steak tartare but scrambled eggs it is. 'Fine,' he says.

'You want me to feed you?'

'I still have one good hand. I'm not a complete invalid.'

'Only asking.'

No way is it coming down to that. Spooning the mush into

his gob like he's a baby. There may be things he can't do, but feeding himself isn't one of them.

'I'll be back up after I sort Tory out with some breakfast. He's still in a state.'

Tory's in a state? Christ almighty. She's unbelievable.

A clump of egg slithers down his throat. Lukewarm. Just the way he hates it. He stares at her back as she opens the door, thinks how simple it would be. Saturday night had opened his eyes. Laura'd had it all worked out in a matter of minutes. It had been tiresome having to wait until the party was over but the drink had helped and, once they'd got to work, the whole thing had been taken care of in an hour. He hadn't been able to dig, of course, but he'd watched. Laura had made him, wouldn't allow him to stay in the house. He'd hated the way she got to call all the shots but he didn't have a choice. Any expression of reluctance to follow her orders and she was threatening to call the police and implicate Tory. Implicate Paddy as well.

Jesus . . . It just shows you, doesn't it? You read about this kind of thing all the time. People disappearing. Vanishing without a trace. Someone always knows something. Isn't that what they say? As long as mouths stay shut, the secret remains. And Paddy knows how to keep quiet. Sure wasn't he there chatting away to that nurse like it was business as usual? Not a bother on him.

He'd never have believed it would be that easy.

He shovels more egg into his mouth. Not only is it almost cold, she hasn't put enough salt on it either. He puts his fork down. He can't eat it.

His eyes close. His head sinks back into the pillow.

He has a lot to think about. A lot to consider.

It must be an hour before Marie returns. Paddy jerks awake from his doze as the door opens, and when he sees her, for a second or two, he wonders how it is that she's still here. Has she not left? Wasn't there a note found somewhere? On the kitchen counter, maybe? Most of her clothes taken, her passport, the stash of cash they kept hidden in that brick of a book about Monet. They'd had an argument, wasn't that it? A shouting match. Worse than any they'd had before. He'd said things. She'd been upset. Crying, she was. In a mess. Yes, he'd probably been insensitive but how was he to know she'd up and leave? If only.

She speaks, halting his fantasy. 'You didn't eat your egg.'

'You know I can only eat it piping hot.'

'And how would you suggest I keep it hot between the kitchen and here?'

'Heat the plate, maybe? Cover it? I don't know. I'm not the expert. Use your head.'

'I'll look into it.'

He bares his teeth in a false smile. 'Where's Tory? Some concern he's showing. He's barely registered my presence since I got home.'

'Give him a break. What do you expect? He's in bits. Think about what we witnessed the other night.' She lowers her voice. 'A murder. A fucking *murder*, Paddy. And we're accessories. How do you think that's going to impact on him? On all of us? He needs our support. Regardless of how it came about, Tory had a relationship with that girl. He had feelings for her. He went up to that place with a girlfriend and came home with dirt on his hands after helping to bury her dead body in a bloody hole.'

'I know, I know. You don't have to spell it out for me. Hard as it might be to live with what happened, that's exactly what he has to do. What we all have to do. Live with it. Okay, Marie? Just. Fucking. Live with it.'

Tears spring from her eyes. 'You know why he hasn't come up to see you? Because – because he feels you don't give a shit about him. Or about me.'

'Why? Because I'm showing some strength? Because I'm not in a snivelling heap? This has nothing to do with how we feel about each other, Marie. This is about survival.'

'You don't have to be a bloody blockhead about it. Showing sympathy isn't negative. It's not a sign of weakness. A girl was killed! Show some consideration of that fact, at least.'

Paddy laughs. 'Less of the holier-than-thou attitude. What? Like you gave a damn about Mollie? You showed as little concern for her as anyone else in that room.'

'I protested! I didn't want her to be thrown in the ground like that!'

Paddy rolls his eyes. 'It's not what any of us *wanted*, woman. Desperate times call for desperate measures. Ever heard that expression? We went along with it because we'd no other choice. End of. And crying about it now doesn't make you any less of an accomplice.'

That shuts her up. Paddy shoves himself to the side of the bed, kicks back the duvet, plants his feet on the floor, wriggles them into his slippers. When he stands, the room spins and it feels like the bones in his legs have gone soft.

Marie frowns. 'Where are you going? There's no need for you to be up.'

He waves her aside with his good hand once his head stops reeling. 'Can a man not go for a piss without facing an inquisition?'

'Well, don't be thinking of wandering about the house. Those painkillers you're on make you light-headed. I don't want you falling and breaking something else.'

'Cluck, cluck, mother hen,' he mutters, shuffling out of the room.

It's not easy in the bathroom, trying to do everything with one hand. He can manage, just about, but he's in his pyjamas now. Buttons, zips . . . That'll be another matter. He groans. He'll have to get trousers with elastic waistbands, slip-on shoes. He doesn't want Marie tying his shoelaces and fiddling with his flies. He takes a good look at himself in the mirror, lifts his chin, turns his head left, right. He's looked better, even he has to admit that. His stubble is heading into beard territory; his hair needs some bounce. He'll shower later. If he can figure out a way to do it himself.

To hell with what Marie said. He can take a walk along the landing, can't he? His legs are less spongy now, though it seems like they're not fully connected to his body. As he reaches the studio, he hears her footsteps behind him. 'What did I tell you?' she calls. 'Go back to bed. There's no need for you to be up.'

He pushes the door. 'I'm stretching my legs, not climbing Mount bloody Everest. I'll be the one to decide what I can and . . .' he pauses before finishing the sentence to allow what he's seeing to fully register '. . . can't do.'

Jesus Christ.

Another canvas.

Just like one of his again but it's one of hers. Sitting on the easel like it's fully entitled to be there.

'So this is why there's no need for me to be up,' he says, taking a long, hard look at the painting. 'And there was me thinking you were worried about me.'

'It's not . . . I didn't . . .' She moves to enter the studio but he doesn't budge from the doorway.

'Must've used a whole tube of my cerulean. And the same of my Naples yellow.' He turns to her. 'Am I right?'

'Maybe. I don't know. I wasn't measuring.'

'Just squeezing it out like it was fucking toothpaste.'

'It's paint, Paddy. It's our bread and butter.'

'And I'm the one who earns it.'

She nods at his bandaged fingers. 'Not at the moment, you're not.'

'Rub it in, why don't you?'

'For God's sake.'

'No, Marie. For *my* sake. You couldn't leave it, could you? Bad enough that I'm out of action for a while without you muscling in. I thought I made it clear the other day.'

'Made what clear? That you're in charge? That what you say goes? That I'm not allowed express myself creatively but you are?'

'Give me a break. *Express* yourself? Last time I checked, creativity was something unique to the individual who's fucking well creating it!'

'It relaxes me, okay? And I may as well be productive if I'm wide awake in the middle of the night.'

'Productive? How is this productive? Oh, let me see. It's for your own . . . relaxation?'

Marie folds her arms. 'Simon Keyes. You've hardly forgotten. Fifteen by the end of next month. And that's on top of five the Gorlan have asked for.'

'And? I'll tell them what happened. They'll just have to wait.'

'We have to live, Paddy. When he's feeling okay, Tory will go back to college. The money has to keep coming in. We've no idea how long it'll take for you to recover. It could be weeks. There's no need for them to wait. I can take over.'

Paddy's eyebrows couldn't get any higher, his eyes any wider. He stares at her, incredulous. 'Are you seriously suggesting . . . I mean . . . I can't believe you're . . .'

'It makes perfect financial sense. And it's only until you're back on form. No one has to know. No one *will* know. We don't have to say a word to anyone about your hand.'

'But I can't just—'

'Yes, you can. Things have changed. We've done something over this weekend that we never, ever would've thought we'd do. And we'll have it hanging over us for the rest of our lives. This won't stop me thinking about it but it'll help to occupy my mind. You can see I'm perfectly capable of . . .'

Her words drift. Paddy can see her lips moving, the tip of her tongue between her teeth, but it's like someone's turned the sound down. His pulse throbs in his ears. He feels strangely disconnected from the space around him, as if he's not really here, as if his mind has separated from his body. He stumbles past her, unsteady, frantic. Bed. He needs to get back there. The pain. Dear Lord, the fucking pain.

THIRTY-TWO

Frank appears in the hall as Laura carries her suitcase downstairs. 'You have everything?'

She squints against the late-morning sun that streams in through the open front door. 'Yep. Not that I brought much.' She hasn't packed the clothes that Laura Karlson wore. She threw them in one of the bin bags the cleaning guys took away yesterday. The black dress was ripped beyond repair. Obviously shit quality despite the hefty price tag. Fair enough, it wasn't exactly the kind of thing you wear for a night of grave-digging but, even so, it shouldn't have split so easily. As for the skirt and blouse, they served their purpose. It's not like she's ever going to wear them again.

She'd tipped the paintings Skellion had left into rubbish bags too, after she'd torn them to shreds. Several thousand euros worth of crap on their way to landfill. Sweet.

Mollie's phone she'd smashed with a rock. She'd flushed some bits down the toilet and distributed the others between the various bin bags, along with the letter-opener, which Frank had cleaned with bleach.

Richie waits at the front door, watching for Bruno, bag slung over one shoulder. He went to his room at two o'clock yesterday afternoon and stayed there till nine this morning. Laura's not sure if he actually slept. The few times she'd checked on him, he'd been awake. But she's grateful he kept himself out of sight. He turns his washed-out face as she wheels her case over the tiles. 'You okay?' she asks, as brightly as she can manage. 'All set?' God, she sounds adult. He nods. She puts her arm around his waist. 'Everything's going to be fine,' she tells him. 'You've nothing to worry about.' She feels his muscles tense and the way he strains hard to keep an inch of space between his body and hers. 'You'll feel better once we get home. I promise.'

'Your sister's right,' Frank says, laying a palm on Richie's back. 'Things will look a whole lot different when the plane touches down.'

Richie stares straight ahead, blinking hard against the sunlight. Last time Laura noticed, he was about a half-inch shorter than her. Now, it's the other way around. She takes a moment to study his profile: the slant of his forehead; his long, straight nose; the sharp jut of his chin. Exactly like their father's.

Gleaming chrome sparkles through the trees. 'Time to go,' Laura says. 'Bruno's here.'

Richie breaks from her clinch, starts walking down the path towards the car.

'Wait,' Frank says, as Laura goes to follow. 'I want to give you this.' He pulls a white envelope from his shirt pocket. 'Don't open it until you're in the air.'

'What the hell, Frank? What is it?'

'Just do as I ask, all right?'

She takes the envelope, pushes it into her bag. 'Okay. It'd better be good, whatever it is.'

He smiles, wraps his arms tight around her body. 'It's always good between you and me. Despite everything, it always will be. I mean it.'

'Mean what? What're you trying to say?'

'I . . . I just . . . Look, we'll talk when I'm in Dublin next week. When we've had a chance to think things over.'

'I'm not sure I want to talk about what happened. What else is there to say?'

Frank bends, hefts a miaowing Trudy into his arms. 'Goodness me,' he says, struggling against her weight. 'Must be all the left-over canapés she polished off yesterday.' He leads the way along the path. 'Come along. Let's not keep Bruno waiting.'

Before she gets into the car, Laura looks back at the villa through the trees. It looks like it always has, but it's not the same place that it was. It holds different memories now.

Frank holds Trudy tight to his chest and Laura ruffles the fur between the cat's ears, feels the delicate curve of skull beneath. 'Hey,' she says, 'meant to tell you. I came across Chilli's bones when I was digging.'

'Imagine that,' Frank says. He pauses, casts his gaze skywards. 'I never told you this but Lee always suspected you knew Chilli was in the boot all that time. I put up with so much from him but that was one thing I could never forgive him for.'

Richie sits in the back, Laura up front. She rolls down the window and Frank leans in for a final goodbye. She supposes she could tell Frank the truth about Chilli but what difference would it make now? Accidents happen, right? And that's all it was – an accident. Fair enough, it was one she could have prevented if she'd wanted to. But, as she's told herself more than once before, sometimes you just have to do what you feel is right.

Bruno tests the waters with some small talk about her stay as they drive. Laura answers in flat monosyllables and he shuts up. Once they leave the twisting roads, he puts his foot down and she watches the landscape whizz past in a blur of earthy colours. Soon the bay comes into view and she tries to focus on the wide expanse of shimmering blue. But all she sees is Frank as they'd left him, standing there with Trudy in his arms, his outline neon-bright, even when she shuts her eyes against the sun.

By the time they reach the airport, Richie is fast asleep, his head lolling on his chest, a thread of drool swinging from his mouth. It takes several hard shakes to wake him and, when his eyes open, he stares, unblinking, like Laura's a stranger.

She waves a hand in front of his face. 'Rich. Come on. We're here. We're at the airport.'

He moves, robot-like, and climbs out of the car.

'You will be back?' Bruno asks, taking their bags from the boot. 'I see you again some time?' Laura allows him to kiss her cheek. He smells agreeably of leather and lemon.

'Sure,' she says. Though, in truth, she has no idea.

Richie keeps his eyes downcast as they walk through the airport and ride the escalator up to Departures. In the line for Security, he bumps heavily against an ancient, bony blonde – all silk scarves, bangles and throat-catching perfume. She babbles something in French that doesn't sound understanding and Laura gives her a back-off-lady glare.

She grips Richie by the elbow. 'For fuck's sake,' she whispers. 'Look where you're going. What? You're expecting a SWAT team to swoop in and take you away at gunpoint? No one *knows*, Richie. No one fucking knows.'

At the conveyor belt, they load their luggage into trays and wait to pass through the body screener. Laura looks back for Richie after she's waved on and sees he's being patted down by an official. She rolls her eyes. It's just a random search but he couldn't look guiltier if he tried. 'Oh, my God,' she says, when he's let go. 'Seriously. Get a grip. You've nothing to worry about. The way you look, you'd swear you were still carrying that fucking letter-opener.'

His movements are tight and twitchy as they collect their belongings and a fiery redness blotches his neck and face. Laura waits behind him in the queue for Passport Control, gently nudging him over the line when it's his turn. The guy behind the glass has bulging, frog-like eyes that flit from page to face several times before he lets Richie go. He plays spot-the-difference with Laura too, though in her case, it's justified. Her passport photo is several years old and shows someone even Laura barely recognises as herself.

Spotting a couple of free seats in the small Departures area, she hurries over to nab them. 'Sit here,' she tells Richie. 'Back in a minute. Need a wee.'

But he grabs her arm roughly, pushes her down. They both slap hard onto the plastic seats. Before she can protest, his breath is like hot steam in her face. 'I killed a girl. Don't you get it? I fucking *killed* a girl.'

Laura glances around, unpicks his fingers from her arm, lays his hand on his thigh. She speaks slowly, quietly. 'Calm the fuck down, will you? Don't be such a fucking dick.'

His chest heaves, his knees jerk up and down. 'What am I going to do? What the hell am I going to do?'

'You're not going to *do* anything. We're going home to get on with our lives. We don't have to worry about what happened. It's not going to be a problem.'

'But it was murder. Not, like, self-defence or some shit like that. I could get *life*.'

She places a hand on his left knee. That juddering thing he does is fucking head-wrecking. 'It's under control. I told you. Skellion might be many things but he's not stupid. He'll keep his mouth shut. They all will.'

'But what if . . . if she . . . if it's ever discovered. If . . .'

'That's not going to happen. Who's going to be randomly digging in Frank's garden? Someone would have to be actively searching. And nobody's going to be looking for her. Seriously.'

Richie lifts his hands, pushes his hair back, then presses down on his head.

'And,' Laura adds, 'even if, by some weird, crazy twist of fate, someone *does* come across her, chances are she won't even be identified.'

'But if she *is* found, and they do all that *CSI* shit, they'll figure it out, won't they?' He turns his face to look at her, his eyes glazed with fear. 'I've seen how they do it on TV.'

'Oh, my God, Richie. Do you want to go and find one of the airport police and just fucking well confess here and now? Get it over with? Jesus. You heard what I said to Skellion. If ever the shit hits the fan, it'll be their word against ours. But it won't come to that.'

'This is going to follow me around for ever.'

'Stop. Just stop. Did you listen to a word I said? You're over-reacting. All that is worst-case scenario. The chances of it happening are so small they're practically zero.'

He brings his left hand to his mouth, gnaws on his thumbnail. 'But I killed her, Laura. That's the bottom line.'

'You had reason, Richie. Good reason. Look at the damage she did to all of us. Think of Dad. Think of Lee, for fuck's sake! Think of how she got away with that. We all thought it was an accident. No forensics figured that one out, did they? People are bumped off all the time and no one knows.' She takes his hand down from his mouth, holds it in her own. 'You did us all a favour, Richie. A fucking favour. You did it for Dad. When you grabbed that letter-opener all you were thinking of was him. Isn't that right?' Richie nods, swallows. Laura leans closer, whispers directly into his ear, 'Hold tight to that thought. Carry *that* around for ever. Nobody got punished for what happened to us. And no one cared enough to do something about it except you and me.'

'And Mum.'

'Of course.' She squeezes his hand. 'Though this is *definitely* not what she had in mind.'

He manages a smile, just about. 'Is she collecting us?'

'Told her we'll get a taxi. Texted her last night. Want to put off telling her about my' – she air-quotes – '"meeting" with the Skellions for as long as possible.'

'What're you going to say?'

She pats his knee. 'I've no idea. I'll come up with something on the plane.'

'We won't be telling her what happened?'

'Richie, please. Don't make me start doubting your sanity. Of course we won't be telling her. Or Amy. Or anyone. Six people know about this and that's the way it's going to stay.' She stands. 'Now, if you don't mind, my bladder's about to burst.'

'Wait a sec,' he says. 'It's weird but . . . it's kind of easier now to see why Skellion did what he did. You know, making sure Tory got away with it.'

Whatever way the light is falling, it shows how his green eyes are made up of patches of yellow and blue. She knows what he's going to say but, still, she asks, 'How do you figure that?'

'Cos you're doing exactly the same for me.'

They pass the waiting time in near silence. When their gate number shows on the screen, they go downstairs to stand in line before boarding the bus that takes them to the steps of the plane. Richie carries Laura's case and she notes that his shoulders aren't as slumped and he gives the cheery flight attendant a half-audible 'Hi.'

The relief when the doors are closed and no one has taken the aisle seat beside them. Richie slips into it, leaving the middle seat free, and flicks through the inflight magazine. Laura is grateful for the distance. They each need some space.

The plane takes off, roars into the sky, climbs over the unbelievably blue Bay of Angels. As it swerves right, away from the coast, she scans the dry, hilly landscape they left barely three hours ago. She knows roughly where the villa is, which hill and what area, though there's nothing visible from this far up except a dense expanse of trees.

It's strangely comforting to know what's hidden in there somewhere. Under the cover of Frank's fig trees.

A secret. Nestled safe and warm and dry.

'Back in a minute,' Richie says, once the seatbelt sign is switched off. Laura looks up as he walks towards the toilet at the front of the plane. There's a queue; he'll be a while. She reaches into her bag.

Typical Frank. Stiff, expensive envelope, its corners embossed with little crowns. The paper inside matches. Same ivory-white, same decoration.

The letter is handwritten, with a fountain pen, in Frank's whirling, expressive script.

Twice, three times Laura reads his words. She understands them but . . . they don't make sense. They can't. It's not possible.

How? How can it be true?

She stares out of the window at the clearest, most heavenly blue sky. A wave stirs in her stomach, rolls up into her chest, swells her throat. Jesus Christ. She gulps it down, swallows, again and again, breathes hard and deep until it dissolves. She'll decide when and if she wants to break down. But it sure as fuck isn't going to be while she's sitting here in seat 18A.

Before Richie returns, she closes her eyes, leans her head on the window and pretends she's fallen asleep.

THIRTY-THREE

Angela lays the table. They should be here soon. Laura texted when they landed and that was almost an hour ago now. Amy took the afternoon off, rescheduled her classes so she could help with the homecoming this evening. Angela has made a carbonara. Everyone likes that. And Amy has put together a fruit salad for after.

There's a strange atmosphere in the house. An edgy calm. Angela could talk about things to Amy now but she'd prefer to wait until Laura and Richie are here. It's only fair. Especially since Laura's the one who went to all the trouble. She looks at the folded sheet of paper on the windowsill and her heart lifts, not for the first time since this morning.

'Cream?' Amy says, into the open fridge.

'Are we allowed?' Angela replies, smiling to herself.

'Special occasion.'

'Top shelf. At the back. Take out the wine while you're at it.'

Angela opens a cupboard, lifts four glasses one by one and sets them on the counter. Napkins. It's a special occasion, as Amy said. She'll use the nice grey linen ones she keeps in the living-room sideboard. She leaves the kitchen to get them and, on the way back, stops in front of the family photos on the hall table. It hasn't decreased, the pain. Not at all. It still cuts sharp through her chest when she sees Karl's happy face. But today, maybe . . . maybe it's a little easier to bear. Could that be it? The load isn't any less. But she has more strength to carry it.

Back in the kitchen, Amy concentrates on whipping the cream, the electric mixer's noisy drone filling the room. She glances up at Angela for a second, flashes a smile, but it doesn't disguise the worry in her eyes. Angela feels a bit guilty. Perhaps she should've said something. She doesn't like to see her daughter so anxious about the outcome of Laura's meeting. But it's only for, what, another fifteen, twenty minutes? No. It'll be better to discuss everything when they're all together, round the table, as a family.

She'd texted Richie yesterday, asked how the party had gone, how he was feeling. She'd kept it low-key, casual, hadn't wanted to get into the whys and wherefores of his decision to flit off, nothing like that. He'd said it'd been fine, hadn't given too much away. That's Richie for you. He'd sounded okay. But, then, there's no real telling from a text, is there? She'd done the same with Laura, just texted to ask about the party, how Frank had enjoyed it, and said that she'd collect them from the airport. Laura had been insistent about them taking a taxi, and now Angela's glad she was. And glad too that Laura had wanted to wait until she got home to talk about the meeting. Angela had resisted it at first but now, in the circumstances, it has worked out much better.

Amy switches off the mixer, turns her head, like she's listening out. 'Think that's them. I can hear a car.'

They hurry out to the hall, throw open the door to the falling darkness, the beam of the taxi's headlights showing the fine fuzz of drizzle that has started to fall. Angela sees Richie first, his face at the window, chalky and bloated. Then Laura, her eyes puffy, her cheeks hollow, her movements slower, less decisive than usual as she climbs out of her seat. They walk together towards Angela, both brightening a little when she moves to gather them in an embrace. She hugs them tightly, quickly, wanting to usher them inside, out of the cold and rain. Amy takes their bags, their jackets; Angela guides them into the warm kitchen, pulling out chairs, telling them, 'Sit down, sit down.'

She'd hoped it was the dusk, and the way the shadows had fallen across Laura's face, that had made her look so tired. But now she can see that wasn't the case. The trip has obviously taken a lot out of her. Richie, too, looks worn out. They're both exhausted, in no condition for any kind of in-depth conversation. When she thinks about it, what need is there for that now, anyway?

Amy heaps the spaghetti into pasta bowls, pirouetting around the table as she sets them on the placemats. Probably thinks things went badly, poor girl. Is doing her best to lighten the somewhat sombre mood. Richie is hungry. Angela watches how he wolfs the food, stuffing his mouth with overloaded forkfuls, answering the starter questions she asks – 'Flight okay? How's the weather over there? Were you waiting long for a taxi?' – with nods and shrugs. Laura twirls her pasta round her fork, but doesn't lift it from the bowl. Round and round, collecting spaghetti, losing it, picking it up again.

'This is good, Mum,' Amy says. 'Really good.'

Laura finally tastes the carbonara. 'Lovely. Thanks.'

Amy asks about the party, wonders what the style was like, wants to know what Laura wore. Angela guesses Frank went over the top with the decorations, smiles when Laura assures her that he did.

Richie pushes away his empty bowl, unrolls his napkin, wipes the sauce off his chin. 'I'm knackered,' he says, yawning. 'I might just go and—'

Angela lays a hand on his arm. 'Of course. Not yet, though. There are things we need to discuss.'

Laura puts down her fork. 'Mum, I—'

'It's fine, love. I can see how tired you are. I'm not going to grill you about your trip. I just want to say how . . . well, how proud I am of you.'

Laura tucks her hair behind her ear. 'But I haven't . . . I mean, I didn't . . .'

'You did. Perhaps you don't know it but you did.' Angela gets up, takes the folded paper from the windowsill. 'There's no need for you to tell me how the meeting went. It's clear it had an impact because it prompted this.' She sits down, opens out the sheet. 'It came in the post this morning. I could've told you earlier, called you about it, texted maybe. But I wanted us all to be together.'

'Mum?' Amy asks. 'What is it?'

'Well, as you can see, it's a letter. Addressed to the Pierce family. Strictly private and confidential. I think the best thing is for me to read it out.' She unfolds the sheet of paper. 'Hand me my glasses, Amy, love. They're on the counter.' Amy does as she's asked and, from the expression on Laura's face, Angela knows that Amy must be signalling to her from behind her mother's back. She smiles to herself, sets her glasses on her nose, clears her throat. 'It's from a solicitor. Serena Muldown.

With a practice in, let me see, oh, yes, Woodmount, Navan, County Meath. The letter is dated last Friday. It's postmarked Friday evening.' She looks up at Laura. 'You called to the Skellions in the morning, yes? Friday morning?'

'Yeah. Eleven.' Poor Laura looks baffled.

Angela nods. 'She must've got straight on to her solicitor and asked her to send this ASAP. I don't know what you said to them, love, but whatever it was, this is what's come out of it.'

'Read it, will you?' Amy urges. 'Don't leave us hanging.'

'Right. Yes. Okay.' She changes her voice now, makes it more pronounced. '"For the attention of the Pierce family, The Haven, Rockhill Road, Rathbarton, County Dublin. I have been instructed by my client, Mrs Marie Skellion, to furnish you with the following letter pertaining to an event that took place at the above address on the night of the fifteenth of February 2013."' Angela lifts her eyes to see her children's reactions. The significance has registered. She reads on. '"We are aware that criminal proceedings against Tory Skellion have been dealt with by the courts, however we wish to advise that the contents herein are delivered without prejudice should any further claims relating to his actions on the night in question be pursued."' Angela pauses, looks up at her children. 'I'm not sure exactly what that means but—'

'Just continue, Mum,' Amy interrupts. 'Read the rest of it.'

Deep breath. Here goes. '"Dear Pierce Family, I would like to sincerely apologise to you all for the hurt, stress and pain caused by the actions of my son, Tory Skellion. It's impossible to imagine what you went through that night and have continued to go through ever since. I want you to know that I'm fully sympathetic and am sorry I didn't contact you sooner. As a parent, I realise how distressing the whole experience must have been. I did want to reach out at the court hearing but I was unsure if I should and, if I'm honest, afraid of how you might react. If that makes me sound cowardly, then perhaps I am. I offer this apology now and hope you can accept it. I know it can't alleviate the devastating consequences of that night but I hope it might help in some small way. Yours sincerely, Marie Skellion.'"

Richie leans towards Angela, tries to get a look. 'Is that it?'

Angela pushes her glasses onto her head, frowns. 'It's not enough?'

'It's a bit . . . generic, isn't it?' Amy says. 'Wishy-washy.'

'How on earth do you make that out?' Angela asks.

'I dunno. She doesn't mention Dad or anything.'

'You spoke about your father?' Angela asks Laura. 'They know he's . . .'

Laura nods. 'Yeah . . . um, of course.'

'I'd say she got the solicitor to write it,' Richie says. 'It sounds too, you know, legal.'

'Well, she probably advised her,' Angela says. 'But that's understandable. You have to be careful.'

Amy pulls a baffled face. 'When you're apologising?'

'You know what I mean. It's a sensitive issue.'

'It's just from her, though.' Amy takes a sip of her wine. 'There's no mention of the father. Or the son. *They're* obviously not sorry.'

'We don't know that.' Angela turns to Laura. 'How did the father seem when you spoke to them?'

'He was . . .' Laura runs a hand through her hair. 'I dunno, he was . . .'

'It's all right, love. I know it must've been difficult. It doesn't really matter what he said, how he came across.' She waves the letter. 'What matters now is this. This piece of paper.'

'You'd think she'd have mentioned Laura's visit, though, wouldn't you?' Amy asks. 'Maybe given her some credit for going over there to talk to them.'

'Solicitor probably told her not to go into any details,' Angela says, 'just to stick to the point and write a plain, straightforward apology.'

'Maybe she already had it written,' Amy says. 'You know, ages ago.'

'Well, I suppose that's possible. She might've been thinking about apologising for some time. And just asked the solicitor to send it after Laura left.'

'Maybe the father knows nothing about it,' Amy says. 'That's why his name isn't on it. He didn't want anything to do with it.'

Angela sighs. 'We can speculate till the cows come home and never know the truth of it. The main thing is, she went to the trouble of writing it and having it sent. And I, for one, am happy she did.' She doesn't bother trying to disguise the annoyance in her voice. If she's honest, she's disappointed with their attitudes. She thought they'd be delighted. Instead, all they're doing is picking holes. Well, Amy is, Richie not so much. Laura's noncommittal. Perhaps she shouldn't expect them to feel the same as she does. They're entitled to their own feelings. 'It might not be life-changing,' she says, 'but it's a gesture of sympathy and that's all I was looking for.'

She casts her eyes over the letter again. Richie knocks back his wine. Amy pours more. Laura stares at her food. It'll take a while, that's all. She herself has had the whole day; they're still digesting it. Everyone reacts differently. In time, she's sure they'll appreciate what it means. She glances at Laura. The last time she saw her so wrung out was at Karl's funeral. It could be the after-effects of the party – no doubt she was up till all hours. But the meeting is bound to have been stressful too. All in all, the last few days have been an ordeal for her. And what she clearly doesn't need is her mother making her feel bad because she's not doing high kicks around the table. And Richie. She shouldn't be too hard on him, shouldn't have assumed he'd be over the moon. To him it's a few lines on a sheet of paper. He's too young, still too hurt to understand what they mean to his mother. This is a young man who took off without telling any of them, without considering their feelings. He's not capable of seeing things from anyone's point of view but his own. That will come with maturity. For now, it's all about himself. Just as it is for any eighteen-year-old. She'll park it now. Revisit it tomorrow. 'Amy made dessert,' she says. 'Fruit salad and cream.' She stands, starts clearing away their bowls.

'Would it be okay if I have mine later?' Laura says. 'I need to lie down.'

'Of course, love.'

Richie drains his glass. 'Me too.'

'Guys. Please have some,' Amy says. 'It took me ages to make it.'

'I didn't say I wasn't going to have any,' Laura tells her. 'Just want to save it for later.'

'It won't keep. It has to be eaten fresh.'

'It'll be fine. Really.'

Amy blows a sigh from her nose. 'It won't. Really.'

'For fuck's sake, Amy. I'm wrecked. Like, I'm totally stoked you went to all that trouble making a fucking fruit salad. I mean, it must've taken you days. You flew all the way over to France and had a serious meeting about it, did you? You peeled all those oranges and sliced all those bananas so that your family could get over their trauma and get on with their fucking lives?'

Angela puts the bowl she's carrying back on the table, keeps a grip on its edges. This is more than tiredness. Something else must have happened over there. And as much as Laura might not share Angela's joy about the apology, it's still a successful outcome. She should be in better form than she is. 'What's wrong, Laura? Did something happen at the meeting? Something . . . I don't know . . . upsetting?'

'I thought you weren't quizzing me on it? You got your apology. Isn't that enough? You said you were proud of me.'

'And I am. But I'm concerned. I know you're tired but there was no need to speak to Amy like that.'

'And no need for her to go bananas over fucking bananas.'

Amy's eyes widen. '*Me?* You were the one who was going mental. But I get it. You went through hell over there. Talking to people is such hard work. And it's not like you had any down time, is it? Like, you weren't relaxing in the sun or going to any parties.'

'You don't know what you're talking about. You haven't a clue. You weren't there so how would you know?'

'Girls. Please.' Angela sits down again. 'Stop.'

'What do you want, Laura?' Amy asks. 'A gold medal? A certificate of achievement?'

Laura drops her head, rocks back and forth in her seat, like she's trying to withstand pain. 'Just leave it, Amy,' she says. 'Just leave it.'

Angela's chest tightens. Something is up. There's no

denying it. She knows her daughter too well. This is Laura. Strong, capable Laura. 'What is it, love? Tell me. Whatever it is, I'm here to help. I'll understand.'

'No one can help. There's nothing anyone can do.'

Richie says, 'Laura?' hesitantly, questioning, as though he knows what it is she's talking about, as if he's afraid of what she might say.

'It's too late,' Laura says, shaking her head. 'I wasn't going to say anything but . . .'

'Laura, you can't.' Richie's face is ghostly. 'We said we . . .' There's fear in his eyes.

'Something bad did happen,' she says. 'Something really bad.'

Richie shouts her name now: 'LAURA. No! You said! You told me we wouldn't!'

Stinging prickles creep over Angela's skin. A cold surge flushes through her body. 'What is it? What's going on?'

'It's Frank,' Laura says. 'He's dying.'

THIRTY-FOUR

Laura lies in bed, wide awake, though her head is thick with tiredness and it feels like her eyes are stuck with pins. She hadn't intended to tell. Not for a while, anyway. She'd wanted to keep it to herself, contain it, hold it inside until it shrivelled up and disappeared. That was never going to happen but it had been her hope.

It was too much to keep hidden. She was already hiding enough. There was no space for anything else.

It's just after two a.m. The rain pelts down and the wind whistles its way into every gap in the brickwork and roof tiles it can find. It's a whining, moaning sound that Richie had been scared of when he was a kid. Their father had tried to fix it, had brought in some of his men. But despite pumping tubes of sealant, silicone, whatever the stuff's called, into every visible crack, they hadn't been able to stop the noise. On windy nights, like tonight, it sounds like the house is in pain.

She rolls onto her side, taps the torch icon on her phone, slides Frank's letter from under her pillow and reads it for what must be the twentieth time.

My dearest Laura,

Here I go, once again. This is my third attempt. It's just so difficult to know how to start.

You'll have left when you read this, which is how I want it to be. I thought about telling you face to face but, in the end, I couldn't, ridiculous coward that I am.

This is not about what happened. Not primarily, anyway. But the events that transpired have inevitably cast things in a different light. You're strong, Laura. That was evidenced by how swiftly you dealt with the whole episode, and how soon afterwards you got – as you would put it – your shit together. But I do worry about the long-term effects. Who knows what repercussions there might be? The thing is, I have the luxury of knowing that I won't have to deal with any of that.

You know I wasn't on top form while you were here – sniffles, not sleeping, etc. – and while those things are, in themselves, merely minor troubles, it's what they stem from that's the issue.

I received my diagnosis six months ago. Three weeks before your father died, in fact, though I didn't trouble him with the details at the time as I knew he was under a lot of strain coming up to the court hearing. I intended to have the conversation at some point in the future. A future which, for him, alas, never came. I've left it till now to tell you, partly because I didn't have the heart to say anything in the wake of his death and partly because I was hoping – against hope, it now appears – that I might recover.

It's cancer, my darling girl. Pancreatic. Untreatable. Terminal. In the beginning, I was sure I could beat it, but now, well, if this is a battle, I'm well and truly on the back foot. I don't have long. A month or two. Possibly mere weeks. But I've accepted it now. There's nothing more that can be done.

The party was a last hurrah, so to speak, though none of the guests knows about my condition. The evening turned out to be rather more eventful than I had anticipated but we dealt with it. That's not to say I wasn't shocked by what transpired and I'm still not sure how I truly feel about it. Finding out the truth about what happened to Lee, that was – is – extremely upsetting. And I know two wrongs, etc., etc., but, in this case, all I can say is that I sympathise completely with Richie's impulsive actions.

You know I'm not a religious man, but what proof do I have to the contrary that I will not meet your dear father, or Lee, for that matter, when I depart? They both left this world suddenly, without saying goodbye, whereas I have been afforded the privilege of being able to tell you of my leaving myself and to spend time with you, which I intend to do when I return to Dublin for good next week to put my affairs in order.

And so, my dear, when I next chain the gate on Notre Rêve it will be for the very last time. I shall not return.

It will, of course, be yours when I'm gone. You may do what you choose with it. And with all that it contains.

I've made arrangements to bring Trudy back too, and I know I can count on you to look after her when the time comes.

Please don't call or text. We'll talk when I'm over next week. I wanted you to be the first to know but I don't expect you to relay the news to the rest of the family unless, of course, you wish to. I will disclose it to them myself if you prefer.

My love, as always,

Frank

Cancer. Fucking cancer. He'd allowed Laura to have her own way, had gone along with everything she'd wanted, and all that time he'd been suffering. All that time he'd kept it to himself.

She could be angry with him for only telling her now, when he has so little time left, but she understands his reasons: as always, he'd put her feelings first.

She didn't mention the letter to any of them, just said Frank had spoken to her about his illness. He hasn't spelled out what happened but there's enough in it to fuel a cross-examination from Amy and Angela.

She realises now that it must have sounded to Richie as though she'd been about to blurt out their secret, but she hadn't been thinking of his fears at that point, hadn't been thinking of anything. When she heard *It's Frank. He's dying*, it seemed as though the words had been spoken by a stranger.

Their mother had assumed Richie also knew – what else was she to take from the way he'd pleaded with Laura? – and that he'd had the cop to go along with it, 'explaining' to Amy and Angela that he'd thought Frank hadn't wanted anyone else to know.

There were tears. Not just her own. Amy's had been the fiercest, probably because she felt guilty about the argument they'd just had. She'd thrown her arms around Laura, sobbing dramatically into her neck. But her grief was – is – genuine, Laura understands that.

Her mother's face. The shock. First her husband, now the man who'd been such a support, such a friend for so many years. She'd shaken her head, refused to believe it, had wanted to call him straight away. 'No, Mum,' Laura had insisted. 'Not now. It wouldn't be fair on him. He'd end up consoling you.'

She pushes the letter back under her pillow, turns off the phone's torch, lets the darkness soak into her eyes and the noise of the wind and rain to lull her half to sleep.

A weight. Warm and heavy. Pressing on her chest, pushing breath from her lungs. A voice comes through the black. *I'm scared, Laura. I'm scared.* A hand scrabbling at her arm. Fingers searching, clasping, squeezing, like they'll never let her go.

'Laura.' Clearer now. Louder. But still soft.

She reaches out. Touching. Feeling. Damp hair. Clammy skin. 'Richie?'

'I can't sleep,' he whispers. 'Can I stay in here with you for a while?'

'Sure.' She makes room, he lies beside her, his hand still gripping hers.

'That noise. I hate it. It's like something's trying to find a way in.'

'Yeah. It's called the wind.'

He doesn't laugh. 'You scared the shit out of me earlier. I thought you'd lost it or something. Thought you were going to tell what we did.'

'Sorry, I – I wasn't thinking.'

'It's okay, I get it. But why didn't you tell me about Frank when he told you?'

'I only found out on the plane. He gave me a letter, asked me not to read it till we took off. I snuck a look when you went for a pee. I wasn't going to say anything to anyone for a while. But I got upset, I guess. I didn't intend to just blurt it out like that.'

'A few months? That's all?'

'Yeah. Maybe weeks.'

'Jesus. Wonder what it's like to know you're going to die.'

'We're all going to die, Richie. What's better, do you think? The way Dad went. Sudden. Without warning. Or like Frank, with time to say goodbye?'

Richie leaves a pause, doesn't answer. Instead he asks, 'Do you think she knew, Laura? I can't stop wondering about that.'

Laura rolls onto her side to face him. 'No, Richie. It was instant. Don't be torturing yourself. She wouldn't have known a thing.'

He leaves a longer pause this time. Laura can just about make out the rise and fall of his chest, the quiet in-and-out of his breathing. 'What are the odds of that apology being sent the same day you went to see the Skellions?'

Laura shrugs. 'Dunno. Pretty high, I'd say.'

'If she'd sent it earlier, a couple of days, everything would be different. What happened wouldn't have happened. I wouldn't have . . .'

'You don't know that. Mum would've had her apology but Mollie would still have been guilty. It doesn't change that.'

''You probably wouldn't have gone, though. Mum would've said there was no need to go over to talk to them.'

'But I'd have been going over for Frank's party anyway. And I wouldn't have wanted to waste the opportunity of playing Laura Karlson and sticking it to Paddy fucking Skellion, would I? Remember, the apology doesn't have his name on it.'

'I suppose. Do you think she's sorry she sent it now?'

'Who knows? Must've been a shot to the heart when she discovered who I was. And she kept quiet about it the whole night, which makes me realise now that Paddy mustn't have known anything about it. He'd have used it as a bargaining chip if he had.'

'Why didn't she?'

'Cos she obviously did it behind his back, didn't want him to know. He's an arsehole, Richie. A fucking arsehole.'

'But maybe she's not so bad. If she apologised, I mean.'

'It's too little too late, if you ask me. But Mum seems happy with it so I suppose that's something.'

'Everything is so effed up.'

'I'm not looking at it that way. I don't consider things to be fucked up. They're all nicely taken care of.'

'I wish I was as strong as you.'

'Bullshit. You're giving yourself no credit. You dwell too much on the negative, that's your problem. Focus on the fact that you did something productive. You discovered all that stuff about Mollie's involvement, you followed me out to Frank's, you . . . Well, you know what else you did. And don't think about what-ifs. It's a set of circumstances you can't change.'

'Can I read Frank's letter?'

'Sure,' she says, taking it out. 'I'm not showing it to Mum or Amy, though. Too much information.'

Richie lies motionless as he reads, his eyes gleaming in the light of her phone. 'Long-term effects,' he says, when he's finished. 'Repercussions. Frank's right. He doesn't have to worry about any of those.'

'Jesus, Rich. You sound like you're fucking jealous.'

'It's true, though. It's not his problem. It's ours.'

'So, what're you saying? You'd prefer to be dead?'

'I'm not sure.'

Laura settles onto her back, grits her teeth. He won't be

like this for ever. He can't be. He'll settle down. He won't forget about it, she's not expecting that, but he'll find a safe place for it in his mind. He'll lock it away and only think about it occasionally, while he's getting on with the rest of his life. This is just a blip, first night home and all that. She'll make allowances. For now.

'I'm not sure it's enough,' he says, after several moments of silence. 'The way we hid . . .'

'Richie, you're being paranoid. We did a good job. I should know – I did most of the fucking work.'

'I think we might have to do something more, though. Just in case.'

THIRTY-FIVE

September 2015

Paddy still can't believe it. Not even when he holds his hand in front of his face. It's like he's hallucinating. He's waking in the night now, time and again, drenched in sweat, shaking. The relief when he tells himself he was only dreaming; the sheer dread when he realises that, no, this is for real.

He'd always been of the opinion that they let him go home too soon after the operation. He should have been kept in much longer. Should have been monitored over a couple of days. He's thinking about suing. Fucking sure he is. *Oh, infection after this type of surgery is rare but not unknown, blah-blah-blah . . .* They'd said it like it was nothing. Like he should have been expecting it. The antibiotics they'd prescribed were obviously a load of shite. Had no effect whatsoever. And all their guff about not every patient having the same capacity for healing, that he was just unfortunate. Were they taking the piss? *Unfortunate?*

This is catastrophic.

He still can't understand how it happened. And he'll never accept it. How can he? He's had to watch Marie standing at his easel day after day, week after week, using his paints, his brushes. Painting *his* pictures. But it was supposed to have been temporary, just to tide him over until he was able to use his fingers again. He hadn't been happy about it but what choice did he have? Keyes is a stickler for deadlines. If he says he wants fifteen canvases by such-and-such a date, he expects them to be delivered bang on time. And as much as Skellions are obviously a big money-spinner for him, if Paddy failed to fulfil an order, Keyes could very easily start looking around for another artist to fill his available wall space. God knows where that could lead: the other artist starts selling well, he or she doesn't demand such a high price or COD and, before you know it, Paddy's pushed out on his ear. He might be overthinking it but it could happen.

There'd been no complaints. From Keyes or from the Gorlan. They'd accepted Marie's paintings as his with no comment and Keyes had even remarked that this new work seemed more 'affecting', for fuck's sake. And, Jesus, the sly smile on Marie's face when she'd checked the account online. 'Money's been transferred,' she'd said, all cock-a-hoop. 'Told you you'd nothing to worry about.' Christ. The only thing that had kept him sane at that moment was the thought that he'd have to put up with her smugness for, at tops, a couple of months.

But that certainty had been short-lived.

He'd worn a path to the hospital, he'd been back so many times. When the infection was found, they'd tried this, they'd tried that, they'd tried the other. It had got into the bones, taken hold, and that was that. No getting rid. He'd actually thought the doctor was joking when she'd started talking about amputation. It was so far removed from reality he couldn't conceive it as even the remotest possibility.

His index finger.

His middle finger.

Disaster.

Doctor made out he was lucky it was 'only' two fingers. She'd known people who'd lost whole limbs to bone infection. That was supposed to make him feel better?

He'd resisted. Of course he had. But the pain was unbearable. They'd swelled like balloons. He couldn't move them. And then there was the fever. Nausea, headaches, feeling like shit. In the end – six weeks ago – the decision was made.

The wounds have healed – just about – but what good is half a hand? Over the last fortnight he's tried. It's no use. He can just about hold a brush between his thumb and last two fingers but not with anything like a proper grip.

He's here in the studio again this morning, having another go. Marie was hovering around earlier, fiddling with his stuff, but she disappeared after Paddy let a roar out of him. Since when did paint tubes need tidying? Spying on him, she was. Waiting to see him make a hames of things. What does she think? That he's lost his marbles as well as his fingers? As if he wouldn't notice. She'll sidle back in later, of course, to inspect his efforts, humming and hawing, bending her head this way and that. But he won't have her looking over his shoulder while he's struggling.

Using his left hand, he squeezes out a squirt of flesh tint, a bubble of Vandyke brown. He drizzles the blobs with linseed, mixes them together – again using his left hand – with his knife. Easy enough. No real skill required. It's when he tries to use the colour, that's when the problems begin. He can't paint with his left hand. He'd had a crack with that after he'd had the surgery. The result was a mess. A piece of canvas covered with patches and mucky daubs. Not a painting. He has to keep at it with his right. What remains of it.

He manages to take a flat brush from the jar, to stab it into the paint, to lift it up to the canvas. It wobbles, flips out of his weak grasp, flies across the room, clatters onto the floor. *Fuuuuuuck.*

For the best part of an hour he tries, dropping his brush again and again. He succeeds, eventually, in applying paint to canvas, but his strokes are too light and too feathery, far too laboured. Where's the spontaneity? The confidence? There's no flow to the composition, no cohesion. It's a fucking joke. He stands back now to take a proper look, his focus moving from his canvas to one Marie completed yesterday. Hers is exactly like a Skellion.

His looks like someone tried to fake one. Badly.

Here she comes now; he hears her steps on the stairs. She walks across the room without looking at him, one hand in her trouser pocket, the other tucking her hair behind her ear. Her I'll-try-not-to-gloat pose.

She stands in front of his effort, tilting her head, as if looking at it sideways might somehow make it okay. After a long pause she says, 'Did you think any more about the prosthesis?'

Is she for real? 'Jesus. You know how to make a man feel good.'

'I'm only asking. They said you should consider it.'

'I will, I will. When I'm ready. I need time to get used to

the fact that I've only half a hand. When – if – I come to terms with that, then I can start thinking about turning into the bloody Terminator.'

She rolls her eyes. 'It's not that bad. Probably take a while to get used to but it's amazing what they can do. I looked them up online. Electrically powered fingers. Work just like real ones, apparently.'

'I doubt very much a yoke like that will allow me paint the way I used to. Being able to pick up a mug of tea is a lot different to holding a brush or a knife and producing a competent piece of art. It's a delicate process. You'd be asking a robot to copy a complex human movement. I can't see how it'd be possible.'

She sniffs. 'Well, I'm happy to continue for as long as it takes.'

Paddy moves away from the easel, walks over to the windows. She's revelling in her new-found power. She knows as well as he does that those things won't work. Maybe for simple, everyday tasks. But not for anything subtle. How could you replicate the dexterity required for deft brushstrokes or the skill needed to paint with a palette knife?

Glancing behind at the sound of movement, he sees her putting his recent effort on the floor, turning it in towards the wall. He watches from the corner of his eye as she selects a clean, newly primed canvas and bolts it onto the easel, then swishes a brush around in a jar of turps. Let her get on with it.

He gazes out over the bay. The late-September sky is clear, except for a rash of plumy clouds on the horizon. He follows a plane as it takes off and climbs steadily in the wake of another already high in the air.

He can't leave her now. Can't get rid of her.

What would he do? How would he survive? Painting is all he knows. He has no other way of earning a crust. Even if he still had full use of both hands, he's too old now for bricklaying. The control he had is gone. In every sense. Marie's in possession of it now. And Laura Pierce. Christ al-fucking-mighty. It's like he's in bloody prison. Every which way he turns, he's thwarted.

Tory's playing the sympathy card. He's back to college now, after the summer break, and making out he can't focus properly, expecting special handling because there's a price hanging over his head. Marie's falling for it every time. And what does it translate as? Money, naturally. He needs so-much for this, and so-much for that. It'll make him *feel* better, take his mind off things, allow him to *enjoy* himself. For Jesus' sake. He's not the only one in the shit. They'll all have dirt on their hands if anything ever comes to light. Pierce said she'd make sure of that. But, as far as Tory's concerned, *he's* the only one affected.

How can they be sure he'll keep his trap shut? They'd warned him not to be drinking much. One word in the wrong ear and they could all be going down. Paddy would fight. Sure as hell, he would. Deny it all. It'd be her word against his. But, as she so nicely pointed out, she's very convincing. She's the best liar he's ever come across.

All his plans. Earlier in the year, he had himself out on his own by this time. Free and easy. He'd been thinking about it a lot. How he was going to extricate himself, head off somewhere, do things on his own terms and to hell with anyone else. He'd been planning to tell Marie about his other flings. The ones she doesn't know about. Had imagined the fight they'd have. Him listing them off one by one, and her storming off in a rage. Who knows if it would've worked? If it would've been that easy? Wishful thinking. Is that all it was? By God, he's not going to tell her now. It pains him to admit it, but he needs her. How else is he going to survive?

'I've been thinking,' he hears her say. 'You could start priming the canvases. You could do that easily with your left hand. Might make you feel more . . . useful. For the time being anyway.'

That was always one of her jobs. She'd continued to do it over the last six months even though she'd taken over the painting, but, come on, how insensitive can you get? Heat rises to his cheeks. 'That's all I'm good for now?'

'I'm only trying to help, Paddy. You'd do well to listen to me more.'

He contains his anger, feels as though there's a rope tied tight around his chest.

'Look,' she continues. 'I know this is all a big mess but we just have to muddle through as best we can. I'm doing my bit. It's only fair you do yours.'

He clenches his teeth. 'That's easy for you to say. You haven't come out of it as badly as I have.' He holds up his hand. 'Look what they did to me. Look what those people did to me! And to think you wanted to apologise to them! Bloody glad I put my foot down. Bloody glad.'

She's silent for a long time. Paddy turns back to the view. That's telling her. She might be the breadwinner now but that doesn't mean his opinions count for nothing. 'Maybe you'd still have your fingers,' she says to his back, 'if I'd gone ahead and sent an apology when I wanted to. Did you ever think of that?'

'You seriously think an apology from you would've been enough?'

'I don't know. But maybe one from the three of us might.'

That's as far as it goes. Neither of them says any more.

Paddy opens the window, sticks his head out to feel the soft, cooling breeze. *Maybe one from the three of us might . . .* Maybe this, perhaps that, possibly the other.

He doesn't care what she says. He's sticking to his opinion. Does she not get that saying sorry wouldn't have made any difference? Especially since it was that Yankee bitch who was behind it all. At least they found that out. Surely Marie would agree that was one good thing that came out of all this.

By Jesus. It's just as well the kid brother did what he did. Because if Paddy had ever seen that stupid cow on the street any time after that night, he'd have mown her down himself.

'I'm exhausted,' he says, as he walks towards the door. 'I'm going back to bed for a rest.'

Sleep comes swiftly. He falls deep into its sweet, black abyss. It holds him, creeps around him, dry and cold. The weight of it covers him. Earthy, gravelly drops.

One by one. Layer upon layer. Thick and hard and heavy.

It fills his eyes. His nose and mouth and throat.

He can't see. Can't breathe. Can't move.

Panic squeezes tight around his neck. Choking. Suffocating. Tight, tighter, until something wild and raging wrenches him awake.

He bolts upright. Gasping. Sucking in air.

Fucking hell. What was that? Some kind of attack?

He opens his eyes, looks around, takes a sip of water from the glass on the bedside table.

He sinks back onto the pillow, lets his eyelids droop, waits for his heart to stop racing, his breathing to find its normal pace.

Then he realises.

A dream.

That's what it was. He'd been dreaming.

But . . . it was Marie who was shovelling the earth. And it wasn't Mollie lying in the hole.

It was him.

THIRTY-SIX

The chain is heavy and ancient, its dull links warm to the touch when Laura lifts it. The padlock also: a weighty lump of a thing; blackened-iron, with worn-down rivets and a heart-shaped brass keyhole cover. It's the first time she's had to unlock it. And the first time she's come to the villa without Frank trotting down the path, calling a cheery greeting.

She opens her bag, fishes out the key – three inches long and swinging from a length of violet ribbon. Frank had given it to her like that, and she allows herself to smile, slightly, at the memory. It doesn't turn easily in the lock. She struggles to twist it, pulling it to the left like Frank had said, but it won't budge. She curses under her breath. Then out loud into the humid afternoon air. 'Fuck's sake.' More rattling, wiggling, twisting until, eventually, she feels a clunk. She lifts the shackle, unhooks it from the links and pushes the gate open just enough for her to slip through before locking it again behind her.

She could have called Bruno to pick her up from the

airport – Frank had made sure to leave her his number. She hadn't, preferring to take a regular taxi with a driver who didn't already know her. Bruno would have asked questions that Laura's not ready to answer. When she told the driver he didn't need to bring her through the gate, that she'd walk the rest of the way, his chunky-lipped leer and raised eyebrow made her almost wish she'd taken Frank's advice. Not that she was scared of the guy. Just that she might have preferred a familiar face.

Jesus, the noise of her case trundling over the gravel. She stops, picks it up by the handle to carry it instead. It seems more . . . respectful. Mad, really. It's not like it makes any difference. It was the same in the airport, going through Security. She'd informed them, of course, had all the necessary papers – death certificate, certificate of cremation – and they'd made sure to put on sympathetic faces. But it felt wrong, somehow, to see her case being handled, X-rayed, scrutinised.

On the plane, she'd stashed it in the overhead compartment, like you're supposed to, as soon as she got to her seat. But then she kept thinking about it. Up there. Over her head. So she'd stood up and rooted around, taken out the urn and held it on her lap for the duration of the flight. The bug-eyed woman sitting across the aisle didn't try to hide her curiosity. Laura gave her a what're-you-lookin'-at glare straight off, which worked. For a while. After the snack trolley passed, Bug-eyes was sneaking sidelong glances each time she took a sip of her hot beverage. Laura knocked back the mini bottle of cava she'd ordered, leaned over and said, 'I'm sure if you had a daughter, friend, whatever, who was taking a loved one's ashes to their final resting place, you wouldn't want some nosy old crone making her feel uncomfortable on such a sensitive occasion. Would you?' She visibly shrank. Laura was able to see only the back of her head for the remainder of the journey.

She turns onto the path. Walking up towards the villa, the enormity of Frank's absence falls on her like a sack-load of sand. This place is nothing without him. Notre Rêve *was* him.

It's not where Laura should be. Not now.

She certainly never intended to come back to the villa so soon. And definitely not on her own.

Frank had intended her to stay at the Negresco, had given her a hefty sum to cover it, and Laura's told her mother that's where she'll be. 'Typical Frank,' Angela had said. 'Nothing but the best.' She'd questioned Laura's insistence on going alone, wondering if she should take Amy, perhaps, for company.

'No, Mum,' she'd said. 'I'd prefer to do this myself. I'll be fine.'

The Negresco. Laura wishes. She'll treat herself one day. But not now. She has to stay here, at the villa, this time.

She has a job to do.

Six months of neglect have taken their toll on the grounds. The grass must be a foot high, the shrubbery is overgrown and weeds peep through the gravel. This isn't what Frank had intended. He'd explained to Laura that he'd originally asked his gardener and odd-job guy to keep coming once he'd left, had set up direct debits to pay them for the next year. After that, Laura was to take over arrangements herself: the place was always going to be hers once he'd gone. But then circumstances had changed. After what happened, he couldn't take the chance. How could he be sure the men wouldn't discover what was hidden under the fig trees? He'd had to cancel his plans for the upkeep, chain the gate and leave the place to its own devices.

He hadn't known how long he'd last when he left; when, exactly, Laura would be travelling to Nice to carry out his final wishes. *A month or two. Possibly mere weeks*, he'd said. Turned out it was four months. A lot more than he'd expected. But a lot less than he'd hoped. When he'd come back to Dublin, he'd been feeling better, he'd said. The improvement continued and he'd become more confident about his prospects, thinking he might confound the doctors and give his cancer, as he said, 'the old heave-ho'. He'd taken them all on a trip to London. Five nights at the Connaught, to hell with the expense. They'd had a ball. Shopping, shows, the very best of food. Must have cost him twenty grand. Nothing gave Frank more pleasure than treating his friends. Or, in this case, the family he'd adopted as his own.

But the decline was inevitable. And the end, mercifully, quick. He'd stayed with them at The Haven until they were unable to provide the level of care and comfort he deserved. It was late July when he entered the hospice. Laura sat beside his bed for hours each sweltering day, looking out through the glass doors to the well-tended rose garden but not able to open them even a crack for fear his shivering would start again. She'd left her job at the restaurant. It was shit pay for shit hours anyway. Spending time with Frank was more important than greeting loud-mouthed dickheads and their rubber-lipped dates, showing them to their tables, and having to smile and be pleasant while she went about it. Angela wasn't surprised when she told her she'd quit, but was almost speechless when she said she'd decided to

go back to art college. If Skellion can make it with the crap
he churns out, there's no reason someone with actual talent
can't either. Frank's birthday present, which, in the end, she
never got to give him, had been a portrait of Lee. When she'd
shown it to him, unfinished, he'd marvelled at how she'd
captured his likeness and had beamed, but through heavy
tears. She told him she'd have it ready in a couple of days but
she slid it under her bed and hasn't looked at it since. Frank
never mentioned it again.

The front door unlocks a lot more easily than the gate. As
she pushes it open, the villa's emptiness hits her like a rolling
wave. How is it that Frank's absence feels almost stronger
than his presence used to? Her footsteps echo on the tiles,
each one hollow and pitiful as it hangs in the air.

Richie wouldn't have been able for this. Not for any part
of it at all.

She already knew it, but now that she's actually here,
walking along the hall, into the living room, opening the door
out onto the terrace, the fact of it solidifies inside her like
concrete. If she was to fall, she might shatter into smithereens.

There it is.

The place.

She scans the ground under the fig trees, tries hard to spot
any tell-tale signs. But there's nothing. Nothing on the surface
that might give away what's hidden underneath.

So . . . why? Is it necessary? Will it really soothe the fear?

Night after night he'd come to her. Creeping in, sometimes
crawling on his knees. Crying, pleading. She'd tried so hard
to reassure him but her words had made no difference. All
through the summer, every night, she'd hoped, prayed she
wouldn't hear him at her door. By day, he wasn't too bad,

sometimes sullen and withdrawn but that's normal for Richie anyway. There were times he was brighter, more engaged with his surroundings, his family. He'd visited Frank often in the early days of his hospice stay, though never staying long. Towards the end, he'd stopped going completely. Unable, Laura believes, to cope with the prospect of more finality, more grief, more death.

It's darkness that does it. The withdrawal of the day. If he's somewhere she can watch him – the kitchen, the living room – she sees it. A sort of film glazes his eyes, draws fear across his face, ties his hands in knots. He sits there, twisting his fingers, thinking, thinking, always thinking.

She'd told him she couldn't do it. That she felt there was no need. Over and over she repeated herself until, after Frank's cremation (there had been no funeral, at his wishes), she began to consider the idea. His face when she told him. Doubt, at first. Suspicion. Even when she'd convinced him she'd do it, he didn't display relief. That will come, she hopes. But she can't know for certain. Here she is again, out here with a plan, and no real way of knowing what the outcome may be.

Three days she has allowed. Just to be sure. It could be way too much but there were so many theories and conflicting opinions online, she felt it best to play it safe. What's the expression? To err on the side of caution. That's it. Frank left her with details of boat hire; some guy he knew. He'd spoken to him, to tell him she'd be in touch at some point soon.

Last time, it was Frank's party that provided the cover for the plan she'd had; this time, it's the scattering of his ashes. Frank. Even in death, he's ever-accommodating.

Right. She should get to work. It's what she's here for. No

slacking. She takes a pack of cigarettes from her bag. She can spare a few minutes to have a smoke before she starts.

Everyday flammable liquids. That's what she'd googled. Most were pretty obvious – white spirit, lighter fuel, turps. But, she'd been surprised to learn, insect spray, hand sanitiser and moth balls were on the list too. Fucking moth balls. Who'd have thought? She doesn't find any of those in the storeroom off the kitchen but her search yields two and a half bottles of white spirit, a canister of lighter fuel and an aerosol spray with a picture of a mosquito and the word *antimoustique*, which can mean only one thing. In the bathroom upstairs she finds some surgical spirit and a large container of hand sanitiser. Olive oil. That was mentioned too. The extra-virgin stuff, apparently. The only kind Frank would use. Had it delivered specially from some producer in Italy, came in a fancy metal drum. She finds one in a kitchen cupboard and dumps it into a cloth carrier bag with the rest of her haul.

Back in the living room, she roots in the sideboard, finds some gin, pours several inches down her throat, sticks the bottle in the bag. She grabs one of Frank's coffee-table books, tucks it under her arm. Out to the terrace, down the steps, throwing open the storage bin where Frank kept garden tools. There's the spade. The one she'd used. The one she has to use again.

This isn't what she'd intended. She'd thought about it, imagined the process, understood how it would happen. What they'd buried was supposed to lie here, undisturbed. Day after day. Season after season. Year in, year out. Until there was nothing left but bones.

But Richie, he won't wait that long. Won't rest easy until all traces have disappeared.

And she'll do that for him.

She'll do anything it takes.

Shovelling the leaves, the sticky mess of ripened fruit, is too easy, too quick. The layer of earth beneath – dry and crumbling – gives no clues away. How can it just sit there, clean and settled, lying to her face?

A swig of gin, and another. Unearthing. Spadefuls. Ten. Twenty. One hundred.

And then the hit. Form. Shape. Solid but . . . uncertain. Not quite fully there.

Scraping. Clearing. Exposing to the air. No smell. The earth's too dry for that. Probably little decay. Mummification. That's what she'd read online.

Blind for the rest of it. Eyes open but unseeing. Refusing to register what she knows is there. Not wanting to be shown how much is left.

Without looking, she pours it all. Every drop. Walking around, waving streams of liquid from left to right. Then waiting. Just a few minutes. To give it time to trickle down, to fully soak in.

Lighter.

Pages, pages, pages. Flittering down.

Quiet, cautious. Barely there. A short snake of flame.

Flickering.

Dying.

Fuck.

More paper. Again. Again. Page after page.

Brighter.

Stronger.

Catching hold.

Licking.

Bursting.

Leaping.

Heat hits her arms, her face. She damps the flames with the spade, pokes around, evens out the blaze. Tends it. Keeps it under control so that the trees don't catch. Satisfied, she un-blurs her eyes. There's nothing to see there now. Only a warm, golden glow.

She sleeps in the living room, stretched on the chaise-longue. All night. Not waking once. When morning comes, she walks onto the terrace to take a look. Wisps of powdery smoke hang above the smouldering, blackened space. She won't go closer. Not yet. She'll wait. It'll keep burning, reducing, eating its way through. Feeding itself. Until it's spent.

She smokes, drinks black coffee, wanders from room to room. So strange to think the villa is hers. She's not sure if she wants it. The legalities haven't been sorted yet but Frank's solicitor has been in touch. A lengthy process, he'd said. A lot of paperwork. Of course, so he can justify the crazy fee he's going to cream off for himself. Before Frank died, he'd transferred a more than generous sum into Laura's bank account – *To keep you going, my dear* – but has, he told her, left her more in his will. He appointed her as executor, whatever the hell that entails – she'll find out soon enough.

More sleep, to pass the time. More cigarettes and coffee. She hasn't brought anything to eat. It's not a time for food. Not meals, anyway. She finds an unopened packet of fancy French biscuits in a kitchen cupboard. Past their sell-buy date but still edible. As she nibbles them, sitting at the kitchen table, her phone buzzes with a text from Richie. Just a question mark – *?*

:) she replies. He'll understand.

At dusk, she checks. It's just over twenty-four hours now. The fire still smoulders but, when she jabs at it with the spade, it falls in on itself. The job is done. Sooner than she'd thought.

Digging through the heap of black ash, the spade scrapes against something hard. The temperature hadn't been hot enough to burn bone. But she'd expected that. They're manageable pieces, though, nothing to worry about. She heaps it all out onto a patch of ground she has cleared of leaves, spreading it in a thin layer to cool. Only as the hole is almost empty does she notice the pieces of skull, the jawbone. Scooping them up, she drops them on the ground and smashes the spade down hard, letting out a roar so she can mask the sound.

The afternoon busies around her as she strolls through the narrow streets and onto place Rossetti. The smell of crisping dough wafts through the air, outdoor tables are laid and cleared and, in front of the cathedral, a skinny busker in threadbare dungarees croaks his way through a dismal version of 'Freebird'.

She's taking Frank on a final journey – his urn, at least – passing all his favourite places. She'd got out of the taxi at the Méridien, slamming the door on the grumpy fuck since he'd refused to turn on the meter and charged her seventy euro for the twenty-minute journey. Fair enough, he'd probably come from the city to the villa in order to collect her and it's usual to be charged for that too, but still . . .

She'd crossed the road to the promenade, going down almost as far as Castel Plage before crossing over again and through the arch onto the bustling Cours Saleya. It's a hot, hot day and she'd been glad of the market stalls' shady awnings. Had been tempted by the arrays of fresh and dried fruits, cheeses, nuts; the baskets of sweet-smelling soaps – almond, lavender, lemon. But she's carrying enough of a load. A bag on each shoulder.

Turning right onto rue de l'Opéra, she'd approached place Masséna, walking across its chequered tiles to the dancing fountains inside the Parc du Paillon. Kids ran through the swirling, misty spray, squealing like little pigs when the water jets suddenly spurted skywards. Life goes on, she told Frank in her head. Carry on as normal.

Out one of the gates to the right, over the tram tracks and down the steps to the Old Town. Here now, in place Rossetti, she sits at an outdoor café table with a glass of rosé. She places the bag holding Frank's urn on the chair beside her; the other bag she dumps at her feet. The time on her phone reads 3.38 p.m. She can spare another ten minutes: she's arranged to meet Louis the boatman at the port at four. When she'd called him last night, he'd almost been in tears. He'd explained, in clumsy English, how Fronc had been such a good, good man and how sorry he was to hear that the time had come.

'Tomorrow afternoon?' she'd asked, keeping her fingers crossed.

'*Oui, oui,*' he'd replied. 'I very happy I am help.'

He's waiting for her on the quay when she arrives, wearing – as he'd said – a red rose pinned to his shirt 'for Fronc'. His boat – *Fantaisie* – is more a mini-yacht: navy and white hull, shining chrome rails, wooden deck with steps down into a small cabin. He smiles as he kisses her cheek, obvious warmth in his dark brown eyes.

Frank had mentioned something about maybe needing permission to scatter his ashes, informing authorities. But Laura's not bothered. Neither, apparently, is Louis. He doesn't ask for anything, just makes a remark about how *jolie* the urn is, when she shows him. 'He like!' he says, with a thumbs-up. 'Fronc, he like, *non*?' Laura laughs. It's true, Frank had liked his urn. He'd chosen it himself. The most expensive and decorative one he could find. Who the fuck cares where ashes are scattered anyway? There's a lot more offensive stuff chucked into the sea. Louis doesn't ask, either, about the other large cloth bag Laura carries. But, then, why would he? It's not his concern.

He stays respectfully silent as they leave the port and head out into the bay. He steers left and motors some way further, coming to a stop with Cap Ferrat before them and Villefranche to their left. Laura looks at the pretty harbour a few kilometres up the coast. Skellion is up there somewhere, getting on with things but always on his guard. He'll never rest easy. She may have got rid of the evidence but he doesn't know that. She's never going to tell.

It's possible – probable – she'll bump into Tory some day: Richie heard from friends of friends that he'd been seen around. She might be walking up Dame Street maybe, or passing St Stephen's Green. She'll catch his eye, he'll pretend he hasn't seen her. But he'll look back over his shoulder when she's gone.

He'll never stop looking over his shoulder.

Louis turns away, allowing her to say her goodbyes in private. The water is calm. Only the slightest of ripples as, swiftly, she slips the bag from her shoulder, turns it upside down, tips the contents over the side of the boat. Clumps of ash cling to the surface. Bone fragments sink beneath the waves.

Taking the urn, she unscrews the lid, sprinkles the fine grey ashes onto the glittering water, watches them disperse and float away for ever.

'Take care,' she whispers. 'And I'm sorry someone else is muscling in on your final moments. I know you'll understand.'

She doesn't cry. And she won't.

Not now. Not ever.

October

'Aren't we supposed to have a mass or something?' Amy asks. 'I thought that's what you did on the first anniversary.'

'Some people do,' Angela says, as she slices baguettes in half. 'But I'd prefer it to be just the four of us. We don't need to go to church to remember your father.'

'We don't need to do anything to remember him,' Amy says. 'He's in our thoughts every single minute.'

'I know, love. I know.'

Laura opens the drawer, takes out the cutlery. 'Where's Richie? I presume he'll be joining us? It's his birthday lunch, after all.'

Her mother nods. 'Of course. He's outside. His delivery's arriving this afternoon.'

'What delivery?' both girls ask together.

Angela pauses before answering. 'Well . . . he wanted it to be a surprise. But I suppose I can tell you now.' She looks up at her daughters. 'He's going to rebuild the treehouse. He ordered the wood the other day.'

Laura feels the warmth of Trudy's body pushing against her shins. 'The treehouse? What the . . .? I mean, I thought we agreed getting rid of it was the right thing to do?'

Angela frowns. 'I'm not sure any of us ever said that, love. He pulled it down in the heat of the moment. He was so angry. Your father had just . . . Anyway, Richie thought, you know, this being the anniversary . . .'

'We're not kids any more. What do we need a treehouse for?'

'That's not the point, Laura. He feels bad. He wants to fix it. Your father would like that. I know he would. And at least he's doing *something*. That's a good thing, surely.'

Laura clatters the knives and forks onto the table, grabs her hoodie from the back of a chair, pulls it over her head.

'Go easy on him, love,' Angela says as Laura opens the back door. 'Today of all days.'

In the garden, the grass is wet underfoot and layered with fallen leaves. The sky is grey, the air damp and cold. Laura shivers, pushes her hands into her sleeves, wraps her arms around her waist. What the hell is Richie thinking? Why bother? What's the point?

There he is. Under the tree. Gazing up into the branches. She jogs down the path, cold air rasping in and out of her throat. 'What's all this about the treehouse?' she says, when she reaches him.

He lowers his head, shrugs. 'Dunno,' he says to the trunk. 'Just something I want to do.'

'But I thought you were happy you'd pulled it down. I thought you felt it was the right thing to do.'

He looks at her now, pushes his hair back from his forehead. 'Things might feel right at the time, Laura. It doesn't mean they always will.'

She studies his face, his eyes. 'What're you trying to prove?'

His eyebrows come together. 'Don't know what you mean.'

'It won't make you feel better. You'll go to all the trouble but things won't be any different. We can't go back to the way we were, Richie. That's not how it works.'

'You think I don't know that?' He turns away again and she watches how his jaw clenches. How he lunges forward. How he punches the tree trunk. Once, twice, three times. 'You think I don't *fucking* well know that?'

He stumbles a little, drops his hands to his sides. Laura eyes his bloody knuckles. 'Lunch is ready,' she says, and starts walking back towards the house.

Angela tries. She knows they're all trying. They're here, aren't they? Around the table, together, as a family. It's what they're supposed to do. But being together isn't all it's cracked up to be. Less so, as time goes on, it seems. It makes Karl's absence even more acute. At least when they're scattered throughout the house, each in different rooms, they can pretend. Collectively, that's almost impossible. Four is supposed to be five. There's no getting away from that.

And today, exactly one year on, how could it possibly be any different?

Still, they try.

'It'll be nice,' she says to her children, 'to have the treehouse back. When your dad built it, he didn't just have you in mind. He was thinking about grandchildren too.'

'Don't look at me,' Amy says. 'I've no plans on that front.'

'I'm not talking about now,' Angela says, smiling. 'But sometime in the future, hopefully.'

'The future?' Laura asks. 'Does that mean we're staying here?'

'I . . . I'm not sure. Possibly.'

'What about Dad? He wanted to move.'

'I know, love,' Angela says. 'It's not something I can think about at the moment.'

'But you can think about rebuilding the treehouse?'

Angela hesitates, clears her throat. 'It's Richie's project,' she says. 'He's the one doing all the thinking.'

'You must be paying for the materials, though?'

'It's his birthday present. That's what he asked for. Look, what difference does it make?'

'Exactly,' Laura says. 'That's my point. It'll make no difference. To anything. It's a complete waste of time and effort. Pulling it down meant something. Putting it back up is meaningless.'

'I don't know why you're getting so worked up about it.'

'It's a backwards step.'

'Well, you won't be the one taking it, will you?'

'I'll be looking out at the bloody thing, won't I? It's not like I'll be able to avoid it.'

Angela sighs. 'Can we change the subject, please?' What is Laura's problem? She's overreacting. Either that or she's deliberately trying to cause an argument. Today of all days.

A silence follows. Then Richie speaks through a mouthful of bread. 'You can't stand by everything you do. Sometimes you have to be man enough to admit you made a mistake.'

'And sometimes you have to admit you didn't,' Laura says. 'Take ownership of your decisions.'

Richie gulps down his food. 'You're full of bullshit, Laura. You know that?'

Laura's eyebrows shoot up. 'Oh, yeah? Of course, it's easy to say you made a mistake when there's someone else willing to sort it out for you. When you don't have to go to any trouble yourself.'

Angela sees the look Richie shoots his sister. She's not sure what's behind this but she has sensed a growing tension between the two of them for some time now. This treehouse idea of Richie's was never going to go down easy. Laura seems to find fault with everything he does, these days. Or doesn't do. She's always ready to pounce. These past few weeks, she's pulled Richie up on just about everything. It's as if she relishes picking holes. Angela noticed it a day or two after she'd come back from scattering Frank's ashes. Granted, it can't have been an easy trip but she'd insisted on going alone and, now, Angela wishes she'd been more forceful in trying to persuade her not to. It's had an effect. Of course it has. God knows, Laura has never been overflowing with sweetness but it seems like she's been squeezed to the point of bitterness. Losing Frank less than a year after losing her father . . . But none of that is Richie's fault. So why the constant bickering? They were thick as thieves when they came home after Frank's party. Naturally, Laura had been incredibly upset about Frank's illness – they all had – but she and Richie had seemed to develop a bond. Angela had often heard them in the middle of the night. The two of them in Laura's room, mumbling, whispering. She'd left them to it. Part of her had even been glad Richie had run off to Frank's that time. He'd still been Richie – still morose, still spending too much time on his own – but, on the plus side, it appeared he'd become closer to his sister and that, Angela felt, had been a good thing. It's all-change now, though. The attachment has weakened. Maybe even snapped.

Amy looks at Laura. 'If it was something you wanted to do,' she says, 'you'd go right ahead and do it. It's not like it was a snap decision. Richie's obviously given it thought so why don't we just leave him to it?'

'Oh, yeah, because Richie would never do something without thinking about it, would he?' Laura replies, side-eyeing her brother. 'Carefully considers everything. All possible outcomes. That right, Rich?'

Richie catches her glance, then looks down at his plate.

'Let's forget about the treehouse,' Angela says. 'For the moment, anyway. All right?'

'Yeah,' Laura says. 'Let's talk about something way more positive. Like the fact that Dad's been gone a whole year now.'

'Stop, Laura,' Angela says, trying to keep her voice from rising. 'We're all still here, aren't we? We've survived.'

'Really? Is that what you think?'

'What? Of – of course. We're all doing our best.'

'Stop trying to pretend we can just carry on as if nothing happened.'

'I don't think any of us is trying to do that, Laura. But we're getting through things, aren't we?'

'Getting through things. Oh, wow. Like a normal everyday family. Go the Pierces.'

'Shut up, Laura,' Amy says. 'Can we not just eat our lunch?'

'Sure. If we can all acknowledge that things won't ever go back to the way they were. Can we stop pretending?'

Angela feels the heat of tears threatening to flood her eyes. 'No one's pretending, love. We're all just trying to do our best.'

'You think so? Look at Richie's hands. Look at the state of them.'

'Richie?' Angela sees his raw knuckles now, torn skin oozing blood. 'What did you do?'

'His best, Mum,' Laura says. 'Richie's always been good at punching stuff. Though it used to be doors. When we'd end up fighting about what happened. See, no matter how much you tell yourself that we're moving on, that we're doing our best, the fact is we're all still angry. We're all still hurting. That's never going to change.'

'No. You're wrong.' The tears come now and Angela does nothing to stop them. 'This is just a blip. No one said it was going to be plain sailing. No one said it'd be easy. But . . . it's getting better. And a lot of that is down to you, Laura. L-look what you did. If it wasn't for you, we wouldn't have that apology letter.'

'Oh, come on. Please. Like, what difference has that made? Seriously. It's a piece of fucking paper. It's not enough.'

'B-but . . . that's not true. It means a huge amount. It—'

'Means nothing.'

'How can you say that? After all you did to make sure we got it? All the trouble you went to.'

Laura shakes her head. 'It would've happened anyway. With or without me.'

'No. I don't believe that. Whatever you said to them made a difference. There's no way it—'

'You weren't there! You don't know what happened! You've no idea!'

'What? What happened? You've never said. If something bad . . . I mean, if you want to talk about it, just—'

'It doesn't matter.' Laura shoves her plate away, pushes her chair back, stands up from the table. 'It won't change anything. It won't change a fucking thing.' She breezes out of the kitchen, her footsteps deft, swift, on the stairs.

Amy is the first to speak. 'God. All that because Richie wants to rebuild the treehouse. I don't get it.'

'It's just the day that's in it,' Angela says, pulling a tissue from her sleeve, dabbing at her eyes. 'She's upset.'

'We're all upset, Mum.'

Angela looks at Richie. 'Do you know what she's talking about? You were there. Is there something she's not telling me?'

Richie shrugs. 'I wasn't there when she went to Skellion.'

'But after? At the party, maybe?'

Richie shrugs again, shakes his head.

'I wouldn't read too much into it,' Amy says. 'I mean, we're all devastated about what happened, and about Dad. But Laura's lost Frank too, remember. I know we all loved him but he was practically her best friend.'

'That's very true,' Angela agrees. 'No practically about it. She was closer to Frank than anyone, really. Things will get easier for her in time. Once she's settled back into college properly, makes new friends, reconnects with old ones.'

'That reminds me,' Amy says. 'Think I spotted Mollie Teller

in town the other day. Meant to say it to Laura. Haven't heard her mention her in a while.'

Richie's head snaps up. 'It wasn't her. It couldn't have . . . I mean . . .'

'How would you know?'

He fixes his eyes on his sister for a few seconds, then turns his attention back to his food. 'Dunno. Think . . . I heard Laura say she'd gone back to the States or something.'

'Well, that'd be good news, I suppose. She wasn't exactly my favourite person.'

'No, not top of my list either, I have to say,' Angela says. She reaches over, touches Richie's sleeve. 'Make sure you put some antiseptic cream on your hands after lunch, love. You don't want them to get infected.'

Laura stands at her bedroom window. Rain has started to fall. A mesh of drops clings to the glass, muddying the view, but not enough to obscure the tree as it waves its almost-bare branches in the wind.

They don't get it.

It's not about trying to put things back the way they were. It's about cutting out the dead wood so that new shoots have space to grow. It's the only way. All her plotting and planning, and Richie just came right out and did what he did. No messing about. That's why she's so angry. He should be chopping the tree down, not putting back the stupid fucking treehouse.

When she thinks about it, it wasn't so hard. Not really. She doesn't like that she had to clear up the mess, but it had to be done. For Richie. For all of them.

It'll be different this time. She won't be getting her hands dirty. Not in any sense.

They won't be hard to find. If Mollie could seek out scumbags to do a job, so can she. She has the money now. Thanks to Frank.

That warmth against her legs again. Trudy. She bends to pick her up, holds the fluffy bulk against her chest.

'I'll get them,' she says, circling her fingers through the soft belly fur. 'I'll get everyone who was involved. You understand that, don't you, Trudy? I mean it. I'll get them all.'

ACKNOWLEDGEMENTS

This book is wholly a work of fiction but it is, as they say in the movies, 'inspired by real events'. A few years ago, my family experienced a violent break-in during a party at our house. Despite the severity of the crime – the physical injuries, the mental scars, the lasting trauma – and the best efforts of the Garda, only one of those charged received any punishment: a few hours of community service and a small fine. The others walked away. All too often, the victims of crime are the ones who end up paying the price.

Thanks to all those involved in bringing this book to life, notably:
My editor, Ciara Considine, and everyone at Hachette Ireland
My agent, Lucy Luck at Conville & Walsh
Copy-editor, Hazel Orme
Friends, Claire Coughlan and Jamie O'Connell
My husband, my children and all my family.

One Good Reason is Susan Stairs' third novel. She is also author of the acclaimed novels *The Story of Before* and *The Boy Between*. She has twice been awarded a Literature Bursary from the Arts Council of Ireland and was shortlisted for The Davy Byrnes Irish Writing Award in 2009. She is one of the contributors to *The Long Gaze Back - An Anthology of Irish Women Writers* which is the Dublin City Libraries and Dublin UNESCO City of literature One City One Book choice for 2018. She lives in Dublin.

www.susanstairs.com   @Susan Stairs